I0635800

THE GIFT

from

TURTLE

a novel

J.T. ALLEN

This is a work of fiction. Names, characters, businesses, places, events, locales, and incidents are either the products of the author's imagination or used in a fictitious manner. Any resemblance to actual persons, living or dead, or actual events is purely coincidental.

Copyright © 2025 by J.T. Allen

All rights reserved. This book may not be reproduced or stored in whole or in part by any means without the written permission of the author except for brief quotations for the purpose of review.

ISBN: 978-1-966343-00-4 soft

Allen. J.T.
The Gift from Turtle.

Edited by: Melissa Long

Published by Warren Publishing
Charlotte, NC
www.warrenpublishing.net
Printed in the United States

With thanks to Senora Lynch, celebrated North Carolina Haliwa Saponi Indian artist, whose exquisite turtle figurines have blessed so many of us.

ACKNOWLEDGMENTS

This book began as a story about an old beach trailer that stood embarrassingly next to a beach mansion. We've all seen them, and the contrast is quite stark. The trailer idea came from my first novel, *Love, Judie Kate*, which featured a brief time of dating at a small, old, and quaint beach trailer. I thought then the trailer had more to say, and that led to this story.

So somewhere along the way, Bailey appeared, and suddenly, I had to write about a fourteen-year-old teenager. Since I have no children and am far beyond the age of parenting teens anyway, and since there is only so much one can safely research about teens, I needed some help. I contacted my wife's niece, Traci Womble, and asked if I could send her "way cool" (Traci's words) teen a list of questions to help me get into the mind of fourteen-year-olds. Many thanks to Emily Womble—who wore red Converse sneakers at her prom—and her friend Anna Holcombe for answering my questions. (I used their names in the story, but the characters are not like them.) Traci also helped me with some other teen and mom questions as well. Tina Cole, my hairstylist, provided advice on hairstyles and clarified even more issues for me.

Special thanks to my first readers. Arleen Widerman, a retired school music teacher (and the best church choir director ever!) read the first draft and provided many poignant comments and suggestions that made the story better and stronger. Despite being retired, her little red pen still works very well! Neighbor Amy Riley, mother of two teens and also a speech therapist in our school system, helped me better understand the culture of teens, the worries of a mother of teens, and the characters of Bailey and Maria. Her daughter, Olivia, taught me the intricacies of Instagram and Snapchat, as well as the psyche of teens. Since she waits tables, I gave her a cameo appearance in the restaurant scene. (Yes, you will get a big tip the next time we eat BBQ!)

My good friends Bob Blackwell and Janice Schroder always asked about Bailey when we had lunch together, and their observations were appreciated. Janice's daughter, Jessie, gives a new and delightful meaning to OCD, and she inspired many of the quirks Bailey exhibits. I also incorporated my own OCD issues into Bailey as well. And yes, there is such a thing as left- and right-handed food.

The staff at Warren Publishing has been amazing. Thanks to Mindy Kuhn for believing in this project; Amy Ashby for advice and patience on our long phone calls; and Melisa Graham who provided excellent observations.

As every writer—indeed, artist—knows, space, understanding, and patience are needed to work on our craft. My wife of forty years, Jackie, provides such space. I am ever grateful for her love and support.

Last is our "feral" turtle. When we toss veggie scraps over the electric fence for the deer, Turtle slowly crawls up and munches away. I have spent many minutes watching this wonderful reptile leisurely nibble this cuisine. He/she is a Zen lesson in slowing down and living in the moment. Turtle especially enjoys cucumbers, cantaloupe rinds, and … corn cobs. Thus, I dedicate this novel to Cob, our pet turtle.

ONE

Days Gone By

The drive from Greensboro to Banker's Point Island was about five hours, depending on how many bathroom breaks you needed and how many traffic jams there were on I-40 and Highway 70. It was long enough for Maria Gowins to think through the last three years of hell she had lived and review her therapist's suggestions on how to move on. It was either that or count how many Bojangles restaurants there were between Greensboro and the beach.

The questions, answers, and guilt coursed around her head like the incessant speeders zipping by her. How had a simple mountain girl gotten so tangled up in a life of wealth and weekend soirees? Ever insecure, especially about her body, Maria wondered why she had married during college. In therapy, she had realized Blane Simpson was more of a father figure than a husband, more like someone who was cool to hang with than a reliable mate. And to be honest, with the freedom of college, she had been a little loose in her morals. *You reaped what you sowed, Maria*, the old church guilt reminded her.

As the miles passed, she relived—*Does it ever stop?*—their successful life in Greensboro. Blane had gotten a degree in finance and, with his business savvy, quickly became VP of a local bank that was later bought out by a major bank, where he then worked hard to rise to the top once more. He was currently on the fast track to a VP position within the growing company.

Maria's life had been less flamboyant: starting out as a history teacher in a local high school, receiving a master's degree in history from UNC Greensboro, and then settling down as a history instructor at Jameson Community College. She didn't need to work, so why did she? Her friends and colleagues had asked her that often. Blane's salary alone could have fed several families of four, and the couple had lived a good life. Why did she bother with a middling career at a *community* college? No kids to fret over—"Kids just get in the way of having fun," Blane often reminded her—so why not enjoy life? Life in a five-bedroom, six-bath, ten-thousand-square-foot castle with an in-ground pool and three-car garage by the lake on a pristine golf course in a gated community. A castle that had more big-screen TVs than BestBuy.

Living the dream. Or so she thought.

It was the pressure to fit in that Maria sought to avoid through teaching and church work. She was put off by the constant expectation of physical perfection. The perfect body with breast implants, liposuction, Botox, obsessive diets, and hours at the gym. The fruits of which were to be displayed in trendy clothes from expensive boutiques while sipping mixed drinks at the club after golf or tennis while discussing your latest trip to the therapist. It just wasn't her. She had been raised in a small, poor community. Hand-me-downs, family values, don't-get-above-your-head raising. When she married Blane, it never occurred to her he would morph into a status-obsessed corporate type. Soon the Maria he married was not good enough. Why couldn't she be like the other women at the country club?

She wanted children, and twice she had gotten pregnant only to have miscarriages. Maybe that was a blessing ...? Her ob-gyn suggested that stress might have been the issue. Her therapist agreed. Was it the anxiety and stress of trying to meet the expectations of the other women in the country club? The expectations of her husband? Maybe. But now she believed it was the result of repressed emotions and suspicions concerning her louse of a husband.

It had begun when she had an intuition one day. Something was not adding up. How could Blane be making that much money? Through her friends on Facebook, she found out what a typical VP of a local bank made. Blane kept the bank statements—"I am a banker, after all," he always reminded her, laughing—and paid the bills, so she had never really seen what he made.

Memo to Maria: No more letting men control your life.

One day, her computer at home had gone on the fritz, so she'd used Blane's. He'd left the bank statement window open, and when she accidentally tapped on the icon, a document came up. She was shocked. There were several accounts in his name only. The deposit from his bank job seemed normal, from what her friends told her later, but other funds had been deposited, apparently in cash. *I didn't know we had this much money!* Something seemed fishy.

As she pondered this disconcerting evidence, she thought about the changes in his behavior and the sudden, unpredictable mood swings. Though once attentive to her every need after college, he now seemed to work more evenings than before. On weekends, he was often nonexistent. The extremes worried her.

"I know I've neglected you, babe, for the past few weeks, but right now, I see what I've been missing!" He would grab her, and the loving was intense and, yes, satisfying. But he was often cranky, distant, and distracted, and sometimes the sex was rough.

Between the bank statements and erratic behavior, something was seriously off. Having grown more suspicious, Maria hired a private investigator.

Months later, the FBI showed up at their door at six in the morning. There were black vans everywhere, people in tactical gear. They came in and arrested Blane, seized his computer, and ransacked the house while looking for evidence. They took Maria in for questioning that lasted hours.

The charges? Human sex trafficking.

Weeks of embarrassment and humiliation had followed. The trial was on the local news and social media. Some of Maria's friends wouldn't return her calls, emails, or texts. Her "friends" on Facebook became enemies as they trashed her in ugly posts. After the trial and convictions—several prominent local citizens were involved—Blane was sent to prison. Maria sued for divorce, and her feisty female attorney took her disgraceful husband to the cleaners. It was for revenge more than satisfaction. Maria got the house and Blane's investments, bank accounts, and beach trailer, a forgotten leftover from the Simpson family will.

Quite a *settlement*.

But things had not been settled. The neighbors treated Maria like a pariah. Friends who didn't know what to say said nothing. Church folks shunned her. Colleagues, except for her good friend Joe Clark, steered clear of her. People at the country club secretly took her name off the roll. Strangers who had only known her face from TV bites cut a path around her at the grocery store. It was like they thought she had been in on the scheme too or was equally responsible. Perhaps, had she kept her man satisfied, none of this would have happened.

Now Maria was after peace of mind. Looking for a way out, she had decided a new job in a new town was the answer. After several interviews, she'd landed a teaching gig at Coastal Community College on the mainland, not far from the Simpson family beach trailer. Not exactly a ticket to paradise, but …

She had sold the house complete with furniture—thank God the housing market had been hot!—and donated the money to the Monica Center, run by Joe Clark's wife, Judie Kate. Then she'd packed some meager belongings and headed down the yellow brick road to her new life, ironically on Banker's Point Island.

Sixteen Bojangles restaurants later … Maria shook her head to get out of the past. "Enough gloom and doom," she chided herself as she pulled over to a rest stop and settled on a picnic bench. She could practically hear her therapist say, "Don't live in the past, Maria. Don't fret about the future. Learn to live in the present."

"Screw Greensboro!" Maria would shout.

"And work on your anger."

But the gloom hovered over her like a dark storm cloud. No matter how hard she tried, her anger toward her former husband would not dissipate, and it was making her averse to men in general. It had produced a life of instant retorts, sarcasm, and profanity. She was snappy, impatient, impetuous. While she had received a huge monetary settlement, she now deplored the life of the rich. Could she manage that disparity? She hoped the new life at the beach would change all that. That the old beach trailer, which she had never seen, could somehow bring healing to her troubled soul.

Would life fail her again?

As she pondered that question, tears filled her eyes and then fell to the concrete table.

Jason Parker stood on the second-floor deck looking out over the ocean, like a ship's captain at the wheel. The cresting waves looked like the folds of a sequined dress. The serenity of the morning washed over him like a calming breeze. As he stretched his legs, the sun warmed his tan body and energized his soul.

Dressed in gray running shorts, he was about to take his morning run and turn heads as he passed. He was the talk of the island, the stuff of daydreams for women (and some men) everywhere, young and old, with his dark, wavy hair and chiseled jaw. Jason worked hard to stay trim, and he secretly delighted in the attention. But dates were not in the cards because of the gorgeous young woman who occasionally accompanied him on his jaunts about the island. They thought she was his wife. She was, in fact, his only (and lonely) teenage daughter, Bailey.

The beach mansion had been a new gift to himself, a life-long dream actually, but also an escape. An escape from his failed marriage and for his daughter as well. In some sense, it was the hopeful beginning of a new life for both of them.

Jason had worked hard to achieve the success now manifest in his new abode. Born to ordinary parents in an ordinary subdivision, he'd dreamed of more. He'd attended East Carolina University for undergrad, earned an MBA from UNC Chapel Hill, and then worked his bones off as a successful certified financial planner. Starting from nothing, "My parents didn't give me a dime," he often bragged at his entry into the long list of American success stories. "Horatio Alger 2.0," he called it.

His success had demanded a trophy wife, and his had been the envy of men. She'd loved his money and used it well to keep his attention, to fulfill his desires. Trim, tan. Flirty, fashionable, fun. Cute, charming, curvy. And the best part, sexy, seductive, even salacious.

He'd had it all: career, success, and a goddess to boot!

Until she had run off with the pool man, of all people. "Yes, the pool man!" he'd learned to laugh when he retold the story to people. But the hurt, humiliation, and embarrassment of the divorce had translated into an exercise obsession.

He had no appreciation for sluggards or those who asked for just a bit of help so they could have an unearned piece of the pie. The only altruism in his life was he wanted to help others achieve their dream of financial independence. And he did. His wealth was substantial because he managed their accounts well. "I don't make money unless you make money" was the mantra on his business cards and brochures. The three-story beach mansion was another exclamation point in his bulging portfolio. His book, *Rich Is a $tate of Mind*, was in its third printing, having sold over one hundred thousand copies.

His new beach house matched his Mercedes perfectly.

As he turned to go down the steps, the trailer stopped him in his tracks. It was like an ugly corn on a foot, a wart on otherwise unblemished skin, spider veins on tanned legs. In other words, it was an eyesore. Faded somewhat, rusted in some places, weeds all around. Obviously, the aluminum shack had not been occupied in years. Most importantly, it diminished the stature of his home.

Why don't they just tear it down? The lot itself would sell for a hundred thousand easily.

Arrogantly and selfishly, Jason constantly worried what people thought of him when they looked at it. "Oh yeah, you're the guy who lives by *that trailer.*" It was how they said "that trailer" that made him wince.

On his run, the past tried to overtake Jason like a runner out to pass the leader of the race. His wife had wanted no part in raising their daughter in her new life. Maybe it was the fact that her daughter was about to hit those awful teen years. Maybe it was selfishly not wanting anything to cramp her carefree lifestyle. Hormones, mood swings, boys, sports, mall trips, cyberbullying. Who wanted to deal with that?

Then Jason reminded himself of his success in the financial planning field, his hard work ethic, his best-selling book. How the beach house was both an investment and a getaway from the loss. How he planned to use the house as a second office to host financial planning parties on the island, hoping to snag a few wealthy vacationers to start an account. He grounded himself in his goals and resettled into his leading pace.

He arrived back at his mansion and paused in the driveway, panting, sweat dripping onto the concrete drive, and then bounded up the stairs where his daughter stood, looking out into the new day. Still jogging as he cooled down, he looked out beside the mansion and stated, "That trailer has got to go."

"Mr. Parker?" Bailey asked in a mocking tone of voice. "You're acting like a rich snob again." The warm ocean breeze whirled strands of her long hair around her face. When she had morphed from a gangly, goofy thirteen-year-old into a blossoming young adult of fourteen, she'd developed a social justice side that balanced her father's conservative, self-made-man idealism. But from Bailey's exaggerated facial expressions and occasional comments, he sometimes wondered if he'd become more obsessed with wealth than the people he helped. And now he knew that she knew that he perceived the ugly trailer as an affront to his success. Was he her first social justice cause to solve?

When Jason reached out to wrap his arm around his teenage daughter, she stepped back and whined, "Eww, you're sweaty! Gross!" Then she faked a hug.

"You're right, dear. I'm sorry."

She rewarded his contrition with a big smile.

Despite his drive for wealth—okay, maybe it was an obsession—Jason was a doting father who would do anything for his little girl. But sometimes it seemed those "anythings" weren't what she really needed or even wanted. And okay, she was not a little girl anymore either. Getting himself to see and understand the difference, especially now, was the difficult task at hand. Try as he might, Jason was having a difficult time seeing things her way. The thirteenth year was bad enough, with latent hormones emerging from their childhood sleep, accompanying out-of-nowhere attitude swings. She needed a mom, but that was out the door after the divorce. Her aunts lived too far away to be of any maternal help. And there were just certain topics that … well, that he felt embarrassed to talk about with someone else, especially a woman. The beach mansion was yet another attempt to fill a void he could not fill or comprehend.

"What time do your clients arrive tonight?" Bailey sighed in a weary, somewhat whiney, tone.

"Around four-thirty," Jason answered. "Can you play host again?"

In the real world, the wife usually played host to the husband's parties, but Bailey would have to do it now. It was a grown-up job she could handle effectively. It was just that, for reasons known only to her, she did not want to do it. But she would do nearly anything to please her father.

She took a long moment to respond, twirling her hair several times. "Guess I'd better pretty up for the folks."

She started to walk away, but Jason pulled her close again and placed his strong hands on her soft shoulders. "Thank you, Bailey. You know I love you."

"I love you too, Dad." And Jason knew she meant it.

She walked inside, wondering what she would wear tonight. That was one of the reasons she didn't want to play hostess. Nothing really fit anymore.

In just a few months, Bailey had emerged as a beautiful butterfly from the cocoon of adolescence. She was tall with waist-long chestnut-brown hair, deep-green eyes, long lashes, full, pouty lips, and cheeks that highlighted an angular face that said "model" all over it.

And embarrassingly large breasts. Just like her grandmother.

TWO

The Beach Trailer

Maria stepped out of her white Toyota Land Cruiser, the hot engine clicking as it cooled from two hundred miles of late-May heat. She stood with incredulous anticipation at the back of the old mobile home, stretched, exhaled the stress of the drive from Greensboro, and sighed. "So this is it, huh?" Frankly, it was a bit disappointing.

The worn and seemingly weary 1950s beach trailer was wrapped like a repurposed gift in horizontal layers of aluminum panels. From the top, the metal domicile flowed down from a faded, oxidized yellow into a large band of weathered white and then into faded yellow once more down to the bottom. The white band was occasionally discolored by splotches of light yellow that had seemingly drifted south, and the lower yellow strip was smudged with similar white migrations. Maria thought of icing oozing down the side of a donut. Louvered windows, encrusted all over with a patina of salt and corrosion, punctuated the walls. The roofline at the front angled upward for a sliver of a skylight and then abruptly dropped to continue the flat roof to the end. Two doors graced the long side facing the sandy driveway, one with a large window about a third of the way from the front end and the other featuring a smaller window near the back end. Three dirty windows, front, middle, and rear, also faced the driveway. The siding had a bit of rust, oxidation from years in the sun, and small sand pits and debris dings from hurricanes and northeasters. Overall, the old trailer was in good shape. After years of waiting, it just needed to exhale.

"Wonder what the inside looks like?" Maria mumbled to no one in particular.

Continuing the theme, a faded and rusty white aluminum awning stretched from the roof out over a concrete patio. Sandblasted, crusty metal posts held it up. Underneath was a corroded and cobwebbed faded-black light fixture with one pane of glass broken. Maria assumed there was yard furniture somewhere but was not sure where that might be. The trailer had simple underpinning that hid the two-foot space between sand and floor that, on other mobile homes she'd passed on the way down, was filled with lawn mowers, metal lawn chairs, kids' toys, old dogs, and stray cats. Running alongside the underpinning was grass that had needed a good trimming years ago, a few stray flowers that begged for attention, and various oyster shells mixed with sand like bits of shrimp in creamy grits.

"Yummy," she mumbled sarcastically.

She took a deep breath and walked up to the metal door. She reached into her purse, took out the key with the faded and worn tag that read "Beach House," and inserted it into the crusty door lock.

"Here goes."

It took some force as corrosion, like arthritis, impeded the task, but finally, the jiggling key overcame the ravages of beach weather, and the doorknob turned with a scratchy squeak. The hinges, out of shape from years of neglect, warned the inside of the trailer that someone was entering. Feeling a swoosh of stuffy hot air, she paused. It was like the trailer had been holding its breath.

"Oh, there's the yard chairs!" she called out, staring at a pile of corroded aluminum frames and frayed webbing that would be a fine addition to the county dump. She hauled out the mess and parked it on the deck—"I'll get to you later"—and resumed her exploratory journey into the trailer.

Before her was a small living room—or was it a den?—and to her right was a short bar with two stools. Beyond that was a kitchen with windows on three sides, and to her left was a narrow hallway that led into the darker side of the trailer.

"Three bedrooms and a bath in that tight space?"

She set her pocketbook on a small empty plant stand, rested her hands on her hips, and wondered at the space. A well-worn carpet that seemed to have originated from the fifties. "Surely, it is not that old!" A simple vinyl sofa on plain legs. A small cloth chair under a cheap print of the Hatteras Lighthouse before it was moved to its new location. A corner lampstand complete with what could only be called a retro lamp, its pleated shade a blended mixture of aged brown and lingering white. And a tall, slim bookshelf full of worn beach-read paperbacks (judging from the titles) and old *National Geographic* magazines. To her right beside the plant stand rested what looked to be a TV stand, sans TV.

Above the bar were several shelves with beach decorations, mementos, trinkets, and a small stereo with a turntable and two speakers. She wandered into the kitchen and looked toward the built-in stove and matching refrigerator. Dark stained veneer cabinets outlined with lighter, almost yellow, trim wrapped around the kitchen, leaving a gap for the small window over the sink. An old AM radio stood sentinel on the scratched Formica countertop, guarding a layer of dust and an ancient two-slice toaster.

Memo: Need a microwave and air fryer.

Faded yellow polka-dot drapes allowed ample light into the kitchen from the windows that faced right, left, and toward the beach. The blurry view out front was of a large sand dune that had blown up from years of storms, hurricanes, and blustery beach days. To the right, maybe one hundred feet away, was a three-story modern beach mansion. To the left, three hundred feet away just beyond a thin patch of tall seagrass, was a smaller yet just as imposing house.

A clock, whose last gasp ended at 4:23 someday long ago, hung on the wall beside a small cork bulletin board covered with blotchy pieces of paper, business cards, three rusted tacks, and an old pizza take-out menu. Curiosity got the best of Maria, and she poked around in the cabinets. Thick plastic dinner plates of many colors were stacked beside matching saucers and bowls, along with small, large, and very tall cups and glasses, some that were obviously very old Mason and jelly jars people repurposed for glasses years ago. A set of salt and pepper shakers still wrapped in cellophane completed the contents.

In the other set of cabinets, she found sticky old rubber containers of sugar, flour, cornmeal, and something she could not identify from at least forty years ago. Beside them were pots, pans, lids, an iron skillet, an ancient cheese grater, an egg white separator, a juicer, and a very stale pack of Nabs.

Looks like this old trailer fed a lot of people back then!

Maria pulled out the drawers and found assorted styles of tableware, carving and paring knives, spatulas of various sizes, three ice cream scoops, two sets of measuring spoons, three bottle openers, handfuls of corncob sticks, skewers for the grill, a wine bottle opener, and a pizza slicer.

Do I dare open the fridge?

Prepared for a frozen monster to fly out, she slowly opened the door and saw a slight cloud of cold air escape and then stared at a single box of baking soda. The freezer revealed two lonely ice trays covered in frosty crystals ready for the next drink.

The coolness made her aware of the sweat covering her brow. "It's so stuffy in here. When's the last time this thing was opened?" She closed the fridge, reached over a chrome-framed chair, grabbed the gray window crank, and tried to open the louvered glass windows. It took two hands and a Herculean effort, but finally the taut crank broke free and forced the salted windowpanes outward. A burst of humid ocean air rushed inside. She cranked open the other two windows, breathed in, and then headed to the back, drapes behind her now flapping happily like Tibetan prayer flags.

The narrow, claustrophobic hallway to the back side of the trailer passed a small bedroom lit by a lone window, another bedroom that was dark with no windows, and a tiny hallway leading to a small bathroom and closet that held a washer and what looked like a heating unit. All ended with a large primary bedroom with another door facing the driveway. What appeared to be cheap wood paneling—it gave a bit if you leaned on it—covered all the walls.

After all Maria had been through the past year, it was just what the doctor ordered. "Home sweet home," she sighed. Finally, the old trailer had a new resident.

Tired of exploring, she opened all the windows to air out the trailer, removed a board that prevented the outside door in the bedroom from being broken into, and headed to the Land Cruiser. Three travel bags, four tote bags, and one suit bag later, the clothes she brought for the summer were piled on two beds. Toiletries deposited in the bathroom, she headed out once more and retrieved several bags of groceries and one cooler and filled the kitchen with her victuals and wares.

Sweat now dripped off her arms and down her legs.

Bottle of cold water in hand, she stepped out onto the patio, unfolded the one chair that looked stable, and plopped. "Finally."

Greensboro was behind her. The future would have to wait.

A few moments later, feeling more curious than refreshed, she set the bottle down and headed for the beach. The boardwalk leading from the trailer to the beach was an old structure that ascended over the tall dune before stepping back down to the shore. The slats across the wooden joists creaked under Maria's feet. Rusted nails had inched their way up, clawed by many summers of heat, now becoming hazards for unsuspecting toes and cheap flip-flops. Many slats were withered and cracked with age. All were worn, and two snapped when Maria stepped on them.

"One repair job," she muttered in a memo to herself. But the roar of the waves, the salt in the wind, and the heat from the sun sent that order to the bottom of her to-do list. On the sands below the dune were families who, presumably, had come from the public-access path that ran behind a line of tall seagrass behind the trailer. Sparkling waves roiled beyond that, and farther out, a lone fishing trawler chugged a path parallel to the beach.

It was a far cry from Maria's Appalachian youth. She had been to the beach a few times—once for a church youth trip, the other times with girlfriends on a lark or brief vacation—but overall, the beach was still something foreign to her. She just was never a lie-on-the-beach kind of gal. Used to hardwoods, mountain laurel, and twisting roads that took five miles to go one mile, she preferred small, gurgling streams and the soft whispers of the winds gliding over tall peaks for her vacations. The tidal sands and crashing surf were totally different. Very different. Very flat. And right now, it did not matter.

She took a deep breath and sighed again. "I can get used to this." It was more resignation than expectation.

She found a dry patch of sand and sat down, pulled her knees up to her chest, wrapped her arms around her legs, and inhaled. Reveling in the scene before her, she wondered what view Blane had outside his jail cell in the federal prison in Butner, North Carolina.

After a long stroll past squealing kids running from the waves, young girls with bikinis too teeny and cheeky, fat men with blaring red bellies, and occasional whiffs of cigarette smoke, all of which had been serenaded by beach music drifting from an old boom box, Maria realized her shoulders were a little sunburnt, so she reluctantly headed back to the metal relic that would be her home for the next chapter in her life.

As she stepped onto the patio, she spied a sparkling red beach bike—handlebars splayed out wide, a huge white cooler on the front, and a large metal basket on the back—heading down the road. The rider spotted her, slowed, and then wheeled into the driveway, dust from the sand flying in the westerly breeze. He hit the brakes, skidded to a stop, jumped off, stomped the kickstand down, and then walked over to her all business-like, taking his helmet off.

He was stocky, short, muscular, and covered with freckles from head to toe. His long red hair curled in various directions, and based on her knowledge of Irish history and culture, she figured maybe the curls came from his Irish genes on at least one side of the family. Or maybe they simply came from the wind as he cycled about the island. Unkempt but oddly professional, he looked fourteen, maybe fifteen. Maria felt a keen business sense was growing and emerging deep within him, an ability to see the future in many creative and productive ways. A can-do spirit generated an air of confidence that radiated all around him.

"Hi!" he called out. "You're new here, right?"

Maria cautiously stepped forward to greet the friendly stranger. "I am indeed. Who are you?"

He walked up to her, stuck his hand out, and answered, "Most people call me Reddy Freddy."

She saw a glint of something in his eye as she shook his hand. "But ... you would like to be called ...?"

"Frederick, ma'am." He paused. "They call me Reddy Freddy because of my red hair and freckles." His scrunched lips and raised eyebrows showed how embarrassed he was by the description.

"Frederick it is. I'm Maria Gowins. And yes, I'm new here. Just arrived a few hours ago."

"So this is the old Simpson trailer. Nobody's been here for years. Are you kin?" The spunky kid sure did know a lot about the place. Maybe too much? Maria wondered if he saw something in her eyes or on her face. *Quite observant for a teen*, she thought. He followed up his question with another one. "I guess that's a long story, right?"

Maria was caught off guard by how perceptive the kid was. "A very long story, Frederick." She paused and then moved along. "So what brings you by?"

Frederick reached into his pocket and pulled out a magnetic business card. "My mom owns the grocery store up the road. The One and Done. We do online orders too. If you need something, check out our website, call, or click, and I'll deliver."

His pluck was captivating indeed, an odd trait for someone of his …

"Frederick?"

"Yes, ma'am?"

"May I ask how old you are?"

Never pausing, he answered, "Fourteen."

"You are mighty enterprising for someone your age."

Frederick breathed in and told the story. After his father had died, his mother took over the family store. They weathered some storms, financially and meteorologically, but she was making a profit. The delivery aspect was Frederick's idea. After the COVID-19 scare, he realized they could deliver and still stay afloat. The idea caught on; they purchased two golf carts and hired two drivers, but Frederick was not old enough to drive one. So looking for a way to be helpful, he outfitted his bike with the basket and the cooler and now stayed busy, so much so that he was homeschooling so he could still help his mother. Vacationers didn't want to stop and run to the store. Locals took advantage of the time-saving service. They called or bought their supplies online, and he saved them a step.

"I'm not old enough to drive a golf cart on the road, but I can ride a bike! The tips are pretty good ... except for the man who lives there." He pointed to the mansion next door.

"Stingy, huh?" Maria asked.

"His wife looks younger than him, but when she pays the bill, she gives me a tip."

Maria admired him for his entrepreneurialism. "So," she wondered. "I bet you see a lot of cute young ladies in your deliveries."

Suddenly, Frederick's face soured a bit. "Yes, ma'am, but after a while, they all look and act the same. Some treat me like I have a disease. Others act like I don't exist or I'm not good enough for them. Sometimes they answer the door naked and then make fun of me." He paused to catch his breath. "Anyway, nobody wants a freckle-faced boy like me." He paused again, looked down at his feet, and then looked back at the mansion. "But she's different. She's nice. Wish she were my age."

Maria had to admit that his appearance, by the standards she'd grown up with, was a bit off-putting. And okay, he had some muscles from toting groceries and riding his bike, but he was not football-stud material or a surfer-dude bum all the girls wanted nowadays. But his smile was so endearing, and his manner was so mature, maybe girls his age just could not make the connection that he was a burgeoning, fine young man. She could see him owning a chain of grocery stores one day. "Well, when they grow up, they'll realize what a fine catch they missed!"

Frederick grinned widely. "Yes, ma'am, they will!" He pulled his helmet back on and hopped on his bike. Making the cell-phone hand gesture, he yelled out, "Call me, Ms. Gowins!" Frederick zipped off down the road, wondering to himself, *Does she know the story behind that trailer?*

Maria looked back across the driveway at the beach mansion. The white Mercedes SUV was immaculate, not a speck of dust on it. The mansion was as imposing as it was impressive. Concrete driveway, three stories, decks all around the first two floors, separate balconies for each room on the third floor, and what looked to be an elevator from the ground up. The yard was like the golf course at an expensive country club: manicured lawn, seagrass-trimmed edges, flowers, sprinklers. Spiffy hurricane shutters. Steps from the second-floor deck tracked down over the dunes to the beach.

"Can't wait to meet the neighbors," she sighed sarcastically. Money had brought her no happiness in Greensboro. Now she was right next door to it again.

She walked back into the trailer and noticed the temperature had not changed much, although the trailer had aired out. Oddly, the aluminum shell felt like it had relaxed a bit. "Hope there's an air conditioner in this thing." She found a thermostat on the hall wall, but there was no cool setting. "Not good." There were no air conditioner units in the windows either. She rummaged around and found a dusty, rusty oscillating fan and plugged it in. "It works!" She took it to the bedroom where she finished putting up her clothes.

Maria then looked at the bed. It was covered by an old, faded, worn quilt. She patted it, and dust rose up, inducing a brief sneezing fit. Holding her breath, she quickly took it off and headed to the door and tossed it onto the patio.

"Out with the old." Back to the bedroom, the sheets had been protected from dust by the quilt, but they were musty and smelled like the old spare bedroom in her grandma's farmhouse. Soon they accompanied the quilt on the patio. Maria worked her fresh sheets over the spongy mattress and then paused to look around.

"Okay, it's not a five-star in the Caribbean, but it'll do."

Then she fell backward on the bed and let the fan breeze cool her off. Soon she was sound asleep.

THREE

The Neighbors

On the second-story deck of the beach mansion, father and daughter leaned on the railing and stared in both open-eyed wonder and apprehension at the spiffy Land Cruiser parked by the eyesore trailer. The contrast between the modern SUV and worn aluminum hovel was too much, like parking the knight's majestic steed next to a peasant's shack. The quilt and sheets on the patio were the icing on the cake, reminding both of the ordinance back home against people putting ugly couches on their front porches.

"Well, at least now we know somebody actually owns that thing," lamented Jason, derisive disgust in his voice.

Bailey was not quite so quick to judge. But the messy bedclothes on the patio did measure high on her Yuck Scale. She wrapped a long arm around her father. "Father Mr. Jason Parker *Snob*," she responded.

The shadows of early evening were etching their way across the expansive deck. Jason Parker, with his financial-planner game face on, was in full form as the guests arrived.

Blue shorts, deck shoes, and a dark-pink pullover tee, all from upscale websites, highlighted his tanned legs and arms and allowed his trim muscles to advertise the results of his exercise regimen.

Bailey did her best to entertain, but at fourteen, she could not really relate to the adult strangers, most of whom mistakenly thought she was an adult as well. Dressed in a dark-red floral sundress that flowed to the floor, she drew looks from the men and nods, jealous and approving, from the women who stood around with drinks in hand, making small talk and trying desperately to one-up each other with their latest exploits, purchases, and travels. Two men stared more than looked, and some women wondered why Jason wanted such a young "thing" until they discovered Bailey was actually his daughter. Ever experimenting with hairstyles, she let a few locks of her long brown hair fall about her face and chest, and the rest was in a thick braid that cascaded down her back to her waist.

The party was actually a marketing ploy by Jason to gather potential clients. On a lark, he had run an ad in the local island's weekly online newsletter, and oddly, some vacationers responded. After a few drinks and hors d'oeuvres, he settled them down on the deck in the shade for his spiel. Bailey walked around, silently picking up plates, refreshing drinks, and pointing to the restrooms when necessary, all while trying to ignore the stares, glares, and occasional pick-up lines. After a brief video on the outdoor big screen, brochures were passed out, and then dinner was served buffet-style inside. The guests were free to sit about and relax as Jason worked the crowd like a politician at a pig picking.

Across the yard, Maria was in a stew. Fresh from her nap, she was about to make a sandwich, only to discover she needed some items from the store. When she stepped outside, she saw all the cars in her driveway and neighbor's driveway. "What the—" She caught herself. One promise she had made after the divorce was to watch her language as she created a new self. The stress, anger, and humiliation had led to a vocabulary that was violent, juvenile, and the envy of sailors. In therapy, she had addressed the issue. The only thing she could control, her therapist had taught her, were her reactions. "Breathe, Maria, breathe." She inhaled. *Five, four, three, two, one.*

Five vehicles were parked all around her SUV, not including the cars in the neighbor's drive. Even with four-wheel drive, she could not get out. She inhaled and exhaled again and then remembered Frederick. She pulled out the magnet he'd given her and saw the website. Now full of control, she rushed inside and pulled out her computer and opened it up but then realized she had no internet. "Blast." She dialed the One and Done number and talked to a raspy-voiced clerk who took her order after Maria explained she had no internet to order from.

"Can you send it by Frederick?"

The clerk's answer was yes.

A half hour later, Frederick pulled up and knocked on the door. "Hi, Ms. Gowins! Got your goodies!" He handed her a gallon of milk and two plastic bags. She handed him thirty dollars and told him to keep the change. You would have thought she'd given him the moon. "Thanks, Ms. Gowins!" He nodded to her and then hopped back on his bike. "Got another delivery to make!"

Crisis solved, Maria finished her home-delivery meal and then headed back to the beach. "What else can I do?" she complained. Then she chided herself. "Maria, millions of people would love to take a walk on the beach right now. What are you complaining about?" Attitude addressed, she sniffed the ocean air once more, lifting her arms then lowering them yoga-style as she exhaled, and took a step toward the salty, slightly fishy, therapeutic aroma that wafted from the other side of the dune.

The rhythm of the waves caught her eyes and ears. In and out, ebb and flow, wax and wane. Crash, thud, wash, ripple. Each receding wave seemed to flow under another incoming breaker. There was a somewhat steady beat to it all, but the beat seemed to be occasionally punctuated with syncopations that, in the long run, all came together in a relaxing vibe. Beach music, Bob Marley, and sea shanties all combined into one symphony.

Sanderlings raced after the receding waves, bills digging into the sand. Then they fled the incoming waves only to turn again and follow them out, bills digging once more. Worries soon faded into wonder as Maria lost herself in the tides.

Then she spied small, dark somethings occasionally emerge from the ocean. "What was that?" she called out loud.

Suddenly, the something jumped high and splashed back into the sea.

Dolphins! It was the first time she had ever seen a dolphin. Ever.

She stared in awe as the pod slowly worked its way southward, a spout of water and then a fin. Spout of water and another fin. Spouts of water and fins.

An affirmation of her new life?

Minutes later, spiritual moment over, she headed back to her new home, full of bright hope as the sun settled into the dark of rest.

As dinner ended, Jason clicked on the big screen on the outside wall over the bar, asked the guests to pull up their chairs, and began his second video presentation about how to set up financial planning to live well. Produced by a professional company, the presentation was like an extended movie trailer.

Bailey lit up the old-style, romantic citronella lamps to ward off the mosquitos as her father waited while people watched. She quietly cleaned up the deck and kitchen area as Jason finished his presentation.

"So folks, that's all. While you are here, enjoying Banker's Point, stop by and let's see what I can do for you. Or if you don't have time but want a great beach read"—he opened a box resting on the deck and dramatically pulled out a copy of his book and waved it around—"get a tan and learn about financial freedom!"

It was ten o'clock when the last guest, a loquacious blonde perhaps looking for more than financial security, wiggled enticingly down the steps, her heels clicking away. Bailey was tired, but she picked up the few remaining plastic wine glasses and half-empty beer bottles while her father tidied up the kitchen. When all was done, she sat out on the deck and listened to the ocean come and go. Jason scooted a chair over to her, and both breathed in.

"Bailey, you looked beautiful tonight. Thank you for your help." He leaned over and gave her a hug.

She enjoyed his attention and affection, but lately, she was not sure of his assurances of her beauty. In this stage of her life, with her new adolescent body, fourteen and beautiful meant boys saw her as nineteen and a challenge, men saw her as twenty-five and available, and women and girls saw her as a threat. She just wanted to be fourteen, but she could not think of a way to explain this to her father. "Daaaaaaad, two *men* asked me out tonight."

Jason suddenly perked up. "Told you, you were beautiful tonight." To him, it was a badge of honor for men to see his daughter as pretty.

Bailey was embarrassed and unsure of how to handle such come-ons. "It makes me feel uncomfortable, Dad."

Jason was caught off guard. It was a comment he was not used to hearing and, indeed, did not understand. Another step on the learning curve of being a single father to a fourteen-year-old daughter who had the sudden misfortune of looking twenty-five.

He stood up and motioned for her to come over to him. With no vocabulary to address the conflicted hormonal needs of his daughter, he resorted to the only thing left. He put his arm around her neck, sensing her insecurity, and tried, unsuccessfully, to be a father. "Honey, with your looks, I'm afraid you are just going to have to learn to live with it. We can't un-beautify ourselves, can we?"

Bailey giggled at the new word and looked him in the eyes. "Daaad, 'un-beautify' is not a wooord." Her response revealed an increasingly peculiar side of herself. She could host a party as well as any adult and, in the next instant, revert back to a goofy teenager.

Suddenly, Jason recalled how just a few months ago, she'd looked *up* to him. At fourteen now, she was becoming a woman. Six feet tall, long legs—now she looked directly *at* him. He hugged her close once more and then pushed her back. But in the dim light of the deck, he saw her eyes exude two emotions: one of a loving daughter and the other of fear.

She looked down at her breasts as if in shame. "Those men looked at them all night long." She broke out in tears. "Not at me, at *them*."

He sighed and thought, *This again*. How does a father talk to his teenage daughter about her breasts? He sighed again to himself and finally admitted what he had been loath to say. *Bailey needs a mom, and I need a wife.*

Inside the hot trailer, Maria rinsed off her salty skin in the small shower, dried off with a fluffy towel, and then lay down nude on the bed, the fan blowing warm, stuffy trailer air mixed with a slightly salty aroma all over her body. The beach walk had been good for her soul. Bare feet in the sand, connected with mother earth. The ocean air was like the soothing incense of aromatherapy. The evening sun warmed her like a heated massage. And the last squawks from the gulls were like the bird calls on a yoga CD ... kind of.

Enjoying the air wafting over her body, she recalled her time on the beach. She worked through her negative-positive beliefs to shift her way of thinking. She recalled the yin-yang symbol—the solar side of bright, warm, masculine yang contrasted with the lunar, dark, watery, mysterious, feminine yin. How each side of the symbol had a small hole. Black in white, white in black. Life could be sunny, but within that warmth was potential darkness, and vice versa. The balance of life. Life was not the dichotomy of good or evil. Life was up and down, left and right, inside out.

Like pondering the mystery of a guru's koan, Maria let the layers of her pain and anger fall away until she made sense of her moment. From big mansion, sunny, to small trailer, dark. Or was it the other way around? Was the beach a new chapter, a time of gestation, before birthing a new Maria? Or was the beach the sunny side, warmth and joy? She was learning that life was about *both/and*, not *either/or*.

In her mountain church, it had been about *either/or*. Live in heaven or burn in hell.

Despite the hot and humid air from the rusty fan, for the first time in three years, Maria slept like a baby.

Somewhere in her morning dream of Shemar Moore rescuing her from a demented creep, Maria heard a knock on the door. She shot out of bed, briskly shook her head, and then realized it was not Shemar at the door but a real person. She grabbed a pair of shorts and a shirt, brushed her hands through her bed head, and raced to the front door, hopping on one leg as she pulled on her shorts. When the third knock echoed in the den, she yanked open the door and nearly spooked the two people standing outside.

They saw a disheveled thirtysomething with messy hair, wrinkled shirt and very nonmatching shorts, and wild and bleary eyes, obviously seeing everything in a haze.

"Morning, neighbor!" Jason called out, almost apologetically. "Did we wake you?"

Ever alert for yet another sales opportunity, Jason had suggested that morning that he and Bailey go next door to meet the new neighbor. "We need some help finishing off the leftovers from last night anyway."

Bailey, remembering his comments about the poor people who owned "that trailer next door," had asked a very perceptive, sarcastic question: "Do you really think the *poor* people next door have any *money* to invest?"

Maria collected herself, then realized she must have looked like she'd just escaped the sanitorium. "Well, uh, yes, but, uh, no problem." She ran her hands through her hair once more. "What time is it anyway?"

Jason answered her question despite the awkwardness. "Around ten thirty. Maybe we should come back later …?"

Maria composed herself again and tried to make light of the situation. "No, no worries. I never sleep in this late. I must have been really tired. Where are my manners?" She stuck out her hand. "Maria Gowins."

Jason reached out and shook her hand. "Jason Parker. This is Bailey."

Maria quickly sized them up. They certainly fit her tainted stereotypes of the affluent crowd. He was handsome, in shape, tanned, with an air of sophistication, hints of gray in his dark, wavy hair, and a stubby beard. He wore a tight olive-green T-shirt, dark-brown shorts, and very nice flip-flops. And she … wow, what a trophy wife. She was gorgeous … and chesty. *Do they even make implants that big?* And, of course, her name is *Bailey*. It's always a cute name. Never boring like *Maria*. She wore leggings and a peach cold-shoulder top, and her pretty, long hair was braided on the right side, and on the left the loose strands were held with a nice little clip. Kind of an odd style for an adult though. Why do the trophy wives always look so good even without makeup?

"Good to meet you two! So what can I do for you?" Maria inwardly cringed at her overly friendly tone. She hadn't meant for it to sound so fake, as though she was trying to sell them insurance or a used car.

Jason looked at Bailey and then back at Maria. "Well, we had a little party here last night and had some leftovers. Come on over and join us for lunch. We would love to get to know you better, right, Bailey?"

She nodded slowly, as if she were three sentences behind the conversation.

These kind of men always speak for the trophy wife. "Sure!" she said. *I would love to tell you about the idiots in my driveway,* she thought to herself. "Let me get my act together. Will eleven thirty be okay?"

Jason affirmed the time. "Take the elevator up or just climb the steps to the second-floor deck. See you soon!"

Bailey waved a shy wave and put an arm around Jason as they walked away. Maria closed the door and frowned. *Big hair, big boobs, and ten years younger. Never fails.*

Looking down at her long feet as they headed to the beach house, Bailey chastised her father. "*See?* She was not wearing pink rollers in her hair or a long, faded gown with fuzzy orange slippers. And she had no gaps in her teeth."

"Point made, Bailey."

One shower, a pair of green shorts, and a bright-yellow blouse later, Maria, with her hair as in place as the summer humidity would allow, arrived on the second-floor deck. It did not surprise her that the deck was covered with expensive, all-weather, poly outdoor furniture. She spotted Bailey very, *very* meticulously arranging the food, seemingly to a set of invisible instructions, on a glass-topped table under a canopy that flapped in the breeze. "Hi, Ms. Gowins, thank you for coming over."

Maria wondered about the "Ms. Gowins" part. *Is she trying to make a statement here or showing off her youth?* "Hi, Bailey, thank you so much for inviting me over."

Bailey politely, if slowly—or was it hesitantly, or a Zen thing? Maria wasn't sure—pointed to a chair, motioned for Maria to have a seat, and then brought her a bottle of water.

"Such a nice place here, Bailey. So how long have you and Jason been married?" *Let's get this little mystery solved right now.*

Bailey looked over at Maria with an odd, sheepish grin. "Actually, he's my father, so I guess we have not been married too long." She smiled a shy smile and then continued. "I get that a lot."

Okay, Maria, time to cure your foot-in-mouth disease. "Oh my gosh, I'm so sorry! It's just that you don't ... well ..."

Bailey sat beside her on a chaise lounge, crossed her long legs, leaned forward, folding her arms across one knee, and sighed as if she were tired. "It's okay, Ms. Gowins. I'm kinda getting used to it."

Gulls screeched a welcomed, distracting call overhead in the silence.

Thankfully, Jason appeared before it dragged out too long. "Hey, you two getting to know each other?" Without waiting for a response, he clapped his hands together as if to give the impression he'd just made the meal appear out of thin air. "Who's hungry?"

As they enjoyed the disparate leftovers—crab dip, hummus and pita chips, shrimp and cocktail sauce, pasta salad, and slightly suspicious day-old selections from a fruit tray—served on red plastic plates in the shade of the third-deck overhang, something odd happened. Maybe it was the wine, the warm ocean winds, or the faint laughter of children playing in the surf over the dunes. Maybe it was the awkward grace of the pelicans heading wherever they headed to, the calming fragrance of sea salt, or the barely perceptible white noise of the waving sea oats. Maybe it was simply the adults feeling the need to explain the reasons for their highly contrasting beach domiciles. Whatever the case, the three strangers slightly opened up the doors to their past. Jason began by explaining how he and Bailey had moved to Banker's Point in January to start over after his divorce. He'd homeschooled Bailey after they'd moved and might continue to do so until Bailey felt comfortable going back to school.

While Maria could sympathize with Jason, she was still wary of men, especially those who exuded wealth. But she was mesmerized by beautiful Bailey, who had spent at least two minutes thoughtfully arranging the food on her plate into organized islands that did not touch. Now with three braids braided into one, she was predictably reticent in front of a total stranger, but Maria sensed that she wished to share her hurt over the divorce and had no adult woman to turn to for female guidance. Teacher Maria also surmised why Bailey hadn't really fit in with her peers at school. It was obvious she loved her father very much, and the feeling was mutual. It was also obvious to Maria that there was much more to Bailey than was visible on the surface.

Maria shifted a bit in the white Adirondack chair and breathed in deeply, but then decided it was not the right time to open up. How would they react if they knew she'd grown up in the western part of the North Carolina mountains? Did they really need to know how she'd met her husband at Appalachian State? Why she'd majored in education and history? His arrest? Instead, she focused on the obvious. "Well, I guess you're wondering about the trailer over there."

Bailey subtly rolled her eyes at Jason.

Maria gave the basic version. "A marriage—he turned out to be a louse—an ugly divorce, a few bucks of his money in the bank, and a rusty old beach trailer."

The trio was quiet for a brief moment, as if everyone had exhaled, and their personal shames and anxieties were blown away by the breeze.

"So," Maria said, shifting the conversation. "Jason, looks like I can use your services. I need to invest my settlement into some retirement accounts. Think you can help me out?"

Jason was glad his ploy had worked, and he wondered just how much money a woman in a dilapidated ocean trailer could have, but hey, everybody needed a retirement plan. He jumped at the chance, and they agreed to meet sometime in the following weeks.

As the conversation dwindled, Bailey looked at her father. "Daaaad," she drawled out. "Isn't there something *else*?" She motioned with her eyes at the trailer as she stood to clear the table.

"Yes, dear," he answered in a hen-pecked tone. He turned and faced Maria directly. "Bailey just reminded me that our folks last night parked in your driveway. My deepest apologies. I had used it before, thinking nobody ever stayed in the trailer. It won't happen again. I hope I can be forgiven."

Maria saw an opening, a way to take a jab at the tightwad man. "Why Jason, yes, you can be forgiven. Penance will be the following: From now on, when Frederick delivers your goodies from his store, you will pay him a good tip."

A wrinkled brow emerged on Jason's face. Now she knew more about her neighbor. She could tell that if there was one thing he did not like, it was people telling him what to do with his hard-earned money.

After putting the dirty dishes away, Bailey had emerged from indoors in time to hear Maria's request. "Told you, Daaaaad." She rolled her eyes at Maria and mouthed the word *cheap*.

Leaving the neighborly trait of tact behind, Maria's temper seeped in, stoked by Jason's jerkwad attitude. "He's a hardworking fella who needs to be rewarded for his pluck. He came up with the delivery idea on his own. You know, he actually sounds just like you, Jason."

Jason recalled Bailey's similar castigations. Now it was two women, allied into a feminine force, who were chastising him. After a thoughtful moment, wisely realizing he was vastly outnumbered, Jason surrendered.

Bailey picked up the rest of the food, and while she was inside, Maria stood and turned to look out over the ocean. It was so peaceful up on the deck.

Jason walked over to Maria, glancing between her and the door. "Can I ask a favor?" he whispered.

Maria was caught off guard to be asked such a question by this handsome man who had everything and the money to get even more. What on earth could he possibly want from her?

His face became serious, fatherly, concerned. "Bailey, she's ... I'm a man and ... well, you know, she's at the age where there are, uh, some things that I just—how do I put this?—don't feel comfortable talking about."

Maria knew what *things* he was talking about. The monthly visitor, bras that suddenly didn't fit, boys who thought they were men and, thus, deserved a look inside their date's clothes. Hormones, mood swings, tears from out of nowhere. Stomping feet, rolling eyes, and exasperated "whatevers." All-night texting. Maria had heard these worries in her private talks with female students and seen them in the classroom when she taught high school and even when she taught community college. The gossip at the country club was full of such talk as well. Also, Bailey was a tall and too-tempting twentysomething in a teen's body.

Bailey came back outside and sidled up to her father. Maria was happy to see that despite all they had been through and all that Bailey was experiencing, they were still close. It was a solid father-daughter relationship.

Maria let Jason's request settle a bit as they all quietly enjoyed the view. "Bailey?" she asked, still looking out over the ocean. "I'm here alone this summer, and I could use some girl talk to get me through. If you ever feel the same, let me know."

Bailey's big green eyes, for the first time, lit up ever so slightly. Something deep within her slowly worked itself through the twists and turns in her insecurities and inadequacies and emerged in a slight, cautious, tentative smile. "Hmm."

Maria took that as, "I'll be nice and seem interested, but you're an adult and, well, whatever."

With no clients to see after Maria's visit and all the details of the week settled, Jason relaxed into his office chair and leaned back. Curious, he opened up a browser and typed in *Maria Simpson* and then *Maria Gowins*. Okay, he was internet stalking, or maybe it was just curiosity killing the cat. Or was it something else entirely?

Two hours later, feeling overwhelmed, he closed out the browser.

Newspaper accounts, video clips from TV, an announcement about her new position at the community college. Social media was good and bad, depending on the topic and source.

Now he was more worried than curious.

"What on earth has moved in next door?" he asked aloud, sighing.

FOUR

Welcome to Banker's Point

Was that a neighborly interrogation or a sales pitch hidden in friendly conversation? Maria wondered as she headed out into the hot afternoon to cruise the island and run some errands. In an internet search before she left Greensboro, she had discovered Banker's Point Island was part of the Outer Banks barrier islands off the North Carolina coast. Two stories circulated on the origin of the island's name. One was about the old islanders, the Bankers, who lived a subsistence life on the island for two hundred years. Industrious, fiercely independent, and amazingly resilient, they were so poor that sometimes they would deliberately mislead passing ships with deceptive lights to make the merchants think they were safely offshore only to wreck on the shallow shoals and, thus, flood the beach with supplies, wooden planks, and other wreckage the people used to build their makeshift houses. The other story was that, in the fifties, after the island served its secret purpose for the military in World War II, several bankers bought up huge chunks of island land and developed it into a retirement village called Banker's Point.

Maria's inner historian surmised it was probably a little of both.

The island, accessed by a rusty old swing bridge, was shaped like a long oval or elongated ellipse that continued into a point, like a paramecium with a tail. The village was in the oval portion, and the tail was the long shoreline.

As she drove up Banker's Drive, Maria saw a sign advertising the local radio station. *Why not?* She clicked out of the satellite-radio bluegrass station and soon was wondering about this local station that seemed to play B-side music from odd bands and time periods.

Island vibe filling the vehicle, she took a right and headed out on Sandy Loop Road, which paralleled the ocean. For several miles, she saw the usual beach cottages, beach bungalows, and beach mansions with an occasional old beach trailer serving as the comma between two island-residence clauses. On her left were older and smaller structures that stood in antiquated protest of the modern predilection to ignore the insurance liabilities of hurricanes and build on the beach rather than safely back some distance from it. Occasionally, a small rustic business, store, or stand interrupted the flow of the residences on the left.

As she rounded the curve at the north shore point of the island, Maria headed south and found some modern houses interspersed with trailers like hers, facing the sound. Trendy coffee shops, restaurants with catchy nautical names, boutiques fancied up to attract specific clienteles, and sport-fishing docks lined this portion of Sandy Loop Road. One oddity suddenly caught her eye: All the trailers seemed to be about the same distance apart.

Now at the bottom of the island, she turned back onto Banker's Drive and headed north into the island's business district. Restaurants, a bank, the post office, the One and Done Grocery and Store—"That's where Frederick works!"—the fire, sheriff, and EMT stations, a health clinic, town hall, the community center, the library, a historic house museum, and even more businesses lined the drive. Bike and golf-cart rentals, fishing tackle stores, knickknack stores, a slushy bar, a walk-up sub sandwich restaurant, and one new-age energy boutique led the list of attractions for tourists, alongside go-karts, a kite shop, the obligatory ocean mini golf, two beachwear stores—one featuring saltwater taffy, the other seafoam candy—and a parasail and dive shop. The Beach Read Book Shop and an ice cream store separated three bikini boutiques, one of which was crudely named Cheeks and Thongs. *Seriously?* And looking out of place was the new Dollar General store.

Trucks of every size and make filled the parking lot of the deep-sea fishing businesses. Several stores—more like refurbished shacks—advertised fresh seafood, including crab boils, to go. A beach Christmas store featured original crab pot Christmas trees from Core Sound. It stood next to a duck decoy store and a small coastal museum. Several small hotels, B&Bs, and one out-of-place five-story hotel filled out the view. Sort of a confused mix of the entertainments of Nags Head and Topsail Island with the old-time feel of Ocracoke Island and Harker's Island.

Maria whipped into the post office parking lot.

Shelly—according to her employee name tag—with her gray hair and a tanned, worn face from many years on the island, helped Maria set up her post office box. "So you're gonna flip your zip, huh?"

Maria's facial expression must've spoken the word *clueless* because Shelly then added, "You know, moved here from there. Flipped the zip ... code."

"Oh, okay, I got it now," Maria said with a smile. At least, she had kind of gotten it. Sometimes she could be a bit of an airhead.

When Maria related where she lived now, Shelly paused. "Are you kin to the Simpsons?" Maria said no without offering any details, only explaining she had inherited the place after an ugly divorce settlement. "Doesn't surprise me. They were an odd family anyway, according to the island scuttlebutt." *Does she know the story?* Shelly then said, "Wait a minute, you already have a PO box."

That caught Maria by surprise. "Really?"

Shelly went to the back of the building and brought back a dusty box full of mail. "And you have mail!" She dumped the box on the counter, and a small plume of dust wafted about. Both women coughed and sneezed—Shelly into the air, and Maria into her elbow, as she had learned to do in a required health-safety video she had watched in elementary school—as they waved their hands to get the dust out of their faces.

Shelly explained that, in the past, the family wouldn't have been seen for several years. Then they'd just show up, complaining their mail had not been delivered, even though, legally, old mail was supposed to be tossed after a long absence. So the staff, rather than risk periodic tongue lashings, began tossing the mail into an old box. "There's only so much you can stuff into a PO box, so we just put it in here." Nobody had been in the old trailer in years. Many years. "It's weird though. They keep renewing the PO box. They send cash and a note to renew it. No signature."

Maria paid her bill to renew it in her name and grabbed the box. "Looks like I have some reading to do!"

One task checked off, she drove up to the bank with the difficult-to-pronounce name of Banker's Point Bank and Trust and rushed inside before the humid summer heat found her, like a cloud of gnats or hungry mosquitos. She was directed to a somewhat pretentious Mr. Burns in a bright corner office, where she could set up her new accounts. She advised him that she needed a checking account and two separate savings accounts. His eyebrows suddenly raised up as she handed him the check.

Maria wasn't fazed by Mr. Burns's incredulous yet skeptical expression. In the settlement, she had received over three million dollars. The house itself was worth nearly two. She took the other million and made sure the victims of her husband's ring received compensation. What was left over, she was now placing in the new accounts.

Mr. Burns gave her a look and asked, "You want a hundred thousand in checking, four hundred thousand in savings, and the rest in another account?"

She nodded, never batting an eye at his excitement and shock.

His hand shook as he placed the check on the desk and tried to type on the keyboard. He probably had never held that much money in his hands before. He looked back at the screen and noted the address once more. "Are you connected to the Simpsons by any chance?"

Maria, now frustrated with the "small-townth" degree of questioning, answered curtly, "Divorced from them." Her tone asked the silent question, *You got a problem with that?*

The accounts set up and Mr. Burns's hands now steady, he handed her a new check card fresh from the machine in a back room, which Maria stuffed into her pocketbook. As she rose to leave, she spotted a man with sandy-blond hair curling out from under his frayed and faded hat. Her post-divorce aversion to men suddenly went mute.

Oh my, what a cutie!

She then noticed his shirt advertised a local heating and air business. She briskly walked up to him, learned his name was Deke, and inquired about his services. "I don't want to take up any window space. Is there any way I can get some sort of air conditioning unit? You know, maybe like those you see on the travel trailers?

"You're in luck," Deke answered. "I had a cancellation this afternoon." He glanced down at his watch. "I can be there in thirty minutes." When she told him her address, he nodded and said, "Ah, the old Simpson trailer. My dad worked on that system years ago. I was just a tyke then."

"Great! I'll rush home to meet you," Maria said and then hurriedly walked away.

Deke muttered to himself, "Lord, I hope she isn't one of *them*."

Mr. Burns, overhearing him, nodded in agreement. "Lord help the island if she is."

A few hours later and details finalized, Cutie Deke headed out to his rusty truck, Maria following behind him with her purse. "Okay, my buddy will be here early in the morning to run the wiring. You're lucky he had a cancellation as well. I'll run over to the mainland tonight and pick up two units, one for the front and one for the bedroom area. You don't need to go any longer without something cool. Summer's been hot already, and we're just getting started. I'll be back tomorrow around noonish. I should have them running by suppertime." He added up the costs on his tablet and showed her the total. "I can take credit cards if you need to."

One swipe of her new card, and the transaction was done. Maria thanked him and then plopped into the aluminum chair on the patio as he drove away. "Now I need internet."

After resting for a few minutes, she walked next door, climbed the stairs, and rang the doorbell. Soon Jason was at the door and answering her inquiry about internet service.

Does he always look like those hunks in the cologne ads?

He handed her a card and noted the cable folks could probably tap into his line and save some installation costs. "In the meantime, here's my username and password. You can crib off of our Wi-Fi until yours gets installed." Maria thanked him and turned to go, but he continued. "I hope Bailey will accept your invitation to the girlie talk."

Before she caught herself, her inner feminist, a new empowerment that had arisen from her therapy, corrected Jason. "Let's call it girl talk. 'Girlie' sounds a bit, well, condescending."

Jason looked puzzled and then frowned, seemingly castigated. "I didn't know that."

"Now you do," she responded, inwardly wincing at her too-harsh tone. She tried to ameliorate the uncomfortable moment. "Sorry, didn't mean to sound so curt. Changes often mean a new vocabulary. And"—this was more to herself than to Jason—"a new awareness of inflections as well."

Jason looked lost. Awkward.

"Didn't mean to snap. Still touchy after the divorce. Anyway, thanks for the Wi-Fi."

Lesson over, Maria bounded down the steps, back to the trailer.

Jason watched as she crossed his lush, green yard to her brown weeds and into her trailer. He could clearly see she was still hurt and wary of men after her divorce. But … there was something strangely endearing about her abruptness. "Not my type." Although, for some reason, he watched her until she shut the door.

Internet connected for the moment, it was time to check out Jason Parker the Financial Planner. Utilizing her internet savvy to track down cheaters in her classes, Maria typed in several search words about Jason. Try as she might, she could find no dirt on the man. Nothing. There were ads for his seminars, a newsclip on the success of his book, and several mentions in noteworthy finance magazines. Several likes on his Facebook posts. Even an excellent rating on the Better Business Bureau website.

What about Bailey?

Maria found two news articles dated two years back that included Bailey's name with pics of her soccer team. Tournament winners in travel soccer. But there were plenty of people shaming and bullying her on social media. Interesting.

After a quick bologna and cheese with mayo sandwich for supper—*seriously, Maria?*—she put on faded shorts, a tank top, and a tennis visor and then went out to relax on the patio.

She pondered the disparity of her new life. She had money but wanted to live in this trailer. She had money but was enjoying the simplicity of bologna and cheese with mayo.

What is this self-imposed poverty about?

As best as she could figure, it was all about getting back to her real self, her pre-marriage self. She had never really been the HOA-community type. She and her husband fell into that life more at his bidding (and then hubris) than anything connected to her. The community-college gig kept her grounded in the lives of "real people," as she called her students. The kind of people she had grown up with. The kind of people she had begun to miss as the marriage grew weary.

And I'm gonna get back to the food I love!

Real food, country food, homemade food. The kind her grandmother, Gran, had made and Grumps (who was always grumpy) had loved. Maria smiled to herself as she recalled breakfasts on the screened-in porch back home. She could still smell the country ham and red-eye gravy. Then she thought about the recipes she had brought with her in the worn notebook Gran had given her after the divorce. Corn pudding, real mashed potatoes—the kind you make with a mixer—and Brunswick stew.

Cracklin' bread!

Full of bologna and cheese with mayo, Maria was lulled to sleep by the rhythm of the ocean waves, and when she awoke, it was long past her usual bedtime.

The second night in the trailer was an odd one. Maria suddenly awoke to what sounded like a young person crying. Curious, she walked about the trailer, her bare feet scuffling along the old carpet, and then outside to look around. Maybe a child had wandered off and then got lost on the beach path by the trailer. Finding nothing, she went back inside, remembering to wipe the sand off her feet. As she passed the first bedroom, she felt a sudden swoosh of very cold air that raised goosebumps on her bare arms. "Odd," she remarked to herself as she rubbed her arms for warmth. The windows were all open, and a stiff breeze was stirring outside from a cold front that had passed through during the night. Maria passed off the strange phenomena as an oddity of the metal trailer and new meteorological effects at the beach she was not quite used to yet. "Oh well," she said with a shrug.

After an hour of listening to the creaks and cracks of the aluminum skin on the trailer, she drifted off back to sleep.

FIVE

Home Sweet Home

Someone knocked on the door the next morning, and Maria raised an eyebrow while the other eye stayed closed, still wanting to sleep. Another knock on the door, and both eyes shot open. "Oh my God, what time is it?" She grabbed her phone. It read seven ten.

The electrician!

She bolted out of bed, pulled on a shirt and shorts at seemingly the same time as she hopped down the hall, first on one foot and then on the other, calling out, "Just a minute!" Still pulling her shirt down, she fiddled with unlocking the door and then threw it open. The person before her was a tanned and wiry young temptation who was probably wondering what, exactly, he had just awakened.

"Morning, uh,"—he looked at his notes—"Ms. Gowins?"

"Guilty!" she answered, hoping she had buttoned her shorts. Her sleepy brain couldn't remember.

"I hope I didn't wake you. Deke said he needed some wire run for two roof air conditioners?"

As he unloaded his truck, Maria realized that there would be no electricity for a while, which meant no morning shower, and the trailer would be useless for most of the day.

Thank goodness I took a rinse last night.

Frustrated that the electrician needed free reign over the trailer, she headed to the beach in a huff. Feeling out of control, she centered herself, calmed down, and waited for her temper to recede.

Air conditioning is a good thing, Maria.

In front of her, the breakers rose, waved, then crashed onto the beach. For some reason, it reminded her of a child shouting, "Look at me! See what I just did?"

Noise. The beach was all just noise.

It was so unlike the mountains—or even the gated community—she had left behind. She recalled the tapestries of colors that had draped the hills and valleys: the summer greens that slowly turned into a fall palette of brown, crimson, orange, and yellow against a background of dark evergreens. She thought of how the day "began" at ten and "ended" at three because the sun rose late over the mountain and settled early behind it, leaving the valley bereft of a full day's sunlight. The days when she stood on a mountain in the morning and could look down at the fog blanketing the sleepy valley below and up at the thick clouds, feeling mystically sandwiched in between. Then there was the utter, deep mystery, the odd kind of silence of the wind that filled her soul with a renewed spirit as she sat on top of the world. Add the hardscrabble life, the humbling simplicity built on the dirt floor of antiquated ethnic ways, supported by the stones of the slopes and creeks. Fried apple pies, sorghum molasses on buttermilk biscuits, salty ham, apple cider with a kick, and corn stored in Mason jars. Sweet, homegrown music: ballads, tales, reels, and hornpipes with guitars, fiddles, dulcimers, and zithers. Little white churches everywhere.

That had been her spirit world.

She stared at the ocean for what seemed like hours, and then, breathing in and out, slowly, deeply, she began walking in incremental steps to see the colors of the crystalline sea, like the rainbowed brilliance of a sapphire stone. Settled down, bottom on the wet sand, unbothered by the beachgoers, she began her studies in the class of Ocean 101.

The colors were somewhat muted: brown at the shore, then a perplexing ebb and flow of green, aqua, and dark blue. But then, based on how the sun shone and where the clouds shifted, variations of those colors reminded Maria of jewels, such as lapis, amethyst, turquoise, and emerald. Soon she would learn that ghost ships and spirits haunted the islanders, like the haints that spooked the mountain folk. The beach, the island, had its own version of folk music. Given the flatness of the island, "day" began long before sunrise, and "night" arrived long after sunset.

There were many lessons to be learned. To quench her stress, Maria reminded herself this was just the first day of class. The waves rushed in and receded, sanderlings hard at work, and she realized it was oddly comforting, a rhythmic kind of white noise that brought a soothing peace to a troubled soul, much like the slow babbles of a cool mountain creek.

As two college-age girls walked by, tiny bikinis, svelte bodies, and dark tans calling all boys, Maria wondered what it would be like to be a gorgeous, mythical mermaid rising from the ocean, the hero in the movie reaching out to her.

Ha! Mermaids are a woman's body on a fish tail. Probably slimy.

A growling tummy reminded Maria she had not had breakfast, so she headed back to the trailer. The electrician—*did I ever get his name?*—was in a sweat as she arrived.

"How's it going?" she asked. "Looks like you might be a while."

He stopped and wiped his brow. "Yeah, sorry about that." Then it must've dawned on him that Maria hadn't eaten yet because he added, "If you're hungry, try that coffee place up the road. Lots of women go there. They have that foo-foo coffee and spiffy food that you ladies like."

Before she could catch herself, she shot back, "Some of us *ladies* like grits, sausage, eggs, and gravy biscuits, you know."

He sheepishly tightened his tool belt, took off his dusty cap, and combed a dirty hand through his way-too-enticing curly black hair. "Sorry, my girlfriend gets on me about that."

"Smart girlfriend." Maria got her purse and headed out. "You got my number if you need me."

The Beach Brew was on the left, going up north on Sandy Loop Road. It was more like a shack on the outside with weathered boards and a conspicuously fresh, new, out-of-place deck. A creaking wooden screen door led inside to a décor that was an odd mix of rustic and contemporary, seemingly pieced together after a trip to Goodwill and several yard sales. Tall, mismatched, iron-legged tables with chrome barstools stood in the center of the store, encircled by old-style wooden booths with cushions and tables that looked like refurbished picnic tables. Black-and-white island pictures from yesteryear covered the walls between expansive windows and faded pleated drapes. There were, indeed, many ladies inside, along with one very lost-looking man and two tables with teen girls trying to look adult-like with their cappuccinos and lattes and smartphones.

The menu was expansive—quiche, wraps, bagels, muffins, and plant-based meats on biscuits, brioche buns, and avocado wheat toast. Baguettes this and baguettes that. Gluten-free options were everywhere. On the bulletin board, cards advertised Reiki sessions, tanning salons, massages, and spiritual energy trails and sessions.

The electrician had been right. This was definitely a place for those who were more in touch with their feminine side.

With her plant-based sausage baguette and raspberry-banana smoothie in hand, Maria found a table outside, shaded by an umbrella laced with short tears and small perforations. She took a bite—*hmm, not bad!*—and looked down at her shorts before quickly crossing her legs and turning sideways away from the porch steps and the main road in embarrassment. At first, she was humiliated, but then she laughed out loud. In the rush of waking up, distracted by the romance of the beach and lost in thought, she had forgotten to put on underwear.

How did I miss that?

Breakfast done, emboldened for no reason other than she could not go home and change with the electrician still there, Maria decided to make the best of things and explore some more. She drove up the road, took the first left, turned right on Banker's Drive, which seemed more sand than asphalt, and found Frederick's store.

The One and Done was bigger than she had imagined. Behind the long front porch with sample Adirondack chairs for sale were two sections divided by the entranceway. On the left was the grocery, and on the right was hardware and basic goods. Maria strolled around the aisles, making mental notes of what was available. It seemed like the place had all the hardware anyone could need. Everyday goods like simple clothes—*no underwear, of course*—pots and pans, and cleaning items. The fishing section was obviously extensive. She headed to the grocery area and perused the shelves, familiarizing herself with the wares. Then she stopped at a bookshelf with local books and a few beach reads. There were several local histories, collections of ghost tales, the obligatory Blackbeard tome, one book on coastal birds, and another on how to tie knots. She picked up the one about the history of Banker's Point Island and flipped through the pages.

"That's a good one, but it's old," a voice said from behind.

Maria turned around and saw a red-haired, freckled woman with a smock on. Her name tag said *Fredericka*. "You must be Frederick's mother," Maria said with a smile.

"That would be me," she answered. Reading glasses rested on the edge of her nose, held in place by a rope chain. Except for her freckles, she was otherwise nondescript. Her eyes were fierce, and her demeanor was intense. Yet there was clearly an easygoing interest in her customers. It was obvious where Frederick got his drive from.

Maria held out her hand. "I'm Maria Gowins."

"I've heard," Fredericka replied as they shook hands. "My little Frederick was quite impressed with you." She winked and leaned in closer. "I think it was the generous tip. Thank you for that."

Fredericka related the history of the store, her family, and the rough times they'd had after the death of her husband. "Frederick took it hard, and he has worked overtime ever since. I wish I could get him to slow down, but he thinks we will go under if he slacks off. So I let him work." She paused and then switched gears. "That's a nice little book on the island, but it's thirty years old. Written by a descendant of one of the original bankers. We could use a new one. Maybe one day, someone will write one. Frederick loves the history of this place. He listens to the old people all the time when he makes deliveries. He's full of stories. He should write one, huh?"

Maria's inner historian woke up. "Well, I would love to record his stories one day. Do you think he could take some time off from work?"

Fredericka took her glasses off. "Honestly, he doesn't need to work at all. I'll give him a nudge and let you take it from there. He's a talker!" She put her glasses back on. "Gotta go. The truck comes in soon, and we have a big order to unload."

Like mother like son.

Maria picked up all the local history and ghost tale books, one beach read, and an *Our State* magazine and headed to the register. On her way out, she picked up the free *Coaster* magazine and a real estate flyer on the racks outside on the porch.

Jason and Bailey were heading to the Mercedes for a quick trip back to Greenville to finish up some business when Maria arrived back at the trailer. The electrician was cleaning up, and Deke's truck was parked in the driveway as well. A battered and paint-splattered extension ladder leaned against the trailer, and Deke was about to haul tools and a saw up to the roof. He paused to discuss details with Maria. He would have to cut two holes in the roof, line up the two units, caulk the holes, and then connect the wiring. There would be a mess inside to clean up afterward. He was pretty sure he would be done by suppertime.

Jason called to her. "Maria, looks like a construction zone over there!" He strode over to her, confidence in every step.

He looked so good it was almost unfair. He was muscular in a nice way ... okay, a *sexy* way. He didn't have bulging muscles like the self-possessed lunks at the gym, but it seemed like every muscle he had was perfectly in view. *Striated* was the word Maria had been looking for when she first met him. His dark-brown hair had a bit of a curl to it. Perfect teeth. In fact, everything about him was perfect. Except for his slight arrogant streak that jumped out like an obnoxious yard dog now and then. *Okay, I could live with the body. The rest? Nope.*

"We're heading out for the day. Keep an eye on the place if you will," he said with a laugh. Then he paused. "Wait a minute. You didn't have air the last two nights? You should have said something." He pulled his keys out of his pocket, took one off the ring, and handed it to her. "A key to our place, just in case. Make yourself at home. TV, food, deck. Cool off. Whatever."

There was that generous side of him too. He couldn't do enough for you. And that was *very* attractive.

"Thank you, Jason, but—"

"Now, now," he interrupted, palm facing her. "I don't want that independent-woman thing here. Please, just let me be a good neighbor."

Letting people help her when they didn't need to was another thing on her psychological bucket list she was working on.

Deke called out. "Ms. Gowins, I need you for a second!"

She quickly thanked Jason and then turned around. "On my way, Deke."

"This is not that hard!" She stomped her foot on the floor with a growl-shout. "ARG!"

It had taken Maria an hour to find the vacuum cleaner in Jason's mansion. She looked in closets, rooms, and the storage shed only to find it in what she'd thought was Bailey's room at the end of a makeshift cul-de-sac—piles of clothes in a corner with three changes of clothes hanging on the handle. She then hauled it to the trailer to clean up what Deke's Shop-Vac had left behind. He'd done an admirable job, but it did not meet the Mary Poppins standards. So here she was, trying to finish up what a man had started.

At least the air is cool!

When she'd tried to plug in the vacuum, she discovered the outlets were the old two-pronged kind instead of three. A frantic call to Fredrick's store and one quick delivery later, she now had several three-prong adapters, a long orange power cord, one vacuum plugged in, and still no power because she couldn't find the blooming switch!

Frederick stood to the side as she cried out, "What am I doing *wrong*?"

There was a long pause. "Ms. Gowins," he answered, choosing his words carefully. "I think you're freaking out too much."

Maria turned from the vacuum to Frederick to give him a piece of her mind, but suddenly, she realized he was right. Even in his young age, his wisdom was quite abundant.

"Yes, I know. You're quite right." She breathed, composed herself, slowed down, and then started again. "Frederick, where do you think the switch is?"

He perused the upscale German-engineered device in front of him that did not, in any way, resemble what most people would consider a vacuum cleaner. He looked from top to bottom, left to right, front to back. "It should be on the handle somewhere, right?"

"That would be the logical place, wouldn't it?"

"Yes, ma'am." He ran his hands over the handle, moving down to the wheels. There, in the empty place where the cord tied around two hooks, was the nearly invisible switch. He clicked it, and the machine came to life. "Problem solved, Ms. Gowins!" he called out over the noise. He stepped back and crossed his arms with an air of satisfaction.

"Frederick, you're a genius!"

He grinned and looked down in mock embarrassment, then looked back up. "Yes, ma'am, I am!" He beamed that Frederick smile that Maria was coming to adore. "Well, with that fixed, I gotta go now, Ms. Gowins!"

Carpet cleaned to Maria's satisfaction, dust off the shelves and furniture, and another bologna and cheese with mayo sandwich consumed, it was time for a quiet evening by the beach. Lungs full of salty air, covered with a fine layer of briny spray, and wineglass in hand, Maria settled into a chair under the awning and relaxed. She was beginning to understand the island vibe, the flow of life here, the rhythms of the ocean, the voice of the waves, and the heat. However, it would take a while longer to adjust to the humidity and the seemingly ever-present film of sweaty dirt on her skin. She just had to tolerate the constant sticky feeling of the summer.

It was like the rust on everything or the salt corrosion and the awful drinking water.

"Ugh," she moaned sadly to herself. *The drinking water.* It had that odd, alkaline taste. Nothing like the spring water from deep in a mountain. Her inner Earth Day said no bottled water. There were enough bottles in the ocean. "I'll just have to get used to it," she said with a sigh.

Beside her sat the box of letters from the post office. With things now settled in the beach trailer, it was time to see what this was about. She took the first one off the top and looked at the envelope. No return address. Just a Raleigh postmark from March 23, 2022. She carefully ripped open the envelope and pulled out a handwritten letter.

Dear Trailer,

I hope you are doing fine. I was thinking of you today, so I thought I would write. I miss the sand and the sun. I miss the cookouts and shrimp on the grill. I miss the bonfires on the beach at night. Remember the sea turtle? Rabbit in the hole?

Mostly, I miss Peter Rabbit. I hope you are taking good care of him for me. Tell him I said hello.

—Miss Missy

Maria shook her head and reread the letter three more times, trying to make sense of it. "What on earth?" She reached for the next one, postmarked four months before, and read it aloud.

Dear Trailer,

I was walking outside today, and the sunshine made me think of you. I heard there was a storm. Are you okay? Did the sand hurt when it blew on your skin? I remember a storm when I was there one summer. The sand hurt!

Is Peter Rabbit okay? I know it hurts when he comes out of the hole. I hope the storm did not hurt him. Please check on him for me. Thanks.

—*Miss Missy*

Letter after letter rambled on in the same innocent, almost childlike manner. But each one mentioned Peter Rabbit and some allusion to a rabbit in a hole. Whoever Miss Missy was, did she have a pet rabbit on the beach? Did Banker's Point Island even have rabbits?

Memo: Ask locals about rabbits.

Growing bored of the repetitive letters, Maria carefully replaced them in order back inside the box so she could resume where she'd stopped at a later date. In the meantime, she flipped through the *Coaster* magazine, looking for places to shop and eat.

The next day, at the Beach Brew—*underwear, check!*—Maria sat outside on the deck and watched the tourists saunter by. Being from Greensboro, she was not used to the people the locals called *foreigners*. As a child, she had seen them around the old stores and at the usual mountain parks, overlooks, and restaurants. But here at the beach, they seemed a different breed altogether. Oblivious, giddy, often rude, condescending. Of course, some were polite and respectful, but there was an edge to many of them. She had to remind herself she was a "foreigner" as well.

The last three days had been filled with cleaning up the trailer, organizing everything, and getting used to living in less than one thousand square feet rather than several thousand. Windows scrubbed and cleaned, inside and out, carpet deep cleaned with the rug machine from the Dollar General, linoleum floor now shiny, kitchen cabinets wiped, some stained plates and utensils tossed away, dry and canned goods put in their place, cobwebs cleared from the closets and corners of the ceilings. All was coming together. A quick trip to the big city on the mainland landed new sheets and curtains, a microwave and air fryer, some organizers, an ordinary vacuum with an obvious switch, and a big-screen TV that, after another day's wait, was finally hooked up to cable.

The small bath had been a little rough, but a double dose of all-purpose cleaner, spray-foam bubbles, and two scrub pads later, it was full of shine. The bright shower curtain with seashells lit up the room. She replaced all the lightbulbs with new low-wattage LED bulbs. The guest bedrooms were spiffed up with bright new sheets—pictures or wall hangings and decorations would come later—and the primary bedroom was nearly *Southern Living* perfect.

Okay, maybe not.

Anyway, today was Maria's day to pamper herself.

The sun was warm, but soon it would be crazy hot. Under the faded-blue umbrella, Maria sipped her iced mocha and pondered the day. The ocean breeze was so comforting, like sheer, cool silk all over her. Pampered by Mother Nature and calmed by the embrace of Old Man Sea, she was finally beginning to relax.

"Third time this week."

Maria looked up and saw a somewhat wild-maned woman with a beach tan standing over her. She was wearing faded-green shorts with a matching blouse and cheap foam flip-flops, had dirty polished toenails, and looked about fiftyish.

"You've been here three times this week. Thanks for the patronage!" The woman took a seat across from Maria. "That means you're not really a tourist—they move about and sample everything—but since I don't know you well, you must have just moved here."

Maria was not sure how to respond, but her face probably said it all.

"Anyway, I'm Tara. I own the place."

Maria introduced herself and took a cautious sip of her drink.

"Oh," Tara answered. "Are you the one in the old Simpson trailer?"

Before Maria could reply, Frederick skidded into the parking lot, jumped off his bike, and raced up to Tara. "Here you go! Two cartons of cream."

Tara reached into her pockets and pulled out a wad of bills. "Thank you, Reddy Freddy, and keep the change!"

"Thanks, Miss Tara. Oh, hey, Ms. Gowins! Gotta go!"

As he sped away, Tara looked at Maria. "Have you met Reddy Freddy yet?"

Maria nodded and took another sip. "Yup, Frederick found me the first day I moved in. He's an enterprising young man."

"He works too hard," Tara corrected.

Maria raised an eyebrow. "I'm guessing there's a story there?"

Tara nodded. "He probably told you about his mom, the store, his dad, and the delivery spiel?"

The umbrella flapped noisily, agitated by a sudden gust. A small bank of clouds covered the deck with a brief shady respite from the heat. "Hmm," Maria hummed thoughtfully. "Do I hear another version of Frederick's life coming?"

Tara recrossed her thin tanned legs and leaned forward a bit, as if sharing a secret. "When his father died, we all noticed a change in Reddy Freddy. He became serious, as if he had to be the father and husband and store owner all in one. That's a lot for a teenager. He works hard—too hard if you ask me—and I think that's his way of replacing his father, of keeping him alive, so to speak."

"I see." Maria sat back and continued to slowly drink from her cup. "By the way, good brew here, Tara."

Tara thanked her for the compliment. "Imported beans, responsibly sourced from small family farms, so they get more attention and less pesticides."

Maria thought some more as she turned the cup in her hands, savored the last drop, and then rolled the bottom of her cup around and around the weathered and splintered tabletop. Tara's view of events sounded just like what Fredericka had related. "So he doesn't have to work that hard, but he makes it sound like, if he doesn't work, the place would go under?"

Tara nodded. "The store is doing great. Stays busy all the time, even with the competition that just moved in at the far end of the island. His mom does an excellent job stocking. She has a knack for knowing what tourists need, you know? The staff is friendly. Everything's running smoothly, but Reddy Freddy has convinced himself that his mother and the store need him to survive. Again, all in an attempt to keep his father alive."

Maria stopped twirling her empty cup and set it on the table. "You sound like a psychologist."

"Nailed me," Tara confessed. "Twenty-five years of asking people how something made them feel. After a vacay down here, I decided that I could do better serving a cup of joe and having a nice, normal conversation. Toss in some mindset rethinking, some Buddhism and Taoism, and a prescription of coffees, smoothies, and wholesome snacks in an office with sun for light and a breeze for air conditioning and watch their attitudes change."

Maria nodded, already feeling better after a cup. Tibetan prayer flags flapped in the breeze. It was then she noticed the spirit tree limbed with multicolored bottles standing by the deck.

"So how long have you been a teacher?" Tara asked.

Maria raised an eyebrow. "That obvious, huh?"

Tara shrugged. "Most of my clients were teachers."

Maria smiled, relaxed, and then asked, "What's the deal with the Simpson trailer?"

Tara, not quite ready to spook a new resident who seemed to be a genuine addition to the Banker's Point citizenry, deflected the question. "Let me show you something. Come inside for a minute."

On the back wall—underneath a weathered sign that read **FISHERY →**—were several photographs of a nearly barren Banker's Point Island. Tara perused them until she saw the one she remembered. "Look at this one."

Maria moved closer for a better look and then stepped back. "Is that mine?"

Tara nodded affirmatively. "Look how far out the ocean is from it." As if reciting from a textbook, she commented about how the ocean was taking over the beaches in a way that made it seem as though the seas had been robbed of their sands. "Look at the old car beside it. And there's no Parker Palace either."

Maria leaned back in for another closer look. The trailer was surrounded by a nice garden. Shrubs stood in pots on the corners of the patio. A wrought-iron table and chairs were under the awning.

About that time, someone hollered out, "Need the cream *today*, Tara!"

"The answer to your previous question, my dear, will have to wait until the next session," Tara said. As she walked away, she wondered to herself, *Does Maria know what she's gotten herself into?*

SIX

Fourteen

Maria stood in the kitchen in the quiet of the morning and listened to the clicks of the aluminum trailer shell as it expanded with the new morning's heat. Those freaking clicks. All night long, off and on, she heard clicks and taps and what seemed to be the very quiet sound of drawers closing. She was obviously still not quite at home in the trailer. "Not as solid as my brick home back in G-boro, that's for sure."

She thought about her new neighbors. For the last several days, Bailey had shown up at different hours of the day to check on her. It was like a stray kitten coming up the back porch, wanting food but still shy and skittish of the one handing her the bowl of milk. "Father Mr. Jason Parker wants to know if everything is okay," she'd say. "If you need anything." The very fact that Jason was concerned about his new neighbor brought an unseen smile to Maria's still-hurting heart. *Why does he care about me? I'm just the new girl on the block. He doesn't even know me well.* It was a far cry from her ex-husband. And something about Jason's attention to her needs was very welcoming, inviting, desirable.

Maria was also beginning to see that Bailey had a quiet, subtle humorous side. After a few visits, Maria had taken a dare and mimicked it back one day. "Thank you for asking, Bailey. Tell Neighbor Mr. Jason Parker that all is fine."

Bailey had laughed, waved shyly, and began to walk away before turning back around. "Ms. Gowins, can I see the inside of your trailer? I've never been in one."

After a brief tour—it was only so big, after all—Maria had invited Bailey to sit awhile. Bailey's eyes grew wide at the invitation. It would mean sitting on old vinyl furniture, and clearly she was not sure about that. "Never seen vinyl chairs and Formica countertops and tables before, huh?" Maria confirmed.

Bailey smiled cautiously.

"We had these where I grew up." Maria sat down in the kitchen and patted the chair next to her.

Seeing that everything seemed safe, Bailey wiped off the chair (just in case) and settled down. "Where was that, Ms. Gowins? Where did you grow up?"

Ah, a breakthrough, Maria thought. "In the mountains, somewhere west of Boone. My grandmother had this kind of furniture, so it's kind of like moving back home."

Bailey took it in and then seemed to buffer a bit. Then her face assumed a slight "eww" look. "So this is your new *home*?"

Maria answered yes.

"It's kind of small."

Maria had then realized that Bailey had never been poor nor seen a middle-class house others would call "normal."

Maria smiled as she recalled that first real encounter with Bailey. Sometimes, Maria would spot Bailey on the deck looking over at the trailer, as if wanting to visit but not sure if she should.

One time, Maria had made up an excuse to see her, so she walked over to visit with the shy teen. "Bailey, can I borrow a cup of sugar?"

The next time, Maria had called out to Bailey and gotten a wave. Encouraged by the gesture, Maria invited her to go shopping, but Bailey just thanked her and said no. Maria didn't take it to heart since Bailey's clothes had always seemed to say, *Don't look at me.*

One evening, Maria had looked out and saw the Mercedes gone, but Bailey was standing on the deck alone. Maria walked over and stood by Bailey who seemed to be miles away. "Bailey, are you home alone?"

"Dad's out on a date or something." She'd rolled her eyes, but they looked teary, and her face was sad.

Maria had seen an opening. "You up for a pizza? We can get one delivered."

After a few silent minutes, Bailey's loneliness had overcome her shyness, and her cautious eyes slightly lit up. "I'm kind of picky."

The pepperoni and extra-cheese pizza had arrived forty-five minutes later. Pepperoni on one side, extra cheese on the other. Precisely cut into six slices. The conversation was slow, sometimes tedious, like pulling teeth, but Maria coaxed out some simple talk. Once the pizza was finished, Maria, not wanting to wear out her welcome, said she needed to head back to the trailer. "Feel free to stop by anytime, Bailey."

As Maria turned to leave, Bailey had called out, "Thanks for the pizza, Ms. Gowins!"

Maria decided on another metaphor: Bailey was like a shy dog who needed some space to figure out if it was safe to be petted. She remembered Robert Redford in *The Horse Whisperer,* who sat in the corral all day until the wild yet shy horse finally gave in to curiosity and came up and stood by him.

Patience, Maria. It was another trait to develop in her therapy. Bailey was certainly good for that.

The next morning, Maria rose much earlier than usual. She took her favorite ugly-face Seagrove pottery mug out of the single-cup coffee maker, stirred in sugar and real cream, and headed to the door. Outside, she settled into her new Adirondak chair on the patio, cup of brew in her hand, the morning sunshine teasing the island awake. She sipped and smiled. *Just right.*

A sudden noise caught her attention, and she glanced over at the Parker Palace, as she now referred to it. Remembering Jason had been on a date last night, she figured he had probably arrived back late. *Maybe that was what I was hearing during the night?*

She saw Jason in the carport under the mansion. *Oh my.* While there was something off-putting about him, she had to admit there was also something that seemed promising, inviting, and … okay, attractive.

What she was witnessing now did not help.

Jason was stretching, leaning over, and touching his toes. The flimsy (and quite short) gray running shorts induced another *oh my.* Then he used his left arm to pull his right one across his chest, then vice versa.

He was also shirtless, his body way too enticing.

That body. *Oh. My.*

Jason was obviously in shape ... *very* good shape! Taut, wiry muscles called out to her from his lean frame. He turned and looked out to the road but did not see Maria staring at him. His core was not that impressive—a tight six-pack that could be gained via a muscle pill, according to the ads—but it was indeed strong, *abs*olutely strong. His chest exuded ... Maria couldn't find the right vocabulary—she would need a sexy thesaurus—but his pecs could tantalizingly fill out a tight T-shirt. He was not a bulky meathead from the gym, but every muscle, tendon, and ligament was defined under his summer tan.

No, he's ... what is he? Does it matter, Maria?

As he flexed and stretched, each awakened muscle continued calling her name like a siren. His legs, taut and sinewy, rippled with a subdued strength. Calves, thighs, quads, and those glutes. The shorts were tight enough to, well ...

I need to stop this wishful thinking right now.

She didn't.

He grabbed onto a bar hanging from the floor trusses and began doing pull-ups. His arms rippled, and his back tensed into a triangle of flexed perfection. Thirty done, he plopped down on the concrete and then pushed himself up Maria's man-gauge fifty times. Then it was squats and rippling thighs.

Maria stared, ogled, dreamed, and fantasized as the routine was repeated three more times. Then, as swift as the god Mercury, Jason headed over to the dunes for a morning jog.

The exercise show disappointingly gone, Maria sipped her coffee. It was cold.

Late that afternoon, Maria woke up from her nap under the awning with Bailey standing in front of her, her long hair now just hanging loosely, blowing freely in the breeze.

"Oh my!" Maria called out, embarrassed. "How long was I asleep?"

She jumped up as Bailey laconically answered, "Not too long."

"How long have you been standing there, Bailey?"

The answer took a moment, as if Bailey were actually adding up the time increments. Calculations over, she finally answered, "Awhile, maybe two whiles."

"Have a seat," Maria offered, still not quite sure how to handle such measured, whimsical humor from a fourteen-year-old girl.

Bailey brushed off what appeared to Maria as invisible sand but was probably millions of life-threatening germs to Bailey on the otherwise new chair. Chair now sanitized, Bailey settled herself into it and crossed her long legs.

Maria felt a small tinge of jealousy emerge within her. Compared to Bailey, she was just so, *so* boringly ordinary. Oh, to have thick hair and long eyelashes, the whole package. Instead, she had wide hips, plain shoulder-length hair, and fair skin. Not to mention, she was as flat-chested as a little girl. "So what brings you out on this wonderful evening?"

Bailey leaned back and looked as if she were pondering quantum theory. Then she said, "Ms. Gowins, when I asked Father Mr. Jason Parker what *girl talk* was, he said, 'Look it up,' but all we got was 'women talk about women's stuff.' Then he said to come over here and ask. Is there something else to it?"

It was clear Jason was wanting Bailey to come to Maria for girl talk. "That's a tough one. I may have to take a walk on the beach while I mull that over. Want to join me?" When Maria stood up, Bailey, amazingly, followed suit.

As they headed up the boardwalk, Bailey asked, "Ms. Gowins, what does *mull that over* mean?"

The two of them headed north up the beach, the waves crashing in and then swooshing back out, each time carrying away parts of Maria that needed to be tossed overboard—anxiety, anger, stress, fear, and even lingering shame. There were those sanderlings again. The sun was starting to fade, and the dune shadows were lengthening, coloring the sands with different hues of browns and tans and grays.

The women walked slowly, casually, more so because it seemed to be the fastest speed Bailey was capable of. It was like she was always lost in thought or maybe just perpetually stuck in a mental Zen garden. Or maybe she was afraid to get to where she was going because it might be new and different …?

Maria had learned a lot about Bailey just from looking at her clothes. While other girls seemed to prefer next to nothing, especially at the beach, Bailey was the opposite. She wore a very loose, long-sleeved shirt and modest frayed jean shorts. At first, Maria had wondered why Bailey never wore booty shorts or bikini tops to get that tan going, but she soon learned why.

It came out as they discussed school, fashion, and friends. The one sad theme in the conversation was Bailey's embarrassingly large breasts.

"They call me *Chester, Double-D Bailey, Booby Bailey, Busty Bailey, Bailey Boob, Ditsy Titsy.* I get so tired of it, and those are the *nice* names." Bailey rattled off others from bullies who had claimed to be her friends on Snapchat and Instagram. They would take selfies with her, post them, and make crude comments or edit them into grotesque images. Boys would save them and share them all over social media. She got calls for hookups from people she hadn't met, many of whom suggested doing some very improper things to a teenage girl. Once, she even received a package containing a skimpy Hooters's "uniform" along with an address to the sender's house. A note tucked inside the "shirt" read, *I bet this won't fit, LOL.*

Plus, nothing ever fit the poor big-chested girl. "Crop tops, tank tops, backless … they don't consider big-boobed girls like me at all," Bailey complained. "Now it's all about going around *braless*. Seriously? The weight is killer on my back. If you're thin and have tiny breasts, then the fashion fits. The rest of us are just out of luck and style."

Maria had noticed that Bailey's move from reticent to loquacious showed just how much thought she had put into the topic and how much pain came from not being able to dress the way she wanted. She had to wear extra large to fit her chest, which made her look fat, pregnant, like she shopped at Goodwill, or like a waif in a Dickens novel. Cue more name-calling.

To keep boys and men from hitting on her, Bailey had begun to wear anything that made her look ugly, out of style, or big to turn them off. It didn't help. The come-ons were as crude as always, and *everyone* stared at her.

Maria noticed that even with the large shirt on, it was still obvious Bailey's bra was too small. *Poor girl. Probably scared to buy the next size because she'll have to admit she's getting bigger.* Maria had the opposite problem. She could fit right in with the day's fashions, except for braless.

No way.

Maybe …?

Nope.

"I used to play soccer and was quite good, but then *these things*"—Bailey pointed at her chest—"grew, and wearing a sports bra hurt. Now they want me to play volleyball, with my height and all, but … it's embarrassing, Ms. Gowins. So now I just stay to myself." Maria could hear Bailey's sniffles over the waves. "And I don't want to say anything, but Father Mr. Jason Parker's no help either."

Wondering at Bailey's sarcasm—or was it just a teenage, whimsical use of multiple names and titles for Jason?—Maria answered, "What do you mean? You two look like you're real tight."

They walked awhile as Bailey seemed to be working up the courage to talk about things that, at this point, were off limits. "He's the best father I ever had." She laughed at her own humor, which Maria was slowly getting used to. "He loves me, and he hugs me, but that's one problem. He has always hugged me tight, but now it hurts. He doesn't want to talk about my boobs, and I don't want to hurt his feelings." She paused for a moment and then continued. "And on top of that, he asks me to do things, like be the host at his parties. Sometimes, it's like I'm his secretary or something."

The waves ebbed and flowed as the tide slowly changed from low to high. Gulls squawked overhead. Sanderlings ran from the waves as they crashed in and chased them as they subsided back out. A lone sand crab crept sideways back to his hole. Late-evening beachgoers nabbed shells to take back home.

Eventually, Maria asked, "Bailey, can I make a suggestion?"

Aware she had opened up and really wanted some answers from Maria at first, Bailey was suddenly not sure about the whole girl-talk thing. It just meant someone else to get in her face and lecture her about something. She breathed in, like a penitent child awaiting her punishment. "Okay, sure."

"Let's not call them 'boobs' anymore. That's crude locker-room talk, not to mention degrading. *Breasts* seems kind of sterile. To me, *tatas* seems demeaning. Some of us ladies call them *girls*."

Bailey paused, stopping to glance between the sea and Maria, not quite sure what to make of what Maria had just said. Her pouty lips opened and closed as she struggled to find the right words.

Before she could, Maria continued, "Giving them a name you prefer puts *you* in charge instead of your detractors."

"Detractors?"

Maria forgot Bailey was still a teen. "People who speak ill of you."

Bailey just hummed in response, processing the word and idea, which seemed to take an inordinate amount of time. She observed her surroundings as she thought. Several waves crashed on the beach in the interim, and a lone fishing boat raced back to the docks on the other side of the island. Then a slight grin rose to meet her now-devilish green eyes. "I think they're a bit too big to be called *girls*."

Once more, it took Maria a moment to understand Bailey's dry humor.

As Bailey considered more options for what to call her breasts, the clock seemed to pause. Maria wondered if Bailey was just tediously slow, introspective, or maybe even learning impaired. Finally, the wondering wheels came to a halt. "What if I call them *ladies* instead?"

Maria approved of the new name. "Yes, more classy than *boobs*, huh?"

Bailey nodded her head, now smiling more and feeling a bit affirmed. She assumed a medieval tone of voice as she said, "Felicitations, me ladies."

They both laughed and continued their walk.

After a few minutes, Maria observed, "Sometimes, changing the nomenclature, the perspective, really helps."

Bailey was not sure what *nomenclature* meant, so Maria explained, "A different name."

Bailey, ever learning new words from this wise older woman, filed the definition away for future reference.

Suddenly aware of the lengthening shadows and how far they had walked, they turned around and headed back home. They dodged evening beach walkers distracted by their phones, retired women fast-walking over the sand with their arms flailing back and forth, and people bent over with plastic bags and small buckets, searching for unbroken shells.

Soon Maria had a question for Bailey. "What would you like to be most in the world?"

Bailey thought the question through as if she had never considered it before, although she had, time and time again. The problem: Was she ready to disclose that to anyone, and if so, was Maria that someone? She took a dare and said, "A writer." Her tone was an odd mix of shame, embarrassment, and hope that someone would not question her dream.

"Really? A writer? Why?"

Bailey wasn't sure if the question was disapproval or interest. Was this what girl talk was about? Sharing souls, dreams, and secrets? "I like to create things, explore things. Maybe that's why I zone out so much. I like words, putting them together into sentences. Stories are make-believe, but they tell the truth. Maybe I'd be a novelist or history writer? Something."

Maria asked if she was writing anything now, and Bailey remembered she was writing about a medieval princess stuck in a remote castle. "Just some scribbling, that's all," she answered, embarrassed to admit it yet hoping Maria would approve.

"Well, I would be honored to read some of your writing, if you want me to," Maria offered.

"Umm, we'll see," Bailey responded in a tone of voice that said, *Thank you for being interested.* Then she paused their walk, twisting her long hair, eyes looming larger than usual, lips quivering, as if she would cry any minute. "But honestly … what I would like most in the world right now is to just be fourteen."

Maria was absolutely floored.

SEVEN

Turtle

The next day, Maria, coffee cup in hand as usual, awaited the early-morning Half-Naked Jason Show, only to be disappointed when he came out wearing dress shorts and a shirt, travel bag in hand.

When he saw her under the awning, he walked over to where she was sitting. Out of nowhere, he wondered if she felt lonely. Then another deeper thought surged to the surface. A sort of chivalrous, knight-in-shining-armor duty to take care of the poor damsel in distress. "Maria, I owe you big time. Bailey is a changed woman this morning. She really enjoyed the girlie … uh, no, sorry, *girl talk*. And we had a good conversation during breakfast about, you know …."

Maria looked at him with a you're-kidding-me face. "They're called *breasts*, Jason. It's okay to say it out loud."

Corrected and castigated once more, Jason gave her a look full of embarrassment but also relief. "It's difficult, Maria, in many ways. Thank you!"

Maria smiled and nodded. "Anytime."

At the same time, Maria spotted Bailey heading down the porch steps with the vigor of a snail on a mission, so the conversation shifted immediately. She sported modestly frayed jean shorts, what looked like black Vans sneakers, and an oversized teal Banker's Point shirt, shoulder bag brushing her hip. Her long feet kind of clunked along in a goofy way. "Morning, Ms. Gowins!" she called out with a bit more vim than her usual measured, sedated vigor. Then she methodically, deliberately walked over to Maria and gave her a very unexpected hug. Jason's eyebrows raised, and Maria, now standing on her tiptoes, smiled at him over Bailey's shoulder with an oh-my-gosh face. When Bailey pulled away, Maria saw just a hint of a gleam in her eyes, a lift in her smile, and a bit of confidence in her shoulders.

"We're headed to Greenville for some business," Jason said, slightly interrupting the ladies' moment. "Be back in a day or two." With that, he tossed his travel bag in the back of the Mercedes, and Bailey walked to the other side and elegantly settled into the passenger's seat. "You've got my card with the number on it," Jason reminded Maria. "Call or text if you need anything. And I mean, *anything*." Then he caught himself. What did he mean by that?

Even though the trailer was small, Maria was still finding places that had not been explored yet. The tiny, windowless bedroom was next on her list. There was something odd about it—a weird feeling, sensation, tingle, shiver from somewhere every time she entered it. She had tried three different LED bulbs in the room, each with brighter lumens, yet it still felt dark. She added a lamp and hung bright beach pictures on the dull walls. No change. The new sandy-color beach décor sheets and the matching spread with brightly colored sand dollars and conch shells added no extra light to the room. "It is what it is," she said with a sigh, finally giving up.

Then there was that rustic, antiqued chest of drawers. Maria recalled a time when she'd overheard her parents talking about the fad, as people had bought the kits to craft an antiquey feel to old and even new furniture. Sort of like folks adding a distressed look to furniture today. Even in the old trailer, with the retro décor and vibe, the chest was just ugly. Dirty, white strands between streaks of something that was either gray or green. Maria had emptied the chest of a few girls' clothes, some seashells, and a worn romance novel with dog-ears marking all the sex scenes. But try as she might, Maria could not get the bottom drawer open. She pushed, pulled, and yanked it sideways and up and down. She jiggled and shook it, tried slow and fast jerks. In desperation, she pounded it with her fists. "Ow!"

Nothing would budge the stubborn drawer.

Finally, after she had calmed down, Maria inched it open just enough to get her hand into it. "Maybe there's something stuck behind it." She wriggled her hand all around and could just get her fingers behind and over the back of the drawer.

Nothing.

But as she pulled her hand back, she felt something hanging down from the bottom of the second drawer. She pulled the second drawer back and then wriggled both drawers some more until she could pry the object out. "What on earth?"

It looked like an old, dried-out diary. She sat on the bed and flipped through it. The handwriting was balloonish, like a giddy teenager's script. The first entry was dated June 15,

1995. It stopped abruptly on September 4, 1999, with an entry that was uncharacteristically jiggly:

Dear Diary,
Something's wrong. There's blood and I'm hurting.

Maria grabbed her phone and searched the date. It was Labor Day weekend. Then she flipped back to the beginning of the diary and found entries that coincided with summer vacations at the beach. They all began around early June and ended mid-August with a brief entry in early September. The writing seemed a bit childish at first and then aged with each year, yet it still reflected a simple, almost naïve mentality. The subjects were clearly from a girl's perspective—shells, bathing suits, weather, food, people, games, fun, boys. Each was signed, *Miss Missy.*

"Ah!" Maria exclaimed. "That has to be the Miss Missy from the letters." She pulled out the box of letters from the post office and compared the handwriting. Sure enough, nearly an exact match, allowing for ageing.

But there was one more thing that caught her eye. Searching through the entries, she found there were titles of games played—spades, Chutes and Ladders, Operation, Monopoly, Chinese Checkers, spoons, etc.—but Miss Missy constantly referenced what appeared to be a game (maybe a song) called Rabbit in the Hole. Time after time, she wrote, *Tonight I played/sang Rabbit in the Hole with …* and then noted the other player. Usually, it was someone named Peter— *hah, Peter Rabbit*, Maria laughed to herself—but there were some other people too, all masculine names. A teen's wish for boyfriends at the beach? Cousins? An odd version of spin the bottle? "Interesting."

Curious, Maria grabbed her phone again and searched *rabbit in a hole*. Apparently, it was a metaphor for a journey, generally in a fairy-tale sense, like *Alice in Wonderland*, but also in a mythical or spiritual sense. It could also imply a totally engrossing idea, hobby, task, or topic of deep conversation.

Had Miss Missy and her friends been into fairy tales? Surely kids were not aware of such a term for deep conversations. Whatever it meant, now there were two pieces of evidence for Miss Missy and one other name: Peter. Who could these two have been?

I don't remember them mentioned at those God-awful Simpson family reunions.

What to make of the final entry? The blood could have been from the girl's first period. But why didn't the diary pick back up the next summer?

"Maybe she stopped going to the beach," Maria mumbled to herself.

But then another thought hit her: Was this simple girlie mystery tied into the constant local curiosity about Maria's connection to the Simpson trailer?

"When did the letters to the trailer begin?" She shuffled through them, searching for the oldest one. "Found it!" She looked at the postmark: Raleigh, October 14, 1999.

A few nights later, during Maria's girl-talk time with Bailey on the patio, the topic for the evening shifted to boys. Having figured out that all boys and men were jerks and creeps, the girls moved on to, "If you met one who was not a jerk or creep, what would he be like?"

About that time, Frederick scooted into the driveway on his bike and skidded to a dusty halt. He retrieved a package from his basket and walked confidently over to the patio where he seemed to somewhat stop in his tracks. It was like he had not seen Bailey sitting with Maria.

"Hi, Frederick," Maria said cheerfully. "Come on up! It's just me and Bailey here. You got my goods?"

Frederick walked (uncharacteristically) sheepishly up to the patio. Ignoring Maria, he looked at Bailey and, in his best professional voice, called out, "Hi, Mrs. Parker. How is your husband doing today?"

Bailey rolled her eyes at Maria, as if saying, *Again?*

Maria jumped in. "Frederick, meet *Miss* Bailey Parker, Mr. Jason Parker's *daughter*."

In an instant, Frederick's eyes lit up imperceptibly.

Bailey stood politely, towering over the short delivery boy, and reached out her hand. "Pleased to officially meet you, Mr. Frederick."

For once, a normally loquacious and confident Frederick was speechless as he shook her hand. It was soft and warm.

Bailey sat back down, and Maria continued rowing the rescue boat for Frederick. "Frederick, you got time to join us for a snack? There's plenty to share if you'll just hand me that bag."

Frederick was still caught in the realization that Bailey was not *Mrs.* Parker.

She's so pretty. Bet she's a college girl, he thought.

Maria smiled knowingly as she reached over and pulled the bag out of Frederick's hand. "I'll just put these on a plate while you two chat, okay?"

Sitting down in Maria's now-empty chair, Frederick finally came back to his friendly senses. "I always thought you were Mr. Parker's wife."

Bailey grinned. "Yeah, I get that a lot." She paused a moment and crossed her legs, which took long enough for a nervous Frederick to think of a question.

"What college do you go to?"

Bailey went into sleep mode for a moment then powered back up. "I'm just fourteen. I start high school this year." Then she continued. "So who are you married to?"

Frederick caught her humor immediately and laughed out loud. *You, I wish.*

After Frederick left, Maria looked over at Bailey. "I think Frederick is rather smitten with you. That's the first time I've ever seen him speechless."

Bailey frowned. "Ms. Gowins, I think every male on this island is 'smitten' with me." She rolled her eyes and sank back into her chair in despair but then offered a small smile after a moment. "He *is* kind of cute though. I like his curls and freckles."

The next day, Maria decided to confide something to Bailey. She wasn't sure how Bailey would respond, but it was more sharing than anything else. *It's what girls do, right?* "Bailey?" she started, munching on a cracker with a poor man's pâté—tuna salad spiffed up with celery, chopped boiled eggs, gherkin pickles, and some spices.

Bailey, momentarily distracted by the breeze blowing her loose hair, twirled a stray strand in her long fingers and then eventually looked back to Maria.

"Can I tell you a secret?" Maria asked, picking up the conversation now that Bailey was mentally back in town. She bit into another cracker.

Bailey's face shifted to her barely visible demure smile. After a moment, as if the question had to be processed, she answered, "Okay."

Maria took a breath and dove in. "I've always wanted to go skinny-dipping in the ocean." There. The cat was finally out of the bag. With the confession, Maria felt like *she* was fourteen again.

Bailey's eyebrows lifted slightly, sending out competing, silent responses. One said, *Oh my God, like, you've got to be soooo kidding! What if you get caught?* The other, barely visible in Bailey's eyes, was more revealing—a very hesitant, nearly imperceptible message that said, *Me too ... but I would never do it.*

Another lengthy pause.

Finally, Bailey asked, "In daylight?" Then she reached for another cracker and spread the "pâté" on it.

The idea was momentarily intriguing, but Maria was not that brazen ... yet. Still, something got her thinking about it. Maybe it was the magic spell of the beach, the salty fairy dust sprinkled about by a dirty Old Man Sea, or a teasing, rebellious, sensuous mermaid. "No, silly, I'm not crazy. At night ... in the dark ... in secret." She saw her words simmer awhile in Bailey's measured contemplation.

Sometimes at night, when Bailey knew Jason was asleep, she would slip out onto her balcony and look at the stars, listen to the ocean, feel the breeze, and fade into a dream. Deep within her, seemingly worlds away, incarnations ago, there was a pirate woman. A devil-may-care diva. A she-wolf howling out in the night. A mystical mermaid. She would emerge on the full moon and dance in the nude on the hilltop, like the female worshipers on a mountain at night in the Greek stories of old. She would flaunt her feminine side, sing and twirl, jump and shout. Her long hair would flow with the zephyrs of her whims, and she would drink the elixir of uninhibited joy. Joined with other women of like spirit, her body free from shame, she would hold the hands and arms and bodies of fellow females who found release in being themselves and, if for only a brief moment, were no longer slaves to the expectations of others.

Sometimes.

Then she wondered what it would be like to just slip off her long nightshirt and feel the breeze on her skin.

Only to be caught by her father and humiliated. Or be seen by the neighbors who might have been doing the same thing. Lord knows what they did at night. Or what if the sheriff saw her? Did they patrol the beach at night? Or what if she got stung by a jellyfish *down there?* Or hauled off into the deep by a monster shark? Or caught in a riptide and carried off to the Caribbean? Or ... the possible scenarios were endless in her mind.

But as she sat with Maria that day, discussing the thrill of skinny-dipping, a question stirred deep within her soul, rose slowly like a spring in the woods, filled her heart like a soft breeze, and finally wafted over her face: Was Maria one of *them* too?

Bailey the Therapist grinned and then chomped another cracker.

Back from what Maria was now calling "Bailey Land," mouth full of cracker, Bailey asked her, "What's keeping you from doing it?"

Maria was caught off guard. What *was* keeping her from doing it? She now lived at the beach. She was just a shell's throw away from the ocean. It would only take a moment. Suddenly she was giddy with derring-do, like a crazy teen at the beach after graduating from high school or on spring break with her friends, getting a tattoo on the butt. Impulsive, reckless, adolescent, clearly not thinking of the consequences, totally caught up in the moment.

She smacked the table, spooking Bailey, who dropped her cracker on the floor. "You know what? You're right. I'm gonna do it. No more namby-pamby. Time to grab life by the horns!"

Bailey, having picked up her cracker, was not quite as enthused by Maria's new resoluteness. "Namby-what-be?"

"Namby-pamby. You know, weak, wimpy, indecisive, milk toast."

Bailey's face twisted into a confused grimace, looking puzzled. "Milk toast?"

Maria, having lost the moment, went back into teacher mode. "Weak, timid, ineffectual."

Bailey's face returned to normal, and her mouth resumed its usual beautiful pout. Maria counted the seconds. At forty-three Mississippi, Bailey had made the computations and stored the new terms in her mental vocabulary file with an "oh." She then spread some tuna salad on a new cracker, obsessively making sure the whole cracker was covered right up to the edge, and stuffed the whole thing into her mouth.

With a full mouth, Milk Toast Bailey squinted and asked, "When are you going to grab those horns?"

Maria reached for her phone and looked something up. As she scrolled, her face slowly lit up. "The sky is mostly clear for the next few nights. There is a new moon two days from now, so it will be really dark." She set the phone down and thought some more. "By golly, Miss Molly, I'm going to do it!"

"Ms. Gowins!" Bailey exclaimed, looking shocked and slightly horrified. She could just picture the sheriff hauling a naked Maria to the pen. Or a sea monster pulling her down into the sea.

There was a long pause as both ladies settled down for the moment. Maria looked away, as if the sudden lark had flown by.

Then Bailey leaned forward and whispered, "Can I come?"

"*Bailey!*"

Three nights later, the girls' night started up. Bailey and Maria dined at the Boardwalk Café, Bailey blithely turning heads while Maria prepared to fend off any daring males who took the plunge toward the underage teen. After dinner, back in the trailer, the girl talk turned to a deep discussion about whether Brad and Angelina would still be fighting over the divorce when they went to heaven. Or who Kim Kardashian's *fourth* husband would be. Then they watched Netflix until two o'clock in the morning.

Finally, it was time.

Nervousness was clear on both their faces. Maria was having second thoughts, and Insecure Bailey was in full force.

"We don't have to do this, you know," Maria consoled a stiff-shouldered Bailey. Adult Maria was back in stride, worried about how this would affect Young Bailey, what would happen if they were caught, and Jason's paternal response. Was she leading an adolescent down a dangerous path?

Honestly, Bailey was more worried about Maria seeing her naked. And being pulled under by a monster. Then there was something called *undertow*.

"It was a silly idea," Maria said in a despondent yet responsible tone. "Maybe we shouldn't."

But both heard the faint sound of the tempting siren's call, and soon their hesitation melted into something daring.

"Namby-pamby!" Bailey taunted Maria.

"Milk toast!" Maria shot back with a laugh.

"Let's do it!" each shouted back to the other before taking the plunge.

Wrapped in fluffy oversized beach towels purchased just for this occasion, the girls raced over the dune toward the black, roaring ocean, crescents of white iridescence flashing before they crashed on the sands. Bailey giggled as she paused, looking around for wandering nocturnal beachgoers. A new moon blessed their ritual with darkness except for the sparkles of a zillion stars in a cloudless sky.

The coast was clear.

Maria tossed off her towel, and Bailey, looking around once more, dropped hers too. Maria, full of adrenaline, raced to the waters; Bailey, not quite as stirred up, followed once she was assured no sea monsters had grabbed Maria. Both shrieked as they dove into the cool brine. As each emerged from the initial baptismal waters, they danced in the waves, full of zest and caught up in the moment. Maria threw water at Bailey, who dove underwater to dodge the spray.

The deed done, both raced back to the beach, reluctant to tempt fate any more than they already had. But the moment was not over. Bailey rushed over to Maria and hugged her. They shivered in the evening breeze as the stars sprinkled glitter upon them, and they basked in the baptism of the moon goddess Selene. The moment was spiritual, universal.

And now filled with shivers and goosebumps.

They dried off and giggled some more, laughing at what they had just done, what they had gotten away with, surging with femininity and solidarity.

Wrapped in towels, they scurried back to the dunes when suddenly Maria froze. "Bailey, look!"

Bailey's heart stopped. Had they been caught?

They stood between two thick lines etched deep into the sand. Maria walked slowly toward the dune and loudly whispered again as if not wanting to disturb the sanctity of the moment, "Bailey!"

"What?"

"A sea turtle!"

They stood quietly, wrapped in their towels, and watched the mother turtle slowly, methodically, dig a nest for her clutch of eggs. As they stared in awe, she rested over the hole, her shell heaving lightly as each egg was released.

Maria suddenly recalled the spiritual, mystical aspects of turtles. "Bailey, Turtle is here to be with us. She could have chosen any place, but she chose to nest here near us. This is special. This is a gift, Bailey. This turtle is a gift to us from the sea."

At first, Bailey did not realize the significance of the turtle. "What?"

Maria tried again, reminding herself that Bailey was only fourteen, and spiritual experiences were probably not high on her list of adolescent priorities. "In Native American lore, each creature has a spirit that can inspire humans, if we allow it. They say the animal comes to us to teach us something important. Turtle came tonight. She is talking to us."

"I thought she was just laying eggs."

"The turtle is about adapting to new surroundings; thus its shell is like a mobile home."

"Like your trailer, right?"

Maria pondered that for a minute. "In a way, yes. Turtle wants us to be open to new terrains, new lands, new lives, but she also wants us to enter these lands at a slow pace. We should not rush into our new lives."

"I can do slow," Bailey answered.

They both watched Mother Turtle in silence.

Then Maria spoke again. "Patience, self-pace, even protection by going deep within ourselves, our personal shells. If we feel threatened, we can recede, even escape, to our personal safe places deep within our souls. While inside, we can seek peace, imagine, and connect with our intuition."

"I can write!" Bailey whispered in excitement.

"And Turtle reminds us of simplicity, of living in the moment, of going with the tides."

"Like tonight?"

Maria nodded her head, excited that Bailey was getting it. And then she saw an opening. "And loving who we are as we are," she said as she put her arm around Bailey's shoulder. "Turtle does not worry that she is ungainly, slow, and unappealing. She does not care that we are watching. She just does what she does. She just lives her life."

Early the next morning, before the beach walkers and joggers and shellers arrived, a crew of volunteers from the local turtle-watch organization found the mother turtle's trail, located the nesting site, and worried over the foot impressions all around the nest.

"At least they didn't disturb the eggs!" Anna called out to her friend Emily.

They took photos and helped with setting up the chicken-wire cage around the nest. When the leader set the warning sign on the fence, they all stepped back. Another nest of hatchlings would be safe from predators and, hopefully, curious and intrusive beachgoers.

Emily pointed out that the footprints led to the walkway over the dune. Leaving the crew, she pulled Anna over the walk and stopped. "Oh … my … God."

Anna gasped and clamped her hand over her mouth.

Emily whispered, "Someone is staying in the old Simpson trailer."

Anna breathed out.

"Do you think they know?"

EIGHT

The Shell

few days after the nocturnal skinny-dip in the brine and the serendipitous encounter with Turtle, Maria was browsing the shelves of Gifts from the Tides and saw a beautiful pine-resin sculpture of a sea turtle. Rising from a bed of real beach sand, Sculpture Turtle looked like a queen—regal, sitting on her dune throne, keeping watch over the deep. Turtle in hand, Maria walked back to her SUV when she remembered she had not seen Jason about her investments. Quickly, she texted and made an appointment.

The next day, she dressed up a bit—*why am I doing this?*—and then spent a moment wondering about it. Was she afraid Jason would look down on her in casual attire? Was she secretly hoping for more than a consultation? Was she giving in to those morning moments when Jason was exercising? She finally, and embarrassingly, had to admit there was an attraction going on. But then she remembered her ex and all his money and ...

She took the steps to the second-floor deck. She paused a moment and took in the view of the beach. The wind was blowing from the east. Cotton-ball clouds dotted the blue sky. Sunbathers were already out in force. Kids screamed as the waves rose high and crashed down like thunder. A shrimp trawler chugged along off the coast. What a nice morning!

Maria took in a deep breath, slowly let it out, then turned and knocked on the glass door.

Bailey appeared in casual attire. *Why doesn't she have on beach clothes?* When she opened the door, she assumed her best administrative assistant manner, complete with a polished voice as she said, "Good morning, welcome to Parker Investments." She motioned for Maria to come inside.

Maria played along, entering the house like a nervous new client.

"I'm Bailey Parker. You must be Mrs. Maria Gowins, here for your ten o'clock appointment. Mr. Parker is on the phone with another client and will be with you momentarily. Please have a seat."

Now it seemed as though Bailey was not playing a part but actually performing her duty as an assistant. Or was she just being her usual quirky, sarcastic self?

"May I get you some water, Ms. Gowins?"

Maria nodded, and Bailey fetched her a bottle from the kitchen.

"Bailey?" Maria asked, taking the water. "Do you work for your dad?"

Thankfully, Bailey came back to her usual self. She carefully, leisurely settled into a chair beside Maria, crossed her long legs methodically as usual, attended to her long sundress until it apparently met some unseen criteria, and still in no hurry at all, leaned forward. Maria waited until Bailey's internal clock caught up with the rest of the moment. The young teen fidgeted with her hair until it seemed in the right place and then rolled her eyes. "Mr. Certified Financial Planner Father Jason Parker likes for me to be the host when he has clients come by. He says it sets a professional tone."

Before she caught herself, Maria spat out, "It doesn't help you to be fourteen, does it?"

Jason, in perfectly pressed shorts and a long-sleeved shirt with the sleeves rolled up his fantastic forearms, emerged from his office like a god from Mount Olympus, full of vigor and anticipation, as Bailey rose up with the deliberation of a sloth. Maria, increasingly indignant, having left her brief time of infatuation behind, stood and headed toward Jason like a doberman guarding a junkyard.

Oblivious to her temper, Jason waved her into his office. "Come in, Maria! I've been looking forward to our visit." He watched a bit too attentively as she walked into the office.

After a few calming breaths, Maria took a seat. *Not your battle, Maria. Calm down.*

The office was appointed with an odd décor: What looked like bamboo matting on the walls with dark-green trim on the crown molding and a mauve carpet on the floor contrasted with the expected beach paintings of lighthouses in Bodie Island and Hatteras and two exquisitely carved and painted duck decoys. Maria just knew they had cost hundreds, maybe even thousands of dollars. Various notebooks with financial titles lined several bookshelves. Two computer screens appeared to be running financial planning apps. A new copy of *The Economist* rested on a small pile of professional journals and magazines.

Jason settled down into one of those fancy, back-massaging office chairs. "So what can I do for you?"

Having calmed down, Maria outlined her goals, planned date of retirement, and dream activities after retirement. She wanted an aggressive growth strategy, preferably socially responsible companies that looked after the environment and their employees. "Ones that treat people with respect and dignity." It came out a little more forceful than she'd meant it to.

Jason gave the standard line. "Socially responsible companies tend to perform less than the major companies. I would—"

Maria snapped, cutting him off with a wave of her hand. She leaned forward, and the angst of millions of jilted people came through her heated words. "Jason, I want no part of any company who stole the pensions from their employees and called it 'downsizing.' I want no part of any Wall Street, MBA-brained, bottom-line mentality that started the lie of bad loans being a good idea, and who didn't see how that policy was going to come back and screw America one day, and the world, with a major recession that caused millions to lose their savings, houses, and jobs. And I want no part of anything that says it is okay to give the rich bastards who created all that mayhem million-dollar bonuses while a lot of people, including their own employees, were let go because the company had lost revenue and had to cut payroll." Maria crossed her legs defiantly. "Capiche, Mr. Certified Financial Planner Father Jason Parker?"

In the stunned silence that followed, Maria heard Bailey snicker.

Jason was caught off guard from this tempest whom, just a moment before, he'd considered to be a convivial and attractive neighbor. "I can see you've done your homework, Maria," was all he could mutter at the moment. He sat back and pondered the possibilities.

But Maria was not done. "I'm an educator, Jason. Homework is what I do." Financial tantrum finished, socially responsible point made, she finally sat back and relaxed.

Jason thought a bit while Maria simmered down and then clicked his mouse a few times. A new screen came up with various options, and he explained them to Maria, offering excellent insights into each fund or stock and making suggestions.

Impressed, Maria responded with, "You are very thorough, Jason."

Now it was his turn for a jab. "I'm a certified financial planner, Miss Community College Teacher Maria Gowins. It's what I do."

Bailey snickered again.

Maria grinned. "Point made, Mr. Certified Financial Planner Jason Parker. Let's do it."

Jason clapped his hands, relaxed from the salvos that had suddenly ceased, and smiled. There was something intimidating yet peculiarly intriguing about this feisty client. "So how much will you be investing, Maria?"

She handed him the check and saw his jaw drop.

Before he caught himself, he blurted out, "Wow, I was not expecting so much. I made those suggestions based on—"

Maria's sensitive short fuse reignited. She was used to the way mountain people were treated by other folks. Tourists were bad enough, but even educated people who had known better saw them as backward and illiterate bumpkins, stock characters from the movie *Deliverance*. The conclusion that a woman living in a trailer might not have enough money to invest was certainly a strong possibility. But for some reason, it felt like an insult.

Assuming a backward twang, Maria put on a good Southern bless-your-heart face and began her response. "Based on whaaaat, Mistuh Pahkah? I done came heeeah wid mah life savin's. Here's mah piggie bank. Iffen you can git me a hammah, we can crack this lil' piggie open." She glared at Jason, clearly offended by his presumptuousness.

Bailey went outside to the deck so she could laugh out loud. The unstoppable force of her father's pluck and initiative had just met its match in the immovable object of Maria's post-divorce defenses.

Jason's face turned red with embarrassment as he tried to apologize. "I—I'm sorry, Maria, it just slipped ... I didn't mean to ... you see, when clients come in, I tend to sum them up by their profession, their looks, their demeanor, or their job history, and, well—"

"And since I'm just a community college teacher on a state salary who lives in a rundown beach trailer, you assumed that I had only a pittance to invest?"

Jason nervously shook his head and tried to explain again.

Maria waved her hand, stopping him once more. "Jason, neighbor-to-neighbor here. You're a loving father, a helpful neighbor, and a professional who obviously cares about helping others achieve their long-term financial dreams. But without giving it much thought, you can be an arrogant ass."

Stalemate.

The silence was not golden.

The real Maria was in full bloom, and she looked more like an invasive, poisonous weed than a soothing, fragrant flower.

So much for therapy.

Based on his flared nostrils, Jason was somewhere between contrite and contentious.

Maria realized she (and her temper) had crossed a line. Jason was obviously not Blane, but she just was not yet sure who Jason really was. "Sorry, raw nerve."

"Truce?" they asked simultaneously. And then they both laughed. The tension left the room, and tentative, if still wary, smiles reappeared on their faces.

Bailey sauntered back in from the deck and stuck her face into the office. "Should I get the bandages and salve, or do I need to call 9-1-1?"

Maria answered, "Better idea. Call Frederick and order a large pizza. I'm buying. Jason, think you can handle the tip?"

Jason grinned. "Why, Miss Maria, I might have to break the piggie bank to do that."

Bailey smiled and left the office, calling out behind her, "Mistuh Certified Financial Plannah Fathuh Jason Pahkuh, should I git the hammah?"

The next morning, after two hours of searching for prospective stocks on the market, Jason took a break and went outside and stood on the deck. Only this time, instead of looking out over the ocean, he stood on the side and looked along the beach. Or was he looking at Maria's trailer? Maybe it was both. He was aware of the change of view but a bit unsure of the reason. At the same time, Maria appeared, stepping out from her door. Rather than heading directly to her vehicle, she paused and looked over at the mansion. Both were caught staring at each other.

Then Jason waved. "Morning, neighbor!" he called out.

Maria waved back, perhaps a bit more enthusiastically than she meant to.

The following day, as Maria dove around the island, she noticed a lot of the old trailers had some nice touchups. Spiffy wooden decks, winding staircases, lots of outdoor furniture—some basic, some trendy—towels drying off on nice custom rails. All in all, an open door to the summer sun and a good view of the ocean.

She thought about her trailer and was inspired by what she'd seen. She'd wanted to fix the boardwalk leading out to the beach and now thought a deck would be a good plan as well. She stopped and asked Tara about any local builders, and together, they perused her bulletin board for possibilities. Through the magic of phone calls, emails, and PDFs, Maria's plans for the overhead deck fell into place.

A few days later, wood was delivered from the lumber company, and the crew arrived early the next morning to begin construction.

The first day, as Maria patrolled the worksite and answered questions from and made suggestions to the crew leader, the columns were set around the old concrete patio in front of the trailer and in the back, and then frame supports were bolted into place.

The second day, the crew set up scaffolding as the frame slowly took shape. Maria stayed next door to work on lesson plans and avoid the noise and occasional horny-man stare.

By the third day, Maria had been cooped up long enough, so she and Bailey scooted out for the day. When they climbed into her car to leave, the crew caught sight of Bailey. As usual, the low whistles and surreptitious stares upset her. "Men are pigs," she said in disgust as they drove off.

"Bailey, always begin with that premise, and you should be fine."

The next day, Maria went to the coffee shop for an early-morning brew before she ran some errands. Tara asked if she had told Maria about her other shop, Island Folk Crafts. "With your interest in history and cultures, you would love this store!"

Finishing her latte and pimento cheese and turkey bacon muffin, Maria dodged morning tourists for two blocks and arrived at a little shack with a unique carved sign out front. It was a weather-worn structure that was obviously the end product of several old-time sheds spliced together, a technique the previous islanders used when they had to make do with whatever supplies—various woods and metals—they could scrounge up, mostly from shipwrecks.

"Now this looks interesting."

Inside, Maria wandered about and admired all the crafts on the rustic pine walls and makeshift shelves. She had seen some of these items in historical works, journals, and even museums. Some she recognized from her Appalachian roots: toys such as corn husk dolls, gee-haw sticks, do-nothing machines, and dancing limberjacks. Then there were more utilitarian items: carved spoons, bread bowls, and intricate cutting boards from other parts of the state. Seagrove pottery was featured in one section. Artsy jewelry crafted from nearly anything imaginable dazzled her eyes. In another section, coastal crafts were featured. Crude duck decoys carved from a single piece of wood, simple wooden toys, sea-glass ornaments and jewelry, African-style masks, and creative textile arts. There were various styles of baskets, but what really caught Maria's eye were the pine-needle crafts and sweetgrass baskets. She turned a corner, and there sat a rotund elderly Black woman carefully weaving one together.

Maria stopped and observed. The woman never looked up.

Just as suddenly, a thinner, younger Black woman appeared out of nowhere.

She called out, "Mrs. Simpson?"

Maria turned to a somewhat familiar voice. Startled, she called out, "Kennedy?"

Former teacher and former student embraced each other. "Fancy meeting you here!" Maria exclaimed.

"Likewise!" Kennedy responded, her long braids wafting around her. Both looked at each other in disbelief before they reminisced about old times. Maria quickly corrected her regarding her last name. Then she listened to Kennedy's story.

Kennedy was the old woman's granddaughter. She'd attended community college where Maria encouraged her to explore ethnic and cultural studies. She'd finished her education with a bachelor's degree in African/African-American Studies with a semester abroad in Guinea. While job searching, she'd seen an online ad for the store. She'd interviewed with Tara, and now here she was, putting her degrees to use. Kennedy pointed to the woman in the corner. "I convinced Grammy to come up for this summer and make some baskets and teach customers about her craft and heritage."

"Ah," Maria said, "you might be interested in David Fischer's book *African Founders*. He does a lot with the African roots of enslaved Americans and how this influenced American history and culture."

Kennedy's eyes lit up, and she nodded excitedly. "I'll put it on the reading list. Thanks!"

"You've got a nice variety here," Maria noted.

"A lot of our inventory is from North Carolina, but I feature the Carolina coastal region, which has some Gullah Geechee roots. Grammy's family has roots in Charleston as well as New Bern." Kennedy paused, walked over to a book shelf, and picked up Catherine Bishir's book, *Crafting Lives*. "Have you read this? It's about African-American artisans in New Bern." She put the book back and continued. "Bread baskets, Moses baskets, fruit baskets. We try to represent all kinds of crafts, but—you know me—I wanted to shift the focus to crafts made by folks with an African or local heritage." She walked behind the register to help a customer with a purchase. "Make yourself at home. Grammy will talk to you eventually. FYI, she's really old school, kind of gruff, but once you get to know her, she's a sweetie."

"Eventually" took about ten minutes. "I'm Hattie," said the elderly woman. After another spell, she actually looked up and stared at Maria. "I think you know somethin' 'bout this." She nodded to her basket and resumed her weaving.

Maria told her about teaching history and related her personal knowledge of mountain crafts and their heritage and traditions. A wisdom emanated from Hattie that one had to really *feel* to appreciate. Her round face, her deep, dark eyes with the etched lines around them, the defiance of her mouth, and her steady posture were all part of the story, but beyond that, if one took the time to look, was a spirit wafting from her and a bright aura surrounding her dark face. It was like she had lived through many generations, manifested many souls, resided in many places. There was a soul that had struggled too much and survived what others would have succumbed to, threaded together into a quilt of shear, blunt honesty and depth that shielded her from any cold storm blowing her way. One could *feel* she preferred her ancient roots to the domesticated ways of modernity. It was quite the contrast to the travelled and sophisticated manner of her granddaughter.

After having sized up Maria, Hattie set her half-finished basket down on the worn, rutted plank floor. "If you pull up that chair over there, I'll share some of my history with you." Hattie paused as Maria set her chair down. "You know," Hattie continued, a wise smile slowly emanating from her face, "in fact, I think you need to learn how to do this." Then she picked up her basket.

Maria smiled as Hattie wove the strands together.

"You're right, Hattie. I think I do."

"It'll help with those troubles in your soul."

Maria leaned back a bit, as if dodging a shot to her face. Then she caught herself. "Hattie, how did you know?"

Hattie's face returned back to its stern look as she concentrated on her basket.

"Hattie know a lot of things."

"*Knows*, Grammy, *knows*," Kennedy called out.

Hattie grinned. "Sometimes I do that just to get her riled up."

Bailey stepped out of the shower, feeling refreshed and energized from an early-morning walk on the sunny beach. Panties on, she remembered that her new, pretty bras she had ordered online with Maria were still at the trailer. Maria had planned to wash her "delicates" and offered to wash Bailey's as well. With her other bras dirty, and being filled with Turtle and Woman Spirit, not to mention the morning's sun and wind and waves from her walk, Bailey felt empowered and bold enough to just bop over to the trailer braless and get her clean ones.

She quietly scooted along the wall to the side window and then glanced outside to see if the coast was clear. It was lunchtime, and no trucks were in the driveway. She buttoned on her favorite shirt her dad had given her years ago, though it barely fit anymore, grabbed her copy of the trailer key, and tentatively stepped barefoot out on the deck. With her dad preoccupied with work in his office, she bounded down the steps and skittered briskly to the trailer.

When she inserted her key, she discovered the door was already unlocked. "That's odd," she muttered to herself. "Maria always locks her doors." Bailey cautiously stuck her head in and called out, "Hello?" Nobody answered, so she stepped inside and headed to the back bedroom.

Then she saw a man standing in the shadows.

Frederick was cycling by on his way home from a delivery, sweating fiercely from the heat and exertion. When he neared Bailey's driveway, he pulled in, hoping to see his new friend. There were no trucks, so he rode over to the trailer, but Ms. Gowins's Toyota was gone as well. Tools lay scattered about, and the generator for the nail gun was idling. The door to the trailer was shut. "Oh well. Guess everyone's out." He turned to leave but stopped dead in his tracks when he heard a scream from inside the trailer.

"No, *stop*! Don't touch me!"

"Bailey?" he hollered then rushed over when he heard more screams, instinctively grabbing the nail gun before throwing the door open.

A man was pulling on a frightened Bailey. Her shirt buttons ripped off. He turned as Frederick yelled, "What are you doing? Let her go!"

With the man momentarily distracted, Bailey was able to shove him away and rushed behind the counter, pulling her shirt together to hide herself.

The wild-eyed man lunged for Frederick, but a barrage of nails hit his legs, and he fell to the floor, crying out, "You son of a *bitch!*"

"Bailey, run!"

Bailey raced out in a blur, screaming loudly as the man writhed on the floor and then stood up, heading for Frederick. Frederick shot at his arms, and the man wailed in pain.

"Call 9-1-1!" Frederick yelled as Bailey fled to her house, holding the flaps of her shirt together. Frederick suddenly realized what he had done and what could happen next. He stood out of sight outside the door. He knew the man would try to run, maybe attack him as well. He put down the nail gun, realizing it was not going to stop the man, and grabbed a long two-by-four.

The man emerged at the door, blood dripping from his bare arms and legs, and his face red with rage as he looked around for Frederick. "Little bastard, I'll kill you!"

He took a step out the door, and Frederick swung with all his might. He heard the man's shin bone crack, and the man toppled with a thud onto the concrete patio. Still full of fight, he tried to stand up, but Frederick swung again and hit him in the head. Again, the man tumbled to the patio.

Frederick picked the nail gun back up and aimed it straight at the man's face as he tried to stand again. "Get up! I dare you!"

Bailey's father careened down the steps, cell phone to his ear, and raced over to the trailer. He saw Frederick standing over the heap of a writhing, bloody, wailing man.

"Frederick!" When he stopped, he realized the assailant was one of the crew members working on the trailer. "Frederick, are you hurt?" Jason asked, taking a hesitant step toward the armed boy, still not sure what had taken place.

"Mr. Parker," a quivering Frederick responded. "I—is—is Bailey okay?"

The work crew arrived back from a long lunch to find yellow tape around the worksite and a sheriff's cruiser and ambulance in the driveway. A deputy waved them away but would not divulge any information other than a crime had been committed, and a young man was wounded. The crew chief called the boss for instructions as to what to do and tried his best to placate his increasingly frustrated and impatient team. Once they realized it was their buddy Charlie, they became restless and increasingly difficult to contain.

Maria, having been called by Jason, skidded into the edge of her driveway, got out of her Toyota, and exclaimed, "What the hell?" When the sheriff tried to hold her back, she defiantly yelled, "That's my home! What's going on here?" The sheriff lifted the tape and escorted her to the scene of the crime. She paused in shock, completely speechless.

Frederick shivered and shook, wondering if he would go to jail for shooting the man. The sheriff was not very reassuring. "Son, we'll have to see how the evidence falls out."

Jason held Frederick close as he gave the sheriff his version of the story. When he was done, Jason assured him, "Don't worry. I'll take care of this, Frederick."

Just then, Fredericka drove up. She hurriedly ran to her visibly shaken son. "Frederick!"

In the meantime, the sheriff needed to interrogate Bailey for her version of the incident, so all moved inside the mansion, but she was locked in her room, crying. Fredericka stood by a still-shaking Frederick, holding him close as Jason desperately pleaded with Bailey to come out. Despite the pleas from Jason, Maria, and Frederick, Bailey wasn't talking.

Maria, well aware of the psychological damage Bailey was suffering, had texted Tara, who suddenly appeared on the second-floor deck. Jason waved her in, and after shooing everyone off, Tara managed to get into Bailey's room, but that was the end of her luck. Bailey was covered in an oversized sweatshirt, leggings showing underneath. New tears paralleled tracks of dried ones down her streaked, contorted face. Embarrassment quaked her body, and no matter what technique Tara tried, Bailey remained silent, too hurt and ashamed to speak. At best, the sheriff could, through Tara, only get nods and shakes of the head, and soon the counselor ended the interview.

"She's too traumatized to speak, Sheriff," Tara said.

The sheriff left Bailey's room and shook his head. "There are just too many holes in this story based on what the accused assailant said, and she's not helping here, Mr. Parker."

"Sheriff, I have security video from the trailer that might help," Maria offered as she pulled out her phone. She had added the security package when she ordered her internet service. She connected to the security company website, tapped in her passcode, and then showed the sheriff the footage. There were three camera views: one from the main entrance looking back into the bedrooms, one from the den looking at the entrance door, and one from the hallway looking toward the kitchen.

After watching the separate videos three times, it was clear the assailant had entered the trailer first without permission and went to the back before disappearing behind the bedroom walls, obviously looking nervous and suspicious. Sometime after, Bailey came in, wearing what looked to be only a long, white button-up shirt. She went to the back, calling out "hello" as she headed to the rear of the trailer.

The sheriff shook his head. "This looks like a rendezvous so far," he muttered.

But then a scream erupted, and Bailey fled up the hallway with the assailant behind her. He grabbed her shirt and pulled her around, and Bailey pushed back with all her might, causing the buttons to rip off. Just then Frederick appeared inside. Bailey backed into the kitchen, putting the bar between her and the assailant. She screamed as he came to the kitchen. Then Frederick fired the nail gun at the assailant, who fell to the floor. Bailey ran out the door, screaming. The camera then showed the assailant chasing Frederick out the door and falling down when Frederick hit him on the shin with a board.

The sheriff watched the video several more times and then asked Maria to send him a copy for his records. "I think these videos will speak for themselves," he concluded, folding his notebook and sticking his pen into his shirt pocket. "At least, it gets Frederick off the hook. The assailant was clearly attacking Miss Bailey, but there is still the question of what she was doing in the trailer by herself."

Maria thought for a moment, then called out to the sheriff in realization as he turned to leave. "Wait! I think I might have an answer. I had washed some of our delicates last night. Seeing no cars in the driveway, she probably came over to get them, thinking nobody was home. She has her own key."

The sheriff nodded his head. "That's plausible, Ms. Gowins, but until I hear it from her, it's just a theory. When she settles down and is ready to talk, let me know so I can finish my statement."

As he drove away, he muttered to himself, "The curse still lives on in that wretched trailer."

Late that afternoon, Maria, incensed by what had happened to Bailey and inside her own trailer, cornered the fumbling, mumbling, and very embarrassed crew chief. "Get your damned boss down here *now!*" When the company's owner showed up later, claiming he was not responsible for what individual employees did, and especially not for some kid shooting nails into "a piece of a trailer," she was in his face instantly, poking him on the chest with one finger, her lawyer on the phone, as she gave him a step-by-step on what would happen if he didn't take responsibility for what had happened.

After that, she then took on the whole crew, spewing venom in the face of each man, one by one. "*No one* enters my trailer without my permission, and get this very clear, gentlemen: When a woman says 'no,' she means *no!*"

Then Maria stared straight into the face of the tall and imposing owner one more time and made something very clear and in no uncertain terms. "The repairs will be free, or I will own your damn company!" she threatened. "Now get these men out of here. I expect to see you here tomorrow."

After everyone had gone, Maria, now shaking all over, looked inside the trailer and assessed the damage. Nails pierced the walls, furniture, and bar. Blood stains riddled the carpet. Chairs lay across the floors. She sat on the threshold and cried. Yes, it was just a trailer, but it had become a lot more to her. Now it was tainted with blood, scars, and trauma. It no longer felt safe.

A question echoed in her head: *Is that the old Simpson trailer?*

Frederick waited in the Parker house, hoping Bailey would come out. Fredericka, assured that her son was okay, had to get back to the store. Frederick said goodbye to his mother and then walked down the stairs to his bike, but he paused when he saw Maria sobbing on the steps. Suddenly he was worried about what he had done to her trailer. "Ms. Gowins, I am *so* sorry I ruined your trailer. I swear, I didn't mean to—"

Maria stood up and motioned for him to come over. She hugged him tight as he started crying and shaking again.

"I was just trying to save Bailey. I didn't mean to mess up your trailer, Ms. Gowins." Reliving the moment all over again, he shook even harder.

Maria grabbed his shoulders, pushed him back, and looked directly in his eyes. Now he was really scared. "Frederick, you *did* save Bailey. And that is all that matters, okay?"

Frederick's sobs subsided with her reassurance, and Maria hugged him tight once again.

"Ms. Gowins?"

"Yes, Frederick?"

"I can't breathe."

Maria laughed and turned him loose. "Sorry, big man!" She looked him over again just to make sure. Then she rubbed her eyes with her fingers. "Feel like helping me straighten up?"

He tentatively followed her into the trailer and then paused. "Ms. Gowins, do *you* need a hug?"

An hour later, sitting on a vinyl chair with holes in it, she pulled out her phone and tapped on Joe Clark's contact. A calming voice answered. "Maria, to what do I owe the honor of hearing your voice today?"

"Joe?" she called out. Then she burst into tears.

Realizing Bailey was not coming out of her room anytime soon, Jason went to check on Maria later that evening. Bottle of wine in hand and cheese, fruit slices, and crackers in a bag, he knocked on the aluminum door and waited.

It opened slightly, and a very fretful Maria peered out. It was obvious from her red face and eyes that she had been crying. Jason wasn't quite sure what to say, and silence spoke of his reluctance.

Maria must've caught on because she said, "Thanks for thinking of me, Jason, and yes, I would like that very much. I'd invite you in, but I think we both know that isn't going to happen. Let's eat outside. The inside is a war zone."

Two red plastic cups of wine later, Maria had calmed down. Somewhat.

Now it was Jason's turn. He was caught between a father's worry for his hurt child and anger at the injustice done to an innocent teen. "He attacked my little girl, Maria. What if he had raped her? Hurt her? Killed her?" Then Jason broke down in tears.

Tears shed, the silence returned. After a moment, Maria got up and walked over to a very distraught Jason. "Up here," she commanded. Jason stood up and was floored. The whirlwind Maria, full of thunder and lightning, the one who took on a boss and crew, the woman who was full of heartbreak and total distrust of men, opened her arms and hugged Jason. "We'll get her through this, Jason." It was as if Maria were his spouse, and they were trying to take care of *their* daughter. The moment ended too fast. "Jason, the brownies I made last night survived the storm. Want one? I've got whipped cream."

Brownies and a third cup of wine later, Jason, perhaps still caught up in the idea of them being married, asked, "Maria, would you like to stay over at my place tonight? You might feel safer. I have a guest room with a TV and separate bath."

Feisty, independent Maria would have said no, but she was not feeling the fight at the moment. It *was* one of those moments when another tight, protective, manly hug, like the one Jason had just given her, would have been appreciated, but maybe that was going too far—

As if reading her mind, Jason asked, "And Maria, if that is out of line, could I at least return your hug with another hug? You look like you could use a second one."

Hug completed and one overnight bag packed, knight-in-shining-armor Jason led the way to the safety of the castle.

The next day, the construction company's owner survived the wrath of Jason Parker, whose lawyer was also looking into the matter. It was man-to-man now. "Let's get one thing straight, pal …"

It was a side of GQ Jason Maria had never suspected to exist.

God, it was sexy!

Standing off at a safe distance, arms crossed in feminine defiance, Maria took her post outside, daring anyone to even try to look at her. The work shifted immediately to renovating the inside of the trailer where the assault had taken place.

Two days later, the renovations and deck were finished. And Maria was free from any more unwanted guests.

It was a silent and trying week for all. Despite Tara's years of experience, she could not get Bailey to crack. After the sheriff came by three different times, he and Tara finally convinced Bailey to write down what had happened so they could proceed with criminal charges. The next day, the written statement appeared out from under her door.

Maria came by often, hoping to lure Bailey out for girl talk, a walk on the beach, a trip to the coffee shop, online shopping, or anything else Maria could think of. Still, nothing but silence. She secretly wondered if this, in some way, had been caused by their nocturnal dip in the ocean and the chance encounter with Turtle. Frederick, who checked on Maria every time he rode by on a delivery run, could not understand why Bailey did not want to thank him for saving her. He was clearly sad, disappointed, and confused. He once told Maria he felt as though *he* had hurt Bailey, not the creep.

On day three, Maria invited Jason over for lunch. She needed some feel-good food, so she whipped up real oven-baked macaroni and cheese and, feeling guilty over the calories, heated up string beans and then made some biscuits.

Jason was wowed by the homemade meal and Maria's hospitality. "Beats that creamy goo they call 'mac-and-cheese' at the restaurants."

Soon the conversation turned to Bailey.

"I don't understand, Maria, I just don't. Why won't she come out?"

Maria, now picking up the dishes, paused to think before looking back at Jason, who looked mighty nice sitting at her table. "I think we have several things going on here, Jason. First, she was *just* beginning to accept herself. Our walks on the beach, the girl talk, the trips into the village. She was

starting to relax and share and even be proud of herself."
Maria didn't dare mention the night of Turtle.

"Okay, so …?"

"Second, with her newfound confidence, she began to feel
… well, maybe a little flirty, sexy, or strong …? I don't know,
something like that. Girls that age do those kinds of things.
It's, like, testing the waters. That would explain why she only
wore a shirt when she came over that day."

Jason turned and looked at Maria with a slight look of
disgust. "What was she thinking?"

Maria sighed. "Jason, she's fourteen. She's becoming a
woman, and at the same time, she's still a teen. Impulses will
come and go, impulses that are not logical but are just part of
the process and the hormones. Sometimes, it's a one and done;
sometimes it's the beginning of bad behavior; sometimes it's
just …" She trailed off, lost in thought.

Jason looked restlessly out the window, as if looking away
from his stress and worries so they would just disappear. "I
hadn't thought of that. I just didn't know that girls would do
that at fourteen." He paused a moment. "She's still just my
Little Bailey, you know?"

Maria thought she heard him sniffle.

"Did you do that at fourteen?" He was clearly searching for
answers and didn't realize the question was way too personal.

Maria looked out beyond the horizon, as if the story could
be found just over the edge of the sea. *Oh, why not?* she
thought to herself, deciding to come clean. *Confession is
good for the soul.* "There was a little dalliance in a hayloft
when I was fourteen." She paused. "And a half." As if that
would make the situation a little more acceptable. "FYI, it

looks good on the country music videos, but hay is kinda prickly when you're naked."

Jason laughed. Suddenly, Stiff-as-a-Board Maria was a bit more intriguing. "I would never have thought that about you, Maria."

Maria was not sure how to respond to that one. *What* do *you think about me?*

They heard footsteps resounding off the deck next door, and then someone knocked on the trailer door. It was Frederick. He was trying to smile and be positive, but the look in his eyes told Maria he was worried on the inside too. She let him in. "Hi, Mr. Parker. Hi, Ms. Gowins." He stood by the door, probably trying to look like an adult. "Did she come out yet?"

Jason looked over at the young man who had saved his daughter, and then he had a flashback to his high school days. He had been in love with a girl two houses down the street. They played football and basketball together often. At a birthday party, they even played spin the bottle. She was his first kiss. Then one day, she didn't come outside to hang out, and at school, she ignored him, as if embarrassed to be near him. He remembered the confusion, shame, embarrassment, and rejection he felt when she refused to explain her sudden change. "Frederick, go back there, let yourself in, and give it another go, okay?"

Ten minutes later, Frederick came back, looking dejected. "I just don't understand."

Maria pulled him close and gave him a mama-bear hug. "Neither do we, Frederick."

His eyes teared up, and Jason gave him a pat on the back. "Buddy, I can't thank you enough. You saved my daughter."

Frederick looked up at the man. "Mr. Parker, I wish Bailey would talk to me." He wiped his nose with his hand, brushing his tears and snot off on his shorts. "I feel like I did something to hurt her. Is that why she won't talk to me?"

Jason looked over at Maria with a help-me-out-here face.

Maria came to the rescue by offering Frederick a tissue. "It's complicated. It's ... well, it's kind of a woman thing, you know?" For once, she was uncharacteristically having a difficult time soothing someone and explaining the situation.

"All I know is that I thought I did a good thing."

Suddenly, Maria saw another new side of Jason emerge. "C'mere, Frederick." He hugged him tight, like the father Frederick wished would come back. "You did, son. You did."

NINE

Nurse Bailey

Bailey, feeling numb, ashamed, guilt-laden, and angry—more with herself than the creep—would slip out of her room at night in her pajama bottoms and oversized shirt when nobody was around, grab a quick bite, and then go back into hibernation. The two days she showered, she refused to look at herself in the mirror.

Jason stayed at the house all week to provide some sense of security for Bailey, but at some point, he needed to focus on work as well. He cancelled two evening sessions that week—*that's a lot of money lost*—to avoid upsetting Bailey. By now, word was all over the island, and in some sense, that was an embarrassment as well. Locals would drive by and pause to look at the "scene of the crime." Jason was devastated, worried, and increasingly angry, something he rarely ever felt toward his daughter. And at night, when he heard her whimpering in her closed and locked room, he cried too. Why wouldn't she let him in?

He did not understand that she felt like she had let her father down.

Frederick, on the other hand, was a hero on the island. Pats on the back, free lunch now and then, a mention in the *Banker's Point Weekly*. But without Bailey, he felt like a failure. Still, every day, he dutifully came by to check on her and ask her to let him in, but Bailey ignored his pleas. She wouldn't even answer any of his texts. Maria tried to console him, but it was to no avail. He would just hang his head and take his bike back to the store and wonder once more what he had done wrong.

Maria tried to help by inviting Frederick over to the trailer to talk about the island's history. She remembered Fredericka's comment about how the island had needed a new, more up-to-date history. After thinking it through and sifting through some books on North Carolina's coastal history, she had an idea to run by him, so she ordered some sandwiches from the deli beside the One and Done. Since the weather was cool for a change, they gathered around the new wrought-iron table on the patio when he had arrived with the delivery, and in between bites, she broached the idea to him. "Frederick, your mom tells me you are into island history."

His face lit up. "Yes, ma'am, Ms. Gowins." Energized by her interest and the question, he swallowed, quickly took a sip of his cola, and continued. "I hear a lot of stories from the locals when I deliver to them. There's a lot here to talk about." He grinned, waiting for Maria to answer.

She stuffed her mouth with chips. "Well, I've got an idea. Want to hear it?"

"Yes, ma'am!"

She paused her eating and told him about the Foxfire Project in the mountains years ago. How a high school teacher had his students go around the old towns, hollers, and dirt roads and visit with folks, interviewing them and collecting their stories, wisdom, craft skills, and lore. How they published their work in many volumes so others could learn about the mountain folks and their culture and ways.

Frederick was all ears.

"I hear you know a lot of stories, and that you like to talk with folks about old island histories."

He was about to pop.

"And I have an old college schoolmate who works for a publisher who specializes in local histories that we can contact if we get enough stories and old photos."

He was leaning so far forward, he had to catch himself before falling on the concrete patio.

"And don't tell anyone, but Bailey wants to be a writer."

Maria picked up her sandwich while Frederick put it all together. "Seriously?"

She swallowed, sipped her cola, wiped her mouth, dipped more chips into the onion dip, and munched away while Frederick tried to keep from exploding at the idea of working with Bailey. "Serious. You in?"

Frederick's eyes looked like that of a child on Christmas morning. "You betcha!"

A few days after what Jason, Maria, and Tara were now calling "the incident," there was a knock on the back glass door of the Palace's second-floor deck. Jason walked to the door and saw one woman and two teen girls standing behind her. Arriving at the door, he sized them up.

The woman was short, a bit stout, maybe fifty or so, not exactly the beach type nor what most weathered islanders looked like. Modest shorts and a blouse suggested the easy calm of the beach yet a business intent. Short black hair and a wise rounded face with deep-brown eyes evinced a depth to her that was not common for most people.

The girls in their shorts and crop tops were tanned, and their faces were slightly mischievous.

Maybe a mother and her daughters wanting to set up an account for college?

He opened the door. "Hi, can I help you?"

The woman stuck her hand out. "Reverend Rebecca Tate from the Methodist Church up the road. This is Emily." She paused while the tall, thin girl with dark-blond hair and blue eyes smiled and reached out to shake his hand. She was the emerging anti-establishment renegade of the two girls. Her keen sense of social justice and a general disdain for the status quo often manifested as breaking traditional norms. Today, it was visible on her feet which featured two different-colored high-top sneakers. "And this is Anna." Anna was shorter, much more filled out than Emily, with dark hair and eyes and an adolescent body that would attract attention from the local boys and tourists. Her heavy eye makeup, red hair, and black boots added together into a confused mishmash of a flirty goth. Jason shook her hand as well.

"I'm Jason Parker. What can I do for you?"

Reverend Tate answered back. "Jason, it's more like, what can *we* do for *you?*"

Emily, looking frustrated with the pleasantries, butted in. "Frederick told us about Bailey, Mr. Parker, and we want to help." There was an eagerness in her voice and eyes that made up for her misguided manners.

"Slow down, Emily," Reverend Tate advised, patting her on the head. She looked at Jason. "She's a bit pushy."

"Tell you what, let's sit on the deck, if you will." Jason motioned to the deck chairs, and after pulling the chairs into a circle, all took a seat. Emily and Anna, sisters in everything but the last name, sat beside each other, looking nervous and fidgety while checking their phones.

Reverend Tate continued the conversation. All three reveled in the lavish environs of the mansion. "We heard about Bailey from Frederick and thought maybe we could coax her out. Offer some support, be a friend, that kind of thing. A little nudge from God won't hurt, I hope."

Jason was not much of a churchgoer. Christmas, Easter, funerals, and weddings. But to be frank, church had not offered much to him, except guilt and embarrassment. He had questions, but the church had no answers except the creeds, doctrines, and hypocrisy. However, with Bailey's situation, maybe it was time to rethink priorities. Nothing else was working. "Well, we have tried everything else. That divine nudge might be worth a try. Prayer would certainly be helpful, I guess. Maybe I should get back into church …?"

Reverend Tate shifted in her seat. She had heard those excuses … how many times? "Actually, I brought in the big guns for this one. Emily and Anna are pretty good at getting people to do things. Maybe we could turn them loose on her?"

Jason was not expecting this. He was ready for the guilt trip, the sermon on how God used events to work out a divine cause, maybe one of those apocalyptic tracts that could be found in mall bathrooms. The Bible lesson that maybe his wealth had distracted him from the simpler life. The love of mammon. Get his priorities right, and God will send blessings. God did not put on people more than they could bear. Even a free Bible. But … two teenage girls?

Jason's doubts must have shown on his face because Anna begged, "Please, Mr. Parker?" She looked like she was about to come out of her skin, and Emily scooted to the edge of her chair in anticipation. "We can get her to come out, Mr. Parker, we really can!" Emily said.

Jason was intrigued at their moxie. *Why not?* he thought. He paused to make sure he wanted to put Bailey through yet another attempt to get her out of hibernation. "Sure, girls. Let me show you her room. Excuse me, Reverend. I'll be right back."

Inside, Emily and Anna both knocked on Bailey's bedroom door and introduced themselves to her. There was no response. They tried again. Silence. Jason stood by as they tried the old shave-and-a-haircut (two bits) knock, but they left out the last two knocks.

Silence.

Then they acted like Sheldon on *The Big Bang Theory*. They knocked three times and called out "Bailey." They did it two more times.

Still no response.

Emily asked if Bailey was on Snapchat. Jason said he didn't think so. Instagram? Again, Jason was not sure.

Then Anna asked, "Can we have her phone number?"

Jason was not sure about that, but he gave it to them anyway. "Are you going to call her?"

"Better," a beaming Emily answered. "There's a story in the Gospel of Luke about a little old lady who annoyed a judge so much that he gave in to her request."

Anna, eyes glistening full of teenage hope, picked up the point. "So we're going to annoy her until she comes out."

They plopped on the floor in front of the door, crossed their legs, and began texting her, thumbs flying. Only it was not texting. It was emojis. Lots of them.

"We're going to get her mind off herself and make her laugh." Emily showed Jason the first emoji message. It was a crab, an apple, and a tree.

"I don't get it," he responded.

"Crab apple tree!" Emily called out. "It will make her laugh when she figures it out."

Jason shook his head. "I don't know, girls, she can be pretty dense sometimes and really stubborn."

Anna typed away with thumbs fast as lightning. She found a canned food emoji and then one where the finger is pointing toward her and then an ear and ended with *me*. She hit Send.

Can you hear me?

"School's out, and we got all summer, Mr. Parker."

In her room, Bailey heard her phone ding. She picked it up and looked at the emojis. Two minutes later, she smiled.

Another ding. She looked at her phone and saw a capital *U*, a canned food emoji, a bee emoji, a smiley face with sunglasses emoji, a lowercase *u*, a play button emoji, and the words *with us*.

It took longer, but she finally figured it out: *You can be cool if you play with us.*

Emily and Anna waited for a bit. And a bit more. Then Emily's phone dinged. She looked down, showed her screen to Anna, who looked back at Emily with a scrunched-up face. "Huh?"

"We can do this. Think, Anna!"

They saw praying hands, two eyes, canned food with *'t* right after it, a bee, the smiley face with sunglasses, a finger pointing to the right, the @ sign, a *t* with a snake, and *mo* with with a coffee cup full of green stuff.

Did the hands mean "thanks" or "pray"? What did the canned food with an apostrophe *t* mean? And a *t* in front of a snake? What was the green stuff in the cup?

The girls talked it out, like on *Wheel of Fortune*. Then they deciphered it at the same time: *Thanks I can't be cool right at this moment.*

The ice had been broken, but Bailey was still not budging.

More texts ensued.

On the deck, Reverend Tate answered Jason's questions about the two girls. "They are ... how do I say this? ... Well, intriguing. Both are somewhat outcasts in their own way. Emily can't stand the establishment, anything related to commercialism, spoiled stars and brats, and on and on. Her grandparents were hippies, and her mother followed in their footsteps. Her father was killed in Afghanistan, so she is antiwar. She even questions the church in many ways. Anna, on the other hand, lives with her aunt and uncle. It's a sad situation—addictions and neglect by her parents. They both see the church as their family, and I guess I am the surrogate mother. Now that they've hit their teens, I can see some changes taking place. Some teen jealousies are emerging. Anna, with her new body and a need to be loved, worries me a bit, and Emily seems headed to any liberal protest she can find. It would not surprise me if she were arrested one day. Still, they both cling to each other like sisters. The cause du jour this summer is sea turtles."

As they were finishing up their conversation, the girls came back outside. Jason looked over at them, hoping for a miracle.

Anna plopped down beside Jason, and Emily took the other side. She showed her phone to Jason, who had no clue what he was looking at. He shook his head, defeated by emojis and teen creativity. "Okay girls, I give up."

Anna was about to pop with excitement. "*Hello?* She texted back, Mr. Jason!"

Emily leaned over and interpreted their cryptic messages for him.

Reverend Tate laughed out loud when Emily finished. "Jason, when these girls make up their minds to do something, it gets done." She related how during COVID-19 they had come up with a plan to keep the church going without people in the pews. Emily's uncle, who lived in Greensboro, was a sound man, and he suggested the church get an FM transmitter and broadcast their service to the parking lot while worshipers parked safely outside. Of course, Emily and Anna took it one step further as the pandemic scare slowly diminished. They found all the weathered and forgotten picnic tables on the island, set them up six feet away from each other around the church parking lot, worked out a plan for local restaurants to provide drinks and small foods, and asked people to bring their radios or get on the church Facebook page. Suddenly, the church parking lot was a large coffee shop and café lounge.

The thing was so popular, the church kept it going long after the pandemic had been declared "over."

"Bailey's gonna be a tough one, but we're tougher!" Anna called out like a coach in the locker room.

"Come on, girls, we got other things to get done." Reverend Tate playfully pulled them along as they headed to the steps. "Jason, you and Bailey come check us out one Sunday."

Jason nodded his head. "Just might do that, Reverend. Just might do that."

The next day, Jason's phone buzzed, and he pulled it out. A text from Maria. *What?* He called her quickly. "How bad? ... He wants Bailey? Why—? ... I'll do what I can." He hung up and rushed to Bailey's room and called out, "Bailey, Frederick's hurt! He's at the hospital. It's bad, sweetie. He's asking for you. C'mon!"

He waited by the door, pacing a bit and thinking she might be putting on her clothes and makeup and twisting her hair into a new style, whatever girls do behind closed doors, but there was no answer. If Fredrick being hurt could not get her out of her funk then ...

"*Bailey Parker!*" he hollered at the closed door. "I've had enough. Frederick's in trouble. *Big* trouble. He's asking for you. He saved your butt, dammit! Now it's your turn. He does not have all day. He may not live. Get going *right now,* young lady!"

He heard the shuffling of feet, what sounded like clothes being put on, something he could not recognize, and then the door opened slowly. Still not talking, still looking scared and withdrawn, head still down in shame with shoulders pulled forward, Bailey silently walked down the hall and headed to the car.

The two of them rushed to room eight in the ER at the mainland hospital. Jason knocked on the glass door, and Maria motioned for him to come in. Bailey stayed behind him and dug her feet in when she saw Frederick lying listless, caged in the huge hospital bed by thick rails. Fredericka, sitting by the bed and holding her son's hand, turned to see Bailey and Jason. Her eyes were bleary with tears, and her face was covered in fear.

Maria brought Jason up to speed as Fredericka worried and prayed over her bruised and broken son. He had been coming back from a delivery that morning when some kids in a BMW with Jersey plates began harassing him. Some tourists riding behind Frederick got it all on their camera phones. The boys deliberately swerved at Frederick's bike several times until he lost control and crashed off the road. Then they sped off. The tourists called 911 while waiting for the EMS and then gave the sheriff the video after he'd arrived.

Bailey, like most teens who've never been in a hospital room, much less an ER, was visibly shaken by the frightening scene before her. There was a machine by Frederick's bed with wires and tubes connected to his lifeless body. A tube around his face and sticking in his nose was connected to some chrome thing on the wall behind the bed. A thin plastic tube was stuck into his arm and covered with layers of tape. The other end of the tube connected to a large plastic bag of fluids hanging from a chrome rack on a pole with wheels. Wires were all over his body, going under the faded hospital gown. More wires were stuck on his bandaged and bruised head. They were connected to a panel behind the bed that looked like a small flatscreen TV. On the screen were squiggly green lines, red flashing lights, and all kinds of numbers. A slight beeping tone kept a rhythm. His other arm was wrapped in thick gauze with some sort of plastic-looking braces protruding from underneath. Bruises and scratches brought more attention to his freckled face and competed with what little bits of his freckled arms she could see. A long yellow tube came out from under the foot of the bed and dripped gross yellow-and-red fluids into a plastic bag resting just above the floor. The thick rails of polished steel and plastic on both sides of the bed seemed to guard Frederick from any more harm.

Bailey was horrified.

"I sure do hope you're Bailey!" an ER nurse called out from the other side of the room. She had thick coils of blonde hair with obvious dark roots in full view. She was average height, no makeup, tanned, and had a kind of stocky build. Her movements were graceful yet deft, decisive, as if every one of them mattered. She was strong in stature, welcoming in countenance, and absolutely in charge in a professional yet courteous way.

As she waited for an answer, Bailey didn't move. The sight of Frederick in the bed after the accident was one thing. The tubes, wires, bandages, and bits of blood here and there were overwhelming. But this was also the first time she had seen him after the attack. He had seen her with her shirt opened and a man grabbing at her, and even though she knew he had saved her from being raped, she was very ashamed he had seen her that way. To get close to him meant she had to reopen those wounds, awaken those psychological pains, the very thing she had tried to stay away from the past week. In a strange way, to be near Frederick now caused the very shame she dealt with every day, the shame she had tried and failed to shut out by hiding all week, to hit her with a vengeance. It was like she could see her naked, vulnerable self when she looked at Frederick.

"Miss Fredericka, let's let Bailey have this seat for a moment, dear." The nurse encouragingly touched Fredericka on the shoulder, as if tapping a button that would release her from the chair. When Fredericka stepped away, the nurse patted the chair kindly yet authoritatively. "Right there, Miss Bailey."

Bailey, who had ignored her father, pushed away a concerned Maria, snubbed the sheriff, and remained mute during a therapy session, slowly obeyed the pushy nurse. She sat beside Frederick looking sad, lost, and scared.

The nurse checked the machine on the pole on the other side of the massive hospital bed and made an adjustment, checked the tube on Frederick's hand, tapped it to be sure, and then walked around to Bailey's side. Bailey stared blankly at the confusing information on the screen.

"So Bailey, you are now Nurse Bailey. Ever since Frederick arrived here this afternoon, he has been asking, 'Is Bailey okay?' We've got him on pain medication, and his brain scans are normal; we don't think there is a brain injury, but he just won't settle down. See those numbers and lights up there?" She pointed to the screen. "With all the stuff he's on, they should be slower than snails. They need to slow down so we can make sure he is ready for the operation to fix his broken arm. The surgeon does not want to do the procedure until he knows for sure that the brain is okay. We think that if you talk to him, he will settle down."

Bailey looked at the nurse then the screen in confusion. Finally, after a long and not very encouraging silence, she spoke for the first time in a week. "But … he's asleep."

Jason flashed a look at Maria, whose eyebrows raised suddenly. Then she quickly put her finger to her lips. Fredericka gasped and then caught herself.

"He looks like he's asleep, dearie. Playing opossum. Watch this." She leaned over Frederick's face and gently said, "Frederick, Bailey's here."

He rolled his face to the voice, smiled slightly, and then slurred out, "Bailey, are you okay?"

The nurse took Bailey's very reluctant and trembling hand and placed it on Frederick's upper arm. "Your turn, dearie." Then she turned to the adults and motioned for them to scoot back. While Bailey worked up her courage, the nurse went back to the computer, efficiently swiped her card, and inputted data, occasionally turning to look at the screen.

Bailey dodged the real issue and Frederick. "What is the tube in his nose for?"

The nurse answered but never looked up. "Oxygen. He has a broken rib and bruised ribs, so it's hard for him to breathe. That helps him."

Bailey paused and then looked at the wires running under his gown. "What are the wires for?"

"Telemetry. They tell us what his body is saying. That's some of those numbers up there."

"Why's his arm so wrapped up?"

The nurse turned around and stared for a moment, as if to say, *Really?* "Broken arm, honey. That's what the operation is for. We need to get him in there soon. It's a bad break."

Fredericka wanted to say something, anything, to get Bailey to talk to Frederick, but the nurse subtly shook her head.

"What's that tube with the yellow and red stuff?"

The nurse coldly said, "Catheter. He had some kidney bruising, so his urine is bloody. We're keeping an eye on it."

Slowly, the ice of shame began to melt deep in Bailey's soul. Her heart warmed up for her friend and savior, and from out of nowhere, she ever-so-slightly rubbed Frederick's arm, first with a hesitant index finger then with her hand.

Frederick groggily looked over at her and smiled again. "Bailey, is that you? Are you okay?" he whispered. "Please, tell me you're okay."

Bailey, her defenses weakened by Frederick's unselfish pleas of concern, breathed in, now ready for the first step in healing herself. She lay her head on Frederick's arm. "I'm okay, Frederick."

Frederick smiled and then winced.

Bailey looked up when he jerked in pain. "What about you? You're going to be okay too, aren't you?"

There was a long silence, as if Frederick had fallen asleep. Then he turned to look at her, and his big, signature grin emerged all over his pale, freckled face. He raised his good hand and gave a thumbs-up. "You betcha!" Then he dropped his hand, rolled his face the other way, and closed his eyes.

"Oh my God!" Bailey wailed. "Is he dead?"

The nurse, always calm and in charge, walked over and rubbed Bailey's back. "Sweetie, look at the screen."

As Fredericka, Jason, and Maria stepped closer to the patient, the numbers changed, the beeps slowed, and the squiggly lines shifted from erratic to measured impulses.

The nurse pulled out her hospital phone, punched in two numbers, and then spoke into it. "He's ready; let's go. Good job, Nurse Bailey," she said, standing up as two CNAs rushed into the room. They readied the bed and patient for transport, Fredericka kissed her son's forehead, Jason and Maria wished him well, and then he was gone.

Suddenly, the intensity of the room vanished, and an antiseptic smell broke the shock of the new silence.

Bailey turned toward Fredericka and warmly, if a bit tentatively, gave her a hug. Then she turned to her father, wrapped her arms around him, and said, "I'm sorry." Then the dam broke, and she wailed.

Jason held his quaking daughter while Fredericka looked on, and Maria stood behind Bailey, rubbing her back.

"That's twice Frederick has saved my daughter," Jason, who was now sobbing as well, said to Fredericka.

She looked puzzled. "How so?"

"First from the creep, now from herself."

TEN

The Fourteens

In the week following Frederick's accident, Bailey finally came out of her room. Now the main task in the Parker Palace was getting her out of the house and back into the world. Maria invited her over for breakfast, like they used to do, but that meant going back to the scene of the crime, so Bailey's mental heels dug in at that request. Girl walks on the beach? Nope. Anna and Emily, still sending salvos of emojis, had invited her out, but Bailey texted back the usual canned food emoji with an *'t* (*can't*). Frederick was healing up at home now but could not ride a bike over to visit. Besides, he had no bike to ride anyway. He tried sending Bailey a postcard (she smiled), emails (she responded with a *thx* and smiley face), and texts (various smiley faces). So for the moment, nothing and no one could get Bailey away from the house. She was either on the deck or inside.

Maria decided to get some advice from Tara. She took Jason as well. For some peculiar reason, it felt like a date. Sort of. In a weird way. "What do we do?"

Jason squirmed uncomfortably in the weathered environs of the trendy coffee shop. "Are you sure this is *food*, Maria?" he whispered in her ear as he pondered the morning menu. "Cauliflower this, cauliflower that." Food now on the table, he was not quite sure of the plant-based thing on a biscuit in front of him.

"It's healthy, Jason," Maria chided. "You know, for your figure and everything." She winked at Tara who fanned herself with a napkin. *It's not the summer sun that has her temperature rising,* Maria thought with a small chuckle.

The ocean breeze was quite brisk, and the flaps on the canopies snapped and clapped in response. Tourists jogged by, some pushing baby strollers, others seemingly trying to impress those who looked their way or passed by. Two boys rolled by on skateboards. Out over the ocean, a parasail pulled by a large boat carried a thrill seeker into a new experience.

"Little steps, Maria," Tara advised before noticing Jason's reluctance to the healthy fare in front of him. "You know, if you actually put it in your mouth, you can decide whether it's good or not."

Jason frowned, but Maria burst out laughing. He reluctantly took a small bite of the biscuit.

"Well, you didn't spit it out, so that's a start. If you come back tomorrow for a second session, I'll teach you how to chew it."

Jason smiled and then swallowed. "Not bad."

Tara looked back at Maria. "Start with you going to her house for, say, breakfast. Get her familiar with you again. Hang out with her on the deck. Get her to look at the trailer, then maybe walk by the trailer to go to the car. Don't forget peer pressure. The kids may have more luck than you two."

Maria looked over at Tara, her eyebrows raised as she pulled out her phone. She texted a long message to Frederick. While Jason was still getting used to the strange food that actually tasted good, Maria noticed that the women and teen girls in the shop were surrounding the windows and staring intently at the gorgeous man at their table. Tara noticed as well and smirked at Maria, who became strangely protective of her man. *Whoa, where did that come from?*

Tara cleared her throat. "Anyway, after a few days, see if she will come over to the trailer to help you out. Eventually, she will break."

Maria shook her head and cited the old adage. "You can lead a horse to water, but you can't make her drink."

Tara nodded. "True, but eventually, the horse will get thirsty and go there herself when she knows it's safe."

Maria looked over at Jason who had quietly finished his breakfast and was, amazingly, still alive. "Okay, Mr. Healthy, breakfast at your place in the morning."

"She'll want her Froot Loops and PB and J."

"That may be what she wants, but they'll stay in my kitchen until she comes and gets them. In the meantime, what she'll get is a waffle with strawberries."

"Good luck with that," Jason answered.

On the way home, Maria got a text back from Frederick.

It's all arranged, Ms. Gowins. My place, tomorrow, 3 pm. C U there?

She texted back a thumbs-up.

The next morning, the Parker Palace smelled like a country diner. Maria had waffles with freshly sliced, late-season strawberries on the table, complete with real maple syrup.

Bailey, hair unbrushed and body covered with an XXL sweatshirt, looked a bit spooked and inquired about her Froot Loops and PB and J.

Maria opened the fridge and reached in for the butter as she answered coolly. "In the trailer, Bailey, if you want to go get them."

Now Bailey was stuck between a rock and a hard place. The rock being her not getting to eat the breakfast she had eaten for, like, forever and being forced to consume something entirely new, and the hard place being her having to go to the trailer and face the frightening memory of being attacked. Choosing the lesser of two evils, she hesitantly sat down at the table as Jason entered the room, though her OCD was off the scale.

Maria forked a waffle and then handed the platter to Bailey, who slowly picked up her fork, poked the waffles as if testing to see if they might explode, and placed one on her plate. Then she gave the platter to her father. Maria, as if demonstrating the new culinary task, spooned some strawberries onto her waffle and handed the bowl to Bailey, who let the juice run all the way off the spoon before meticulously arranging the berries so they weren't touching her waffle. Jason took the bowl from Bailey's slightly shaking hand and spooned the fresh red fruit onto his waffle.

"Smells good, Maria! A fine breakfast for us, right, Bailey?" Jason asked, sounding like the positive and upbeat father in *A Christmas Story*. He reached for the maple syrup, poured some, and then handed the bottle to Maria, who soaked her waffle before handing it to Bailey. Suddenly, breakfast was on pause. Maria and Jason silently watched Bailey think through the daunting task ahead. Calculations were made, a plan drawn up, and then the foreboding, never-before-done task begun. Maria pointed to Jason's expensive wrist watch, and he quietly tapped the timer button.

One by one, Bailey carefully filled each square space in a row, making sure they all had the same amount of syrup, before moving to the next space, finishing out the row and then going back down the next row, one tiny square at a time. Not soon enough for Jason and Maria, each quarter of the waffle now filled with syrup, Bailey ended the tortuous procedure by filling the seam between each quarter. Finally, she carefully placed the bottle down on the table, not making a sound.

Jason tapped the timer on his watch.

Two minutes, fifteen seconds.

With Bailey (still alive) rinsing the dishes and placing them in the dishwasher, and Jason calling clients for work, Maria decided to retreat back to the quiet of the trailer. The chaos of the event had subsided, and renovations and moving in were finally done, so this was the first time she had actually stopped. She settled into a chair in her new den—the old vinyl complete with nail holes creaking and cracking but still holding strong—breathed in and exhaled and then marveled at how the old chair had survived the event.

Without Bailey in the morning, it was quiet. Too quiet. Maria, a bit tired from making breakfast, closed her eyes for a moment but soon was fast asleep.

Big fluffy rabbits circled around the trailer like a merry-go-round, with Maria as the center pole. As the rabbits circled her, she became more and more dizzy. Then ordinary rabbits, still circling, surrounded a young woman sitting on the beach who cowered in fear and began calling out, her cries lost in the crashing of the waves. Then the rabbits grew vicious fangs inches long as they circled an innocent newborn baby. They darted toward the child and snapped their jaws. Suddenly, demonic creatures screamed and burst into what seemed to be a raging river of blood, which then swirled counterclockwise into a black vortex that bored into the earth. Maria's trailer was sucked down into the depths, disappearing amid a blaring roar of screeching voices.

Maria woke with a start, sweating all over, goosebumps everywhere, shivering, cold as death.

"What the hell?" she called out to an empty trailer.

The words *the old Simpson trailer* reverberated in her shaking head.

That afternoon, Frederick, now healed up enough to go out, held a top-secret meeting with Maria, Emily, and Anna at his house. Plans drawn up, the girls scooted away to see if Ja'meel, the latest heartthrob, was working at the pavilion concession stand—"Like, OMG, he uses a pick in his 'fro!"—while Frederick went with Maria to the library. It was an old island house connected by a breezeway to another old house, the local Banker's Point Museum. They both shared archives, and the museum featured a historical collection of local artifacts and pictures, but in the back room were shelves of folders, file boxes, bound materials, and file cabinets filled with who knew what. Maria the Historian felt at home; Frederick, sometimes a patron looking for a book but who normally did his research online at home, looked totally overwhelmed.

"Ms. Gowins, I don't know if I can do this," he said worriedly as he scanned the room once more.

Maria answered, "Frederick, you are exactly right; you can't. That's why we have librarians."

Just then, an older fellow, somewhat bald, thin, and seemingly on his last leg, wandered over. "I'm Clyde Banker, young lady, and I see you have Frederick the Hero with you. You are in good hands, ma'am."

Frederick grinned. "Mr. Banker, you know I'm no hero."

"I think a whole island might disagree with you, young man." He patted Frederick on the shoulder. "How's that arm doing?" Not waiting for an answer, he inquired about Fredericka as well. Eventually, he got back on track. "What can I help you two with?"

Maria introduced herself and then briefly explained their project. "Somebody needs to write a new one. The other is old and poorly written. It sells well, but gosh, it's riddled with grammatical mistakes and misspelled words. Self-published, as I recall. I bet we have a lot of new items that we could add."

They inquired about old pictures, stories from families, family genealogies, newspaper clippings about the island, old phone books, church records, and some old recordings and family film clips.

"Frederick wants to do interviews, and I have a young lady who aspires to be a writer that we are going to use as well. Kind of a Foxfire thing. Think you can help us out here?" Maria inquired. Then it dawned on her that the librarian was a Banker. "Wait a minute, are you from the original Bankers?"

"In the flesh."

As Clyde retrieved folders and files and pictures and old, yellowed newspapers, Maria peppered him with numerous questions. "Clyde, when I drive around the island, I see a lot of old, fifties-style trailers evenly spaced apart. That can't be by accident. Do you know the story?"

Clyde nodded, left the history room for a moment, and then returned with a folder of old advertisements. "This should interest you, Maria." He opened it up, and she saw ad after ad and numerous brochures inviting vacationers to think about moving permanently to the island. "There was nothing here on the island in the fifties except for some old, rundown fishing shanties, decaying duck blinds, and a row of houses, shacks really, built from scraps of this and that, whatever they could salvage from shipwrecks and such back then. The military had some operations here during the second war, but nobody is quite sure what that was about. When the war ended, they left all the buildings and skedaddled. Locals fought each other as they dismantled the buildings or moved them to their properties. The old Black lady's store, the one with the baskets and all, is made from three of those structures tacked together. Anyway, a decade or so later, one store, a small Methodist church, the old seafood operation, and a small—for lack of a better word—hotel was about all that was here. Some fellas from the mainland came in with an idea: They would buy the land from the folks and then build vacation spots with the new mobile homes that were all the rage back then. Patios, plant a few trees, and so on."

Maria was intrigued.

Frederick spoke up. "Mr. Clyde, most of the people in those trailers now are really old. Are they the original owners?"

Clyde looked at the budding historian. "Well now, young man, I have a feeling you are about to find out. Those folks love to talk about the old days."

Maria handed a stack of brochures to Frederick, and then she saw an old newspaper clip. "Simpson Trailer Haunted." The date was September 28, 2002. She tucked it away and then feigned a reason to go to the ladies room, where she read the article. Twice.

What have I gotten myself into?

In the article, locals and tourists reported strange occurrences around the trailer at night. People walking the public-access beach path heard what seemed to be a young girl crying. Some saw a ghostly figure at the end of the trailer, sitting in the sand. Others saw what appeared to be rabbits jumping around at night. Sometimes, passersby thought they saw lights emanating from the sandy yard.

Coming back to the history room, Maria paused and made a copy and then slipped the original quietly back into the worn folder.

Two hours later, the historians had a plan outlined and a list of people to interview.

As they left the library, Frederick paused. "I wish Bailey would have been here."

Try as they might, Jason and Maria, and even Frederick, could not get Bailey in or near the trailer during the week. Maria washed intimates and texted Bailey to come over and get hers. She had Frederick, Emily, and Anna over for pizza and invited Bailey. No Bailey. No girl talk, no sodas on the patio or new deck. No interest in the Beach Brew. No beach walking. No Bailey unless one visited her in the Parker Palace. She would go out on the deck, wearing thick, oversized sweatshirts and leggings, and look seaward for what seemed hours, but she never went to the beach trailer side. But one sign of healing was now obvious: Every day, her long, beautiful hair was washed and fashioned into yet another Bailey coiffure.

Maria, wondering what might pull Bailey out of her trance, for some reason remembered Hattie. The few lessons she had with Hattie had indeed been good for her soul, ameliorating her temper somewhat, and she thought Hattie's artistry, depth, and wisdom might benefit Bailey if Maria could just get her there. She finally cajoled, prodded, and somehow convinced Bailey—who was still reluctant, embarrassed to be seen in public, and covered in shame—to go with her to look at the shops in the village. "I need some shorts and some tops that say 'beach' when I wear them. I might need a consultant." Somewhere along the way, she would introduce Bailey to Hattie.

Two pairs of wide-legged shorts, one spaghetti-strap top, and one daring, for Maria anyway, bikini top later, the shopping list was completely checked off. After much imploring, they enjoyed a smoothie on the porch of the Smooth Sailing Stand. It took a bit, but Bailey finally agreed to the strawberry-banana smoothie if they used only one fruit, not two. Apparently, ice and fruit side by side was okay.

Refreshed with the cool treat, Maria tugged Bailey to the Mermaid's Locker for a look around. One pair of modest high-waisted frayed shorts for Bailey, and it was time.

The walk down the sandy path by the main road was in the sun, and Maria suggested they escape the heat by ducking into the Island Folk Crafts store. "Bailey, I wanted to look at some baskets in here anyway. I saw some the other day: Authentic Southern African-American low-country crafts. You game?"

Bailey's sluggish nod said, "Anything to get out of the heat." Her long-sleeved, oversized shirt and sweat pants probably didn't help either.

The bell on the weathered wooden screen door chimed as both women stepped inside the small store and workshop. Kennedy, finishing up a sale at the register, waved at Maria. The air conditioning was refreshing. Bailey, still just inside the door, cased the whole joint, as if terrorists might appear out of nowhere, or an IED might explode. Convinced all was tentatively safe, she perused the different crafts and was then curiously attracted to the seagrass wall art.

Hattie, attentive to energies with more than just her five main senses and feeling a deeply troubled spirit in the room, looked up from her basket, quickly assessed Bailey, and then surmised the distraught young girl's issues. "Maria, who's this woman with you today?" she asked, continuing her weaving.

Maria introduced a sheepish Bailey, and Hattie pointed a worn and stubby finger to Bailey and then to a chair in front of her as she deftly wove pine needles and straw together. Bailey respectively, if suspiciously, took her seat and, having never seen such a craft, was mesmerized instantly.

Maria gravitated toward some baskets on the other side of the shop as Hattie got to know Bailey. "Bailey, everybody's got a story. Tell me your story." It was more of a command than an invitation to chat. As Bailey assessed the command, Hattie called out, "Maria, I think Bailey and I need some quiet time. Why don't you and Kennedy lock the door and put that Closed sign up for me as you go outside."

Bailey got a spooked look on her face, instantly wondering what she had done wrong. What was Maria up to? More psychology? More "get out of your shell" nonsense? More in-your-face "it's good for you"?

Hattie caught on to Bailey's anxiety immediately. "Child, you ain't done nothin' wrong, so calm down." Hattie's bluntness, though she never paused from her weaving, was disconcerting to Bailey. While she had several Black friends in school, she had never really interacted with an *older* Black woman before, so she was not used to the strength, power, and wisdom in the voice of blunt, matronly authority. When the door clicked shut, Hattie spoke up. "Bailey, tell me about yourself. How old you are? What you wanna be when you grow up?" Bailey thought for a moment as she worked the courage up to respond and then shared her story briefly. Then Hattie continued. "Bailey, in my tradition, we older womens give a blessing to the younger ones. We pass on our spirits to them, hand over our wisdom and our souls to them for the next generation. Some girls and young womens listens and learns. Others toss it out the door. Your choice."

Bailey was still confused, but ever polite and respectful of her elders, she listened attentively.

Hattie saw questions written all over Bailey's face. It wasn't anything she hadn't seen before. "Bailey, we both womens, right? It don't matter our color or where we from. We all belong to the Womanhood, the Sisterhood, and we need to stand together in strength. Got me?" She wove another strand as Bailey soaked in the lesson, one word at a time. Hattie quietly and patiently waited for Bailey to process her words. "Now I want you to listen to me and listen to me good, hear? I believe in a Plan. We all here for a reason. Kennedy asked me to come here this summer for a reason. After I met Maria, I began to see what that reason was. You here today for a reason too. It's part of the Plan. I see how you walk and how you look at yoself, and I know what you feelin'." Hattie, who was very chesty herself, related her insecurities as a child, a teen. How men had mistreated her. "So here's my blessing to you. I want you to listen to me carefully, hear?"

With that question, Hattie stopped her weaving, placed the half-finished basket carefully on the floor like it was a delicate antique, and stared Bailey directly in the eye. It scared Bailey, caught her off guard, but she felt she had to look at Hattie because greater forces were now at work.

The air conditioner in the window hummed, and the scent of pine needles, straw, and old wood wafted about as the drafts cooled the old store. The shop suddenly felt filled with a palpable presence, like a fog, a spirit, a force from far away. Soon Bailey recognized it. She had felt it before. The night she'd skinny-dipped with Maria ... the night they saw Turtle.

Hattie said, "Scoot closer to me and gimme your hands, child." She grabbed Bailey's now-quivering hands.

Bailey felt the coarseness of Hattie's thick, aged fingers, saw the wrinkles in her skin, and then was aware of a glow in Hattie's weathered ebony face. Suddenly, she did not look old. She was radiant. Angelic. Maternal. Eternal.

"Bailey, you is part of the Plan, you understand? God made you for a reason 'cause you part of the Plan. God made you, and that means you is beautiful. And 'cause God made you for a reason, listen to me now, every inch of you is blessed. Do you understand what I'm sayin'? Every, *every* inch of you is blessed." Hattie carefully, wisely, shook Bailey's hands for emphasis. "*Every inch*, Bailey."

Bailey felt currents go through her hands, tingles into her arms, pulses shuddering her shoulders, and then they surged down to her body and electrified her legs and feet. Warmth melted her shame and insecurities. Images of roots and soil mystically appeared through what seemed like a haze, grounding her into the depths of the universe.

"Every inch of you, Bailey." Hattie squeezed her hands tightly, assuredly, lovingly.

Bailey, now empowered by years, generations, centuries of love and blessings and wisdom rooted in a past that was fertilized with pain and grace, slowly understood Hattie's words. The shame, embarrassment, even fear of her body were now transformed into something new. It was not finished; indeed, it would be a while before she gave in to it completely, but the initial spark had been lit.

Hattie waited patiently, wisely, until she saw the nearly imperceptible glint of change in Bailey's green eyes. "Understand me now?"

"Every inch of me is blessed," Bailey repeated slowly, suddenly learning a new mantra. "Every inch."

Hattie let it sink in. Then, blessing achieved, she let go of Bailey's hands.

Empowered by a force she had never felt before, emboldened to a new confidence, Bailey got up, leaned over to Hattie, and hugged her close. "Thank you, Miss Hattie. I understand. Thank you for blessing me. I will never forget this."

But Hattie was not finished. "Now you told me you was a writer. All writers need a story to write. Ima give you mine. Ain't never shared the whole story with nobody before. It weren't part of the Plan ... but it is now. I saw this when you walked in the room. You got a phone?"

Bailey reached into her back pocket and pulled it out.

"Put that on record or somethin'. Now Ima tell you *my* story."

Hattie picked up her basket and resumed her weaving, as if the story came from the pine needles. As she leaned back, she related ... no, moaned and even preached in sing-song fashion her past, her parents' pasts, going back many generations to the lore of her ancestors back in Africa. Her voice was like a song, sonorous, spiritual. The warring tribes, the capture, the life behind fences and in filthy barracoons, sold like cows and goats by her own people to the White men. The dangerous and deadly stench-filled passage across the Atlantic, being worked to death in the humid heat of the Caribbean then sailed against their will to South Carolina to the rice plantations, standing naked on the auction block in Charleston, the generations in slavery, the whip, sold and resold, eventually winding up near coastal North Carolina, the escape from slavery to the Outer Banks at the end of the Civil War, from President Lincoln, Reconstruction, Jim Crow, lynching, church burning, suddenly missing family, ending with her own family and how she came to Banker's Point for the summer.

It was the stuff of Black History Month, but it was the first time Bailey had *heard* the whole story, the *real* story, and *felt* the history, and *experienced* the pain and the hopeful resilience of African Americans.

Two hours later, Bailey had her first real story to write. And what a story it was.

The following Saturday, the blue summer sky was etched by lines of pelicans, punctuated by diving birds and occasional clouds that brought some respite from the sun. Beachgoers laden with chairs, carts, and coolers filed along casually on the walkway behind the trailer. Kids screamed on the beach, men stood by fishing rods, and women tanned and read beach novels all while teens surfed the net instead of the ocean waves.

Behind the dunes, the party was getting started. As far as Bailey knew, it was supposed to be a celebration of Frederick the Hero. Emily, Anna, and Reverend Tate, for the first time, saw the stunning Bailey. Emily and Anna both were instantly jealous—*OMG, she's gorgeous,* Anna mouthed to Emily— but soon their Christian compassion emerged to take care of this wounded victim. Fredericka stood on the mansion deck with Bailey, whose hair featured a short ponytail that became a braid that turned back into a ponytail and then ended with a final braid with a cute bow at the end that matched her new shorts. Maria, in a spaghetti-strap top, played hostess, and Jason, somewhat distracted by the thin straps, was as dapper as an ad in *GQ.* He served drinks, soft and hard, at the bar. "Reverend Tate, would you be offended if we served beer or wine?"

Reverend Tate, wearing cutoffs and a T-shirt that read "God Bless All Nations," looked at Jason with a stern countenance. Suddenly, he was worried. "Jason, if I were Baptist, I would be, but I'm Methodist, and we think that Jesus changed water into wine, not grape juice." She smiled and reached for a beer, and Jason breathed a huge sigh of relief.

The kids wanted to play music and dance, and soon the deck was rocking. Maria, ever the teacher, used Bluetooth to play a song through the speakers and showed them the Electric Slide. Then Anna stepped up, found the appropriate tune on her phone using Bluetooth again, and taught them the Cha Cha Slide she learned at her cousin's wedding. Her boots clunked out the rhythm.

When they got that down to an art, Reverend Tate looked over at Maria and Jason. "Either of you know how to shag?"

Mountain Girl Maria could still clog a bit, but she had not learned the coastal moves. Jason answered yes, and after dialing up "I Love Beach Music," he and the Reverend were teaching the kids the official dance of the Carolina coast. The three girls all wanted to dance with Frederick, who had the smoothest moves of them all. Fredericka and Maria—who annoyingly found herself a bit jealous over Jason dancing with Reverend Tate—stood back and watched the whole show. It became comical when Slow-as-Christmas Bailey, big feet trying to move, danced with the crisp and smooth Frederick. It didn't help that she was a head taller than him. Emily and Anna paired up and soon were singing the lyrics.

Now that they were all danced out, it was time for supper. Jason stood guard over the grill, which was larger than many people's kitchens, and soon burgers and dogs were on the plates with chips and then cupcakes for dessert. Everyone stared and waited as patiently as they could while Bailey meticulously arranged her plate. Ketchup in a perfectly straight line on one side of the hot dog, mustard in a parallel line on the other, neither condiment touching the other. Chips distantly away from the dog, chili on the side, complete with a spoon.

Jason, full of emotions, uncharacteristically asked Reverend Tate to do a blessing. Food blessed, six people watched as Bailey spooned a dob of chili into her mouth and then took a bite of her hot dog. Chewing a mouthful of food, she looked up to see twelve eyes staring in utter disbelief. "What?" she mumbled through a mouth full of food.

After the feast, all settled back with full tummies. Then Emily finally dropped the bomb. "Can we see your new deck, Ms. Gowins?"

Anna chimed in too. "Please?"

No one wanted to look Bailey's way, but all knew what the party was really for.

Maria tried to break the ice. "You know, Emily, it's been adult-tested but not kid-approved yet. I could use some opinions, some thumbs-up, five stars, likes, anything."

Frederick jumped in. "It could be, like, a teens-only thing! No adults allowed, right?"

"Like a club or secret hideout!" Anna shouted out.

"What's our password?" Emily asked. "You gotta have a password."

Suddenly, all were stupefied. Each looked at the other. What would be a cool name for the new secret club?

As each teen thought about it, Bailey's pouty lips, the ones that were once sullen and sad for days, suddenly transformed into a smirk. She painstakingly took out her phone and started texting.

Jason looked over at her. "Bailey, uh, kind of rude there, girl."

But Bailey, traveling the myriad lanes of 5G, never looked up. Soon she made a grand gesture of hitting Send, meticulously tucked her phone into the back pocket of her shorts, smiled, and suddenly everybody's phone pinged. They all looked at their phones, but all they saw was *14s*.

Every face had a confused expression.

Bailey smirked. "Silly, it's easy. The four teens. Get it? We're all fourteen. So the number fourteen with an *s*. Fourteens."

Before the adults knew it, three teens were bounding down the steps while Bailey followed suit at her own measured pace. The teens, including Bailey, now on the deck, checked out the view, sent selfies to friends and family, and then danced to music played through their phones.

Jason, Maria, and Fredericka were stunned, mouths wide open.

Reverend Tate smiled. Another miracle. "The girls never give up," she noted.

"Thank God!" Jason sighed.

"Indeed," Reverend Tate nodded.

The party now over, the sun resting after another long summer day of roasting tourists, and the pathway behind the trailer now deserted, Reverend Tate had taken Anna and Emily home. Maria's deck was now sadly quiet. Bailey and Frederick were sitting on the top step of the deck of the Parker Palace, looking out introspectively over the sea. Inside, Maria, Jason, and Fredericka watched the mismatched pair and wondered what they were talking about.

After a long silence, serenaded by the ocean waves and soothed with the salty breeze, a reticent, pensive Bailey finally asked what had bothered her for days. The very question that had separated her from the one who saved her.

Bailey, looking far out over the ocean, trembled as she asked Frederick, "Did you see me? When that man attacked me, did you see me?"

"Sure, I saw you being attacked," he answered. "I saw you scream and hide behind the counter."

"No, I mean ... did you *see me?*" She teared up, and her voice was desperate, filled with shame and embarrassment.

"Bailey, I don't get it. Why are you crying?" Frederick was having a hard time understanding the question. He remembered opening the door and seeing the man reaching for Bailey, her torn shirt, and the fear on her face.

Bailey was softly sobbing now, quivering, reliving the moment. She calmed down enough to ask once more, knowing she would have to say it out loud clearly this time. She looked down in shame and then looked him in the eyes. "Frederick, did you see my *breasts?*"

In all their time together, Frederick only ever saw Bailey. Even in his hormonal adolescence, he just saw Bailey. He saw her hair, legs, lips, shoulders, hands, hips, smile, laughter, insecurities. And yes, her chest. But it was just part of a greater whole. Mostly, he just saw a friend. It never occurred to him to see Bailey just for her breasts. Never. "Bailey," he answered carefully, thoughtfully. "What I saw was my friend in danger."

Still skeptical, still knowing how boys are, still hurt and even blaming herself and momentarily forgetting Hattie's blessing, Bailey was not convinced. "Are you sure? You're not lying to me, are you?"

Frederick looked at Bailey, hurt now all over his face. "I would never lie to my girlfriend."

Bailey, shock now appearing on her distraught, tear-stained face, slowly looked over at him, and in what seemed a lifetime to Frederick, her quivering lips stilled and then bent into a small, hesitant smile. "Did you just call me your girlfriend?"

Frederick, face growing hot, realized what he had said and what he had revealed and what that implied. "I—I'm sorry, I meant 'friend,' I swear. I don't know—"

She reached out for his hand, the hand that had saved her, still wrapped in a cast, and held it carefully and softly. "I would love to be your girlfriend."

The last row of pelicans for the day flew across the darkening skies as Frederick and Bailey held hands.

The next week, the Fourteens gathered at Club Trailer, raced up to the deck, phones connected to a new wireless speaker, and danced the evenings away. Maria, sometimes with Jason's assistance, would make sandwiches, serve snacks, and refill cups. Otherwise, the deck was now off limits to adults, even if they *did* know the secret password. The third night, it started raining, so the Fourteens decided to go inside the trailer rather than end the party. Anna grabbed the speaker, and then she, Emily, and Frederick bounded inside, but Bailey's eyes filled with fear, and her feet glued themselves to the concrete patio. She wrapped her arms around her chest, as if protecting herself from any harm that might come her way.

Anyone could hear the tension over the rain and feel the fear overtake the humidity. The silence was awkward.

Anna whispered something into Emily's ear. Then Emily whispered something into Frederick's ear. Jason, increasingly impatient, inching toward the door, was ready to haul his reluctant daughter into the trailer. Maria, now at his side, whispered into his ear, "Let the teens figure it out," and then held his rigid, tensed arm.

Quietly, as if in a religious ritual, the teens stepped out onto the porch, Frederick remaining on the last step so he could look Bailey in the eyes. He took his girlfriend's reluctant, quivering hands into his and held them strongly. Emily and Anna stood behind Bailey, removed her hair bands from her two ponytails, and took her long tresses into their hands.

Bailey, nearly quaking, consumed with fear, was now also confused. "Uh, what are you guys doing?" she asked, cautiously looking around.

Frederick, just like Hattie, held her hands tighter, grounding her into the power, trust, and love of friends.

"Samson," Anna replied blandly as Emily pulled Bailey's long locks through her hands.

"What?" Bailey asked, clearly confused.

Emily told Bailey the biblical story of Samson, whose strength came from his long hair.

"We're going to make you strong, Bailey," Anna said.

As the rain continued its cacophony on the aluminum awning, both girls braided Bailey's hair into double-dutch braids that stopped at her neck, where they put one band around both braids. Then they braided the loose ends into a single long braid and then looped it back up and through where the dutch braids came together, folding it over itself and securing it in a loop. Then Emily took out her phone and made a short video of the new style. They showed it to Bailey. Her thick eyebrows rose up as she hummed.

Emily assumed a theater voice and pulled up every big word she could think of. "You are Tressa, the Titan Teen. Before you fight evil powers, you coif your long and beautiful tresses this way. It is your helmet, your armor, your very strength. You are fearless, fierce, and you face every danger with determination and feminine force. You stare down the bad and bring good to the world."

Maria looked at Jason and smiled.

"You break down the doors of despair and empower the weak," Anna chimed in.

Now Jason was smiling.

Frederick looked her in the eyes and said, "Bailey, I was here too. I shot a man. He said he was going to kill me."

Suddenly, the earth stopped spinning. Nobody had been ready for that. Now *he* was shaking as the memories came back, like PTSD to a wounded soldier.

In all the trauma, Bailey had never even considered that Frederick could have been hurt or even killed. In fact, *no one* had thought about the fact that Frederick was dealing with his own fears and feelings. He'd risked his life to save her. Now, for everybody, it was about more than just her.

Frederick took one trembling hand and turned to the trailer. "We can do this, Bailey. Me, you, Emily, Anna. We can do this."

Quivering all over, eyes blinded with tears, Bailey touched her braided hair and then took one tentative step.

And suddenly, the Fourteens were inside the trailer, three hugging Bailey in a knot of adolescent solidarity ... and Jason hugging a surprised Maria in celebration.

ELEVEN

Ship Ahoy

Now that the trailer was safe again, Bailey and Maria resumed their mealtime chats. Today, it was Maria's famous bologna and cheese sandwiches made with her secret recipe—Miracle Whip dressing spread on the outside of the bread and then grilled on the skillet. Straight from the commercial. But she grilled the quarter-inch-thick slices in a skillet, added smoked cheddar cheese, and slathered the bread with deli mustard. At least Bailey ate sandwiches where food touched food. As long as it was in the correct order.

A burger for Bailey was, in order, top bun coated with ketchup, lettuce underneath, and this rested on the burger which had pepper on the top and salt on the bottom. Underneath the burger was the tomato and then mayo on the bottom bun. A hot dog was plain, resting in the bun; the hot dog had to be the length of the bun or longer, mustard on the top of the dog facing her, ketchup on the other side, neither touching. Chili on the side. A fork of chili, then a bite of hot dog. For deli sandwiches, the meat had to be flat, not curled like in the delicious ads, lettuce on top, tomato on the bottom, mustard and mayo together spread *on the meat*. She ate the meat hanging off the sides first, starting at the top of the sandwich, then ate the sandwich sideways, left to right.

And so on.

The question now was how Bailey would eat this one. It seemed each type of sandwich required a different approach and technique for consumption. After a moment, Maria figured out the problem. The issue here was bologna was round and the bread was not.

Sandwich served on a plate, Bailey set out to make it palatable according to her specifications: exactly fifteen chips (sour cream and onion only) on the right side of the plate because they're right-handed food, the sandwich on the left because it's left-handed food, the dill pickle at the top of the plate because pickles require both hands, and none of the individual items touching, of course.

Small talk ensued.

Was she ready for school to begin? "Sort of."

Makeup? "Saw some neat stuff on TV."

New delicates, okay? "Satin feels pretty."

What kind of shoes did she and the girls decide to get to look alike? "Converse sneakers, red."

Maria was curious about Bailey and Frederick. "How's it going with Frederick?" She watched as Bailey bit off the top left-hand corner of the sandwich.

She answered with a mouthful. "What?"

"You know, the boyfriend-girlfriend thing."

She bit off the top right-hand corner. Still talking with her mouth full, she said, "It's not like we're getting married or something." She rolled her eyes.

Maria tossed a chip in her mouth with a crunch. "What does Jason think of this new relationship?"

Bailey was finishing up the bottom right-hand corner. She paused, looking at the bottom left-hand corner. "Got a lecture on no sex, no heavy petting, no real kissing." She rolled her eyes again. "I don't even know what petting is. Frederick's not a dog." Then she took a bite. Now all the corners were gone.

Maria was curious about what came next. "Well, petting is …" She tried not to get too descriptive but then paused.

Now that the corners were gone, Bailey was eating the sandwich in a circle, beginning with the left side, nine o'clock, and moving around in little bites until she reached nine o'clock again, and then she bit deeper and completed the circuit again. And again.

Sandwich done, fingers licked, it was Bailey's turn to ask a question. "Ms. Gowins, think you'll ever marry again?"

In the silence that followed, the metal on the trailer tinked as the sun baked it one more day.

The next day, the midmorning orb shone into the windows in the trailer's kitchen as Maria downed the rest of her juice. She knew Jason should be done with his exercises—it was jog-on-the-beach day—and it would be safe on the beach. It was time to come out of her own turtle shell. A little bit, anyway.

Flannel shorts on, catching herself looking up as if she were doing something naughty, she opened the bag and took out the two tiny green triangles connected with white strings, tied a knot behind her neck, and snugged them into place to hold what little bit of bosom the Creator had blessed her with. Finishing the other knot behind her back, she looked in the mirror. "It's so small." She stood sideways and then looked at her other side. "Look at those tan lines, Maria." She looked at herself again. "What am I doing? I'm not fifteen anymore. I'm not even twenty-five. Okay, thirtysomethings don't do this. Well, some do."

She had lost some of her hips and tummy with the long beach walks, and taking a page from her advice to Bailey, she thought it was time to try something new and daring. She was never going cheeky with the new summer bikini fashions, but the small top was a first step toward a new Maria. And it might give Bailey another shove as well.

"You can do this, Maria," she whispered, peptalking herself. "I'm going to do this." Heading out the door, she looked right and left, making sure Jason was nowhere in sight. For some reason, she did not want Jason to see her like this. *What is that about? Isn't that the point? To land a new fella?* All was clear as she took the boardwalk to the beach.

The sun caressed her skin like a warm bath with body lotion, and the breeze filled her with life. Once she was convinced she was not really naked, she relaxed and soon was carefree.

Sexy.

Where did that come from? It was like she heard a voice. Was Old Man Sea talking? Or was it a mermaid teasing her? Sexy was a new feeling for her. Did the beach do this? *Turtle?*

After she walked about a mile down the beach, dodging an unusually large crowd of morning beachcombers, she saw what she thought was a familiar form running toward her. Maybe it was just a beach mirage. As the man came closer, she suddenly froze. It was no mirage. It was really Jason. Before she could turn around in hopes that he would not recognize her, he slowed down and called out.

"Maria!" he huffed, bending over. "Good morning."

Momentarily not self-conscious, she watched—no, stared at … okay, *ogled*—his too-enticing abs move in and out as he caught his breath. Sweat dribbled off his limbs, and his lean, striated legs called her name out loud. Really loud. Then she remembered her top, and her face grew hot.

He was slowly getting his breath back. "Mind if I join you?"

Maria was nearly out of breath as well. "Sure," she answered, torn between *I didn't want to be seen like this* and *Yes, I'm walking with this god, girls*. Aquaman with short, dark curly hair.

She was not the only one feeling shy. Jason, with all his obsession over exercise and the perfect body, was unexplainably leery of Maria seeing him that way.

Maria was the first to put her foot in the mouth. Or maybe it was to let the cat out of the bag. "You don't usually exercise this late in the morning," she observed. Then it hit her. That meant she knew his exercise schedule, that she looked at him most mornings, that she made time out of her day to watch him. *Does that make me a femme fatale?* "I mean, uh … it's not like I sit out there every morning, you know, with, like, a watch and a calendar or …" She paused, completely mortified.

Fortunately, Jason, still pumped with exercise endorphins, missed the implications. "Yeah, I had no clients or calls today, so I slept in a bit. Now I'm literally running late, pun intended." He laughed. "And Bailey says I need to relax and slow down a bit."

Teacher Maria spoke before she caught herself. "Bailey's right."

Then it was Jason's turn. "Maria, that top makes you look wonderful." Then he caught himself. "I, uh, I'm sorry, that came out wrong … I meant …"

Maria felt even hotter but not from the sun or embarrassment. *So my other clothes don't make me look wonderful? Why is it the top, not just the outfit? Are tits all you boys ever think about?* She was about to unleash.

Jason was still fumbling the ball. What he was trying to say without any success was the ball cap, combined with the big dark sunglasses, gave her a cute and fashionable vibe. Her slimmer body amplified the curves of her wide hips which looked even more enticing as her trendy shorts flapped in the breeze. And the grand finale, with the new, daring top, the whole ensemble brought out her latent beauty he knew was in there. He was glad that, given what she had been through, she was slowly finding confidence in herself. And it was that confidence that made her look wonderful. More importantly, though he would never admit it, it made him *really* look at her.

Maria caught herself before she said anything she would regret. *Breathe, Maria, breathe. Five, four, three, two, one.* "I'll take that as a complement, Jason. Thank you. I'm trying to come out of my shell. This was a huge and scary step. I still don't know if—"

Jason interrupted her. "Maria, it makes you look wonderful."

A quiet ocean wave whispered, *Sexy.*

Suddenly, they were characters in a Nicholas Sparks novel, walking down the beach and making small talk as the sun set. Then her mind wandered a bit further into the beach reads that filled local bookshelves. *Would we make love, have a fight, then get blown away by a hurricane?*

An hour and a slow walk later, they arrived back at the trailer and mansion. Maria's tan lines were now red, and she had walked on the beach with probably the fittest and most eligible man on the island. Jason was relaxed for once, and he had seen a part of Maria he, and even Maria, had not seen until today. Green triangles and tiny white strings were indelibly etched on his I'm Available message board.

Bailey, standing on the balcony as they came up over the dunes, was now smiling and hopeful. Her plan was working. She had told her father he worked too hard and was too obsessed about time, so he should sleep in and do his morning run later. And it just so happened that the time she gave him was the time she knew Maria would be walking up the beach, although she didn't know Maria would be trying out her new bikini top this morning. "Oops."

Jason, energetic once again, bounded up the steps, saw Bailey, and headed her way. "There's my girl!" He opened his arms for a hug.

"Daaad, you're sweaty. Grooosss!" she drolled, stepping back in mocked disgust. What she really wanted to know was how the walk had gone.

"Maria has lost some weight," he observed, faking a hug to his doting daughter. She faked one back with an "eeewww" face. "She keeps that up, she'll get herself a boyfriend."

Bailey took a chance. "Dad, you know, last I heard, *you're* available."

He turned and looked out over the balcony rail as Maria stepped into the trailer. The flittering of her shorts had his attention. Again.

Back to being a financial planner, he answered, "Nah, Bailey, not sure she's my type. I have an image to keep up, you know." He winked at Bailey, but the ball cap, the large dark sunglasses, the curve of Maria's hips that were more accented than that of other slim women, and the triangles all still lingered in his mind.

All day long.

Her trailer kitchen now transformed into a library, Maria watched as Bailey and Frederick stared at the images on the computer screen. They scrolled and looked and scrolled and evaluated. The budding historian and emerging writer were struggling. With Clyde's help, they had located and selected numerous historical sources and then scanned them onto a jump drive now loaded into Maria's computer.

Bailey broke the scholarly ice. "Ms. Gowins, how do we decide? They all look so important."

Frederick nodded his head and then scratched it. "How many pictures will we need?"

Maria found the website of the press her friend worked for, and they explored the picture book option further. Then they began looking at the scans the library volunteer had made of island pictures available in the library and museum. "A hundred, Frederick."

He whistled as Bailey scrunched her lips. "That means I would have to write a hundred captions, right?" she asked.

"Don't forget the brief oral histories and chapter introductions too."

The teens sat back in their chairs, somewhat in defeat.

"Didn't know it would be this hard, huh?" Maria said, also leaning back in her chair. She had been in their shoes before when she worked on her master's thesis.

After a moment, she got up and took out homemade oatmeal cookies, some sans raisins for Bailey, chips (sour cream and onion only), napkins, and drinks. Distracted by the goodies, she let their minds rest a bit.

Historian Maria then went into lecture mode. She explained how writing about history worked. "You have a hunch, or you may have seen or read something that triggered some curiosity. Sometimes, you just realize that there is a hole in the story that needs to be filled." That was part one. "Now no matter which one it is, you start looking at the data, the pictures, maps, old phone books, newspapers, artifacts, other things like oral histories, memories, even tales." The wheels were back in gear. "Frederick, you've been on this island all your life; your family has lived here for three generations. What do they talk about when they talk about their life on the island? What did your grandparents reminisce about?"

The word tripped up Frederick.

Bailey picked him up. "Talk about, remember, or miss."

Frederick looked about the kitchen, as if the old memories were running on the kitchen cabinets like an old drive-in movie theater.

"Bailey," Maria continued. "You're new to the island. What fascinates you when you ride around? What would you like to know as a newcomer?" Back to Frederick. "What do the old-timers talk or complain about when you talk to them?"

"Ghost stories!" Frederick called out.

Not about my trailer, I hope. She shoved a yellow pad of paper to them. "Scribble."

"What?" they both replied together.

"Just write down whatever comes to your mind. A Frederick column and a Bailey column."

Boyfriend and girlfriend moved their chairs closer and scrunched together. Bailey tossed her hair around her shoulder, and it fell on Frederick's chair, touching his leg and setting off quiet alarms he had never heard before. When their knees touched, both wondered what a kiss might be like. Still not sure of the relationship, neither would look at the other.

Maria smiled to herself as the two sidled up to each other. She looked at what they wrote, but it was not much. *Maybe something else is on their minds …?*

Cookies gone, drink bottles empty, and knowing a couple, not historians, was sitting at the table, Maria offered one more suggestion. "Or you could take a walk on the beach and listen to what Old Man Sea says."

Old Man Sea was rather loud and loquacious, as Bailey observed to Frederick.

"Loquacious?" Frederick asked as they walked side by side.

"Talkative," Bailey clarified.

Waves roared, then thundered, then swooshed, then squished as they recessed back into the ocean. Sometimes, there was a loud clap as one wave slammed into another. Other times, the billows were quiet, as if taking a breath.

Shells tinkled, gulls squawked, the breeze whiffed, and their bare feet scrunched in the moist sand or splashed in the remnants and rivulets of the receding waves. Bailey dodged the gross, dirty sea foam while Frederick stomped on it. Since nobody they knew was on the beach, as if it were a secret, both wanted to hold hands, but they were not sure how to start.

"Bailey?" Frederick asked, "Do you ever miss your mom?"

Bailey shot right back. "No."

"Ever?"

"No."

They sloshed their feet in the small pools of water as they walked along. Frederick noticed Bailey's feet were longer than his. And her toenails were red.

But Bailey was not through with the questions. After a while, she finished her answer. "I just wish I had a mom is all."

They walked along some more. Each snuck a hopeful look at the other and then, as if caught, looked back down again.

"Like Ms. Gowins?" Frederick continued. He liked her too. "She's fun."

Bailey, knowing her answer, was not quite ready to respond, so she switched the conversation. "Miss your dad?"

Frederick, ever the talkative one, suddenly was silent. Then he spoke. "All the time."

"Think Miss Fredericka will ever get married again?"

They dodged a beached jellyfish, swished their feet in a little pool, waited on a sanderling to scoot by, and then sloshed forward as sea gulls hung about and squawked over a boy who was learning the hard way that tossing chips in the air meant every sea gull God made would find him in ten seconds.

"Not sure. She doesn't talk about it."

They turned around and headed back to the trailer, dodging little kids digging in the sand, old people bent over looking for shells, and big errant waves crashing intermittently in their way.

Then Bailey finished the question from Frederick. "I wish Ms. Gowins was my mom."

"She's cool," Frederick answered.

As they walked back, Bailey's long steps out of rhythm with Frederick's short legs, their hands accidentally touched and then grasped each other. They looked at each other again, and this time, they smiled.

It was time for the three girls to hit the beach. Maria hosted the beach party at the trailer. Pizza was ordered from what islanders called the "Triple P," but vacationers called it "Pepperoni, Please, Pizza." Sodas were served, and the Beach Boys sang in the background as they awaited their meal.

They were out on the patio when the delivery guy arrived. All three jumped at the sight of the boy with curly black locks flowing over his shoulders like a dream from under his Pepperoni, Please, Pizza hat. He grinned at the instant attention, walked up with a strut, and flirtingly called out, "Who of you *bonitas* ordered the pizza?" His clean, pressed, and very tight T-shirt with the Pepperoni, Please, Pizza logo said "way cool," and his baggy shorts were attention getters. His white teeth beamed between a devilish smile that filled his brown face. His flip-flops made the whole outfit teen approved.

Emily and Anna jumped up and called out together, "We did!"

Bailey stayed glued to her chair, avoiding attention at all costs.

Maria handed Anna the money, saying, "Tell him to keep the change." She watched as the flirting continued.

Ricardo, as the girls quickly learned his name, talked a bit. He was visiting his aunt for the summer so he could work on his English. "We could help you, Ricardo," Anna replied quickly, her budding flirtatiousness now in full bloom.

"Cool," he answered, shifting from one foot to the other. Soon they knew where he lived, who his aunt was, and what times of day he worked.

"Girls!" Maria called out, smiling yet becoming increasingly impatient. "Pizza's getting cold."

Ricardo took the hint. "Better go. Nice meeting you."

Walking to the trailer, Anna and Emily looked backward as Ricardo left the driveway. Emily bent over with mouth wide open and slapped her knees. "Oh my God!" the girls squealed. "He's so cute! His hair! His accent!"

Maria looked at Bailey, who looked back at her and then whined out loud like Charlie Brown's teacher. Maria, laughing hard, spilled her drink.

The day before the party, the three girls had gone into the village to find some new bathing suits for the occasion. Emily and Anna had no problem finding theirs, but soon they actually saw what Bailey had told them before the trip. The two-piece summer fashions showed too much for her comfort.

"I don't want to look slutty or something," Bailey had reminded them. "You know, stuff hanging out."

It had taken some cajoling, but finally, Anna and Emily convinced Bailey a modest tankini would solve the problem. She tried on several and then sheepishly grinned at one as she stood in front of the mirror. Black with deep-blue and rich-red tendrils wrapping around her like a fantasy.

Now, pizza finished, new suits on, and inspired by Ricardo, the Three Amigas, as they now called themselves, crossed the dunes and looked for a spot among all the vacationers roasting on the sands. Children screamed, running from the waves and then dashing back after them. The remains of two sandcastles were now submerged by the rising tide. Three fishermen, eyes on the tips of their expensive poles, hoped for a big one. Blue-and-turquoise sun tents flapped in the breeze, mommies and babies—and at one tent, one large dog—hidden underneath.

On the beach, Emily and Anna sported their new bikinis, which were modestly but still daringly cheeky, following the style for the summer.

"What did *your* mom say?" Anna asked.

"The same as your aunt and uncle did, I bet," Emily responded.

"Too much skin!" they both mocked.

Bailey, after arriving at the same intersection Emily and Anna were in, answered, "Well, there's more bikini than butt, so I think you're okay."

Anna, starting to feel the pangs of rebellious adolescence, muttered, "Cool," but secretly wanted to show more.

Bailey, braving her new tankini for the first time in public, turned around and waited for their approval. Two thumbs up were shot her way.

With towels spread out and sunscreen sprayed on, the Amigas were fast asleep, soaking up the hot summer sun, two of them dreaming of being stranded on a deserted island with Ricardo.

Like the innocent kid in the old tale who stated the obvious as the king walked by in his new "clothes," a child screamed, "Mama, they're naked!"

Emily was the first to notice. Leaving her reverie of Ricardo on hold, she bolted upright and poked Anna, who reluctantly left Ricardo on their date at the walk-up taco stand. "Wake up!" Emily said. Then she turned and shoved Bailey who, thinking a shark had landed on the beach, uncharacteristically stirred into full-alert mode. All three couldn't believe what they were seeing.

Four bronzed and shapely college girls were parading by in their skimpy, barely-there bikinis. When they passed by the Amigas, the bikinis turned into tiny thongs the size of strings.

Emily's face was aghast.

Anna whispered, "Oh … my … God!"

Bailey, initially looking at the ocean, answered, "What?" but then saw the sight and suddenly came on board. "Oh."

All eyes—women, children, and especially men—were aimed toward the brazen display of what amounted to nude buttocks. The girls seemed to bask in the attention as they slowly ambled farther down the beach.

"I guess they don't know, huh?" Anna asked, looking at Emily.

"Know what? That someone replaced their bikinis with dental floss?" Bailey answered.

Anna laughed and told the story.

Several folks on the island had wanted to increase tourism to pull in more money. One of the ideas was to pass an ordinance and then advertise that thongs were allowed since most beaches, including Myrtle Beach, had strict ordinances against thongs in public. The suggestion stalled immediately, since Banker's Point had always been conservatively family friendly. But the majority of the islander's high tide against "public nudity," as they called it, slowly ebbed out among the island commissioners. As discussions and gossip circled the island over the next months, the men on the board, who outnumbered the women seven to four, had a sudden change of heart.

"The owner of Cheeks and Thongs slept with them until they changed their minds!" Emily hissed out. Now full of fury, Emily continued the sordid story.

Going against the public sentiment, the board had decided to designate the far part of the island as thong friendly. A large sign was posted just before that end of the public beach: Thongs Allowed Beyond This Point.

"I guess those four missed the sign," Bailey observed.

"More likely they can't read," Anna answered derisively.

Emily continued her rant. "Her daughter, Riley, the fifteen-year-old slut, wears them all the time up there, just like her mama. She pouts until her folks give in, especially her daddy, and then she buys skin-tight clothes or outfits that show more than they cover up." Emily took a breath while Anna nodded, more in envy than disgust, and Bailey's mouth opened wide. "Her high-waist shorts show more than your bikini bottom." Emily hit pause for a moment, her eyes blaring. "Did you hear she wore a micro-miniskirt to the concert the other night?"

"I heard she *did it* with Jansen," Anna said and paused, a bit jealous. "I mean, he *is* hot."

Emily added, "I heard she *does it* with anybody who looks her way."

The foursome was heading back up the beach, so the girls—indeed the whole beach in a slow wave like that in a sports stadium—paused, turned their heads, and gave them the full attention they begged for.

The exposed entourage now beyond them, Bailey had an observation. "I always thought a thong had *some* fabric with it. Those are just strings." She paused. "That just magically disappear into their rears." She laughed at the rhyme.

Then Emily turned the conversation around. "So it looks like the Amigas are against thongs?"

Bailey nodded, but Anna, suddenly looking high in the blue sky, hesitated. "If it would get me a date with Parker McCollum or Riley Green, maybe …" She paused, her eyes now dreamy while thinking some more.

Bailey, not up to date on country music hunks, wondered who the men were.

"And Liam Hemsworth." Anna faked a swoon.

Bailey followed up. "He *is* cute!"

Emily, full of anticulture angst, shot back, "Seriously? Both of you would? In public?"

Bailey, normally reticent until her brain reached fourth or fifth gear, immediately answered emphatically, "No. I get enough attention on my two trebles. I don't need any attention on my bass."

Emily looked confused. "What?"

"You know, Meghan Trainor? 'All About That Bass'?" Bailey ran her hand overhead and gave a "duh" look toward Emily.

Anna busted out a laugh. Emily stuck her tongue out.

"Not in public," Anna teased.

Emily was astounded. "Anna!"

"Okay, would not." Her tone was not really convincing.

Bailey looked at Emily. "And …?"

Emily fired off. "They get me as *me*, not me with nothing on in public. No way. I would never stoop that low. No way!"

The Amigas paused as the emotions cooled off. They stared at two would-be studs who bumped shoulders into each other in a tough-guy way and began tossing a football back and forth, cocksure their adolescent antics would impress the girls, occasionally looking back at the thonged wonders.

Emily observed, "Boys are so stupid."

Then Bailey, still stuck on the revealed rears of the college girls, humphed with another observation. "I guess their bass only has one string."

Anna and Emily, both thinking the conversation was about the doofuses, looked at Bailey with utter confusion.

Far down the beach, two sheriff deputies escorted four offended and indignant and highly affronted naked women to their cruisers. Wide-eyed children were amazed, appalled women were appeased, and men were aggrieved.

A few days later, Maria sat on the cloth-covered chair at the distressed pine table in the Palace, not quite sure if she was awake, not even sure why she was sitting at the table rather than going back to her trailer to check on the teens. Keeping watch over the kids in the trailer had robbed her of sleep. Had she really seen them on the beach in the night? What time was it anyway? She glanced out the glass door and glimpsed the ocean as it too woke up, a few lone clouds off in the distance moving to the east as if they were shrimp boats going to work.

She drifted off and recalled the breakfast in the trailer two days before. The morning sun had peeked through the back window, filling the small trailer kitchen with the new day, casting shadows from the tall glasses of juice. Maria's plate of eggs, yogurt, and a thick slice of sharp cheddar cheese had been cleaned.

Bailey had carefully assembled another spoonful of Froot Loops and crunched on them while her face looked like it was working on something complex. The quiet waves outside were punctuated with the measured staccato of chewed cereal.

Froot Loops finished, bowl of milk drained, she began eating her PB and J sandwich, carefully toasted on the fifth setting and filled with crunchy Jif peanut butter and generic (only!) strawberry preserves. Finally, she came around to what was on her mind.

"Ms. Gowins?" She ate her sandwich from left to right, like typing on an old typewriter. "Do you think the Three Amigas could have a slumber party here in the trailer?"

The request caught Maria off guard. Not so much the slumber party … but why the trailer? Next door was a huge beach mansion with all the comforts of a luxury five-star hotel. The possibilities were endless. "Here? In the trailer?"

Bailey took another bite, finishing the first row of her sandwich. She hit Return, and it was back to the left again. "It's way cooler than the *Parker Palace*." Bailey rolled her eyes and nodded her head back toward the beach house. "You know, retro and stuff." Mouth full of sandwich, she described her plan that had already been planned by the Three Amigas. Then she asked the real question, one loaded with hopes Maria could not see. Yet. She looked at Maria with her best doe-eyed face. "And maybe you could stay in the Palace while we party all night?"

Maria wondered where this request had come from. What exactly were the girls going to do that required no supervision? But she trusted Bailey, and she recalled that, in her teen years, she wanted no adults around when she and her friends had partied all night during sleepovers. "Might cramp your dad's style."

Bailey rolled her eyes again. That was exactly what she wanted. Maria was becoming like a mother to her, and Bailey secretly wished Mother Maria would marry Father Parker. This was one way to get the boat in the ocean.

As Bailey chewed and ostensibly formed her next sentence, Maria could hear the aluminum siding heating up, seemingly keeping tick-tock time like an old clock. The sound was now oddly comforting.

Bailey, still not quite ready with a sentence, took another bite. "His 'style'"—she air quoted—"is cramping him, but he won't admit it." Second row finished, she licked the oozing jelly off the crusty sides and began the third row of her sandwich.

Maria grinned to herself. *Maybe he would do his exercises for me?*

Bailey saw the whimsical look on Maria's face. "What?"

Maria suddenly felt daring. *What the heck?* "Talk it over with Mr. Parker and get back to me."

Bailey grinned and started the fourth and final row.

Later, the girls were dropped off, and they carried their stuffed backpacks to the trailer as Bailey played host. Maria laid out the rules and showed them the back of the trailer, and the girls giggled the whole time.

"Do all the trailers look like this?" Anna wondered. While the girls had lived on the island all their lives, other than Maria's, they had never been in one of the old trailers.

"Bailey, you were right, it is way cool. Really retro," Emily responded.

Soon the slumber party began. Next door, Master Chef Father Jason Parker had burgers on the grill. Emily and Anna wanted to see inside the whole mansion, so Bailey took them on a tour. Emily was spellbound, and Anna was speechless ... and even more jealous of Bailey. Pool table, indoor and outdoor bars, hot tub on the deck, elevator, paintings (not prints) on the walls, big-screen TVs everywhere, and Amazon Alexa speakers ready for commands. Again, they saw these beach mansions going up all over the island but had never been in one.

The only room not spick-and-span, clean, and orderly was Bailey's. "Bailey, don't you have a closet and drawers?" Emily wondered.

Bailey answered, "They were here a month ago."

Back outside, the teens wanted to dance, and soon the outdoor speakers blared pop and country sounds, and the kids, starting to loosen up, danced away. The Amigas wanted Frederick to come, so since he could not ride his bike yet, Maria paid for a taxi and brought him to the party. The girls loved Frederick, always had fun with him as well, and Frederick delighted in the attention. He grinned as he jumped in, showing off his best dance moves.

"Ooh, Frederick, you go!"

After that, Waitress Maria and Chef Parker played their part, complete with a terrible French accent.

While Maria cleaned up, the four kids went for a stroll on the beach. At their request, and then insistence, Frederick removed his shirt, but when he flexed his arms like a muscle man, all three screamed, "Eeewww" in unison. Frederick just grinned even more.

Later that evening, it was time to close up shop. Maria took Frederick home as the girls settled into the trailer. The Three Amigas, now minus Frederick, kicked into full gear. The stereo was hauled down from the shelf, Bailey found the old records stored in the closet, and soon music from the '60s filled the trailer.

Maria and Jason, the mansion now cleaned up, sipped some wine on the deck as the stars began their nocturnal circumnavigation of the night skies.

"Who's got the first watch?" Jason asked.

"What do you mean?" Maria responded.

"You know, three teens, all alone, no parents … just sayin'."

Maria turned and looked directly at Jason. "Are you saying that you don't trust your own daughter?"

Jason squirmed. This was awkward. He did, but …

"Jason, you've done a fine job raising Bailey. She's good. She's got smarts, respect. I wouldn't let them do this if I didn't trust her."

Jason nodded. "I know, overprotective dad and all. It's just that, after the incident, she seems so fragile, so …"

Maria cocked her foot up and stood it on the toe. She set one hand on her hip and looked Jason in the eye. "Ever ride a horse?"

Jason looked at her funny. "What's a horse go to do with this?"

"Just answer the question."

"No."

"When you fall off a horse, the first thing you do is get back on it."

Jason sort of got it. The wheels were turning.

Maria could see where Bailey got her hesitant smarts from. "Emily and Anna, and even Frederick, are helping her get back on the horse, Jason. Bailey asked me if they could do this. This was *her* plan. She's taking some initiative, trying to get back on the horse."

Jason turned back and looked down at the trailer.

Maria changed the metaphors. "Father Mr. Jason Parker," she intoned, mimicking Bailey. "It's time to let her cross the street by herself."

Meanwhile, the trailer was literally rocking from the dancing. Anna, the more tech savvy of the bunch, connected her phone to the smart TV, and soon the girls were working out the jitterbug after looking it up and downloading the song from iTunes. Then they did the twist to the old Chubby Checker song. Next, it was the monkey and then the locomotion.

Tired of dancing, they twisted weird figures out of Twizzlers. "Aren't we getting too old for this?" Then it was time to play with Bailey's long hair. So back to the internet they went for different types of braids—"Ooooh, look at this site: Braids of the Bad Girls!"—then to Bailey's locks to try them out and then pics and selfies and posting them everywhere. That done, it was TikTok time. After that, it was a brief review of Netflix, but they could not find anything interesting. Last, they got Bailey up to date on Snapchat and then Instagram.

Plopped on the newly installed carpet on the den floor, the discussion turned to boys. Pushed by Emily and Anna, Bailey finally gave a full-length exposé on her relationship with Frederick. "It's cool," she answered in one brief sentence.

"That's all we get?" Emily fired back, eyes begging for more scoop.

"We hold hands and stuff," Bailey answered again with a shrug.

Emily, finally giving up, talked about Blake at the bike rental place. "Like, OMG, his hair is down to his shoulders! And those eyes!" Anna reminded her he was going to college in a few weeks. "Story of my life," Emily sighed dramatically, holding her arm to her head and throwing it back in defeat, then pouting and sniffling like she was crying.

Bailey asked about Anna's "love life." She balked for a moment, then looked shy and finally embarrassed. "There's a guy at the concession stand at the beach bath house—"

Emily excitedly interrupted "Dylan Moore?"

Anna smiled and nodded, and Bailey and Emily both shouted, "Oooh, Anna!"

Anna turned red all over. "He gives me free drinks and stuff."

Emily leaned forward. "And?"

Anna looked down and then answered. "He asked me to play mini golf."

Bailey and Emily squealed.

Then Anna called out, "Have you seen those two new guys at the first lifeguard stand?"

Emily suddenly looked disappointed. "New guys? Lee and Tyler are gone?"

"Off to college and never came back," Anna responded. "But these guys are way hotter. One's got muscles everywhere. And the other ..." She paused as she went off into dreamland.

"Another dream shattered!" Emily moaned, still fixated on Lee and Tyler.

Boys out of the way, they looked up Lululemon on their phones and shared the latest fashions they dreamed of. Bailey noticed they kept saying, "I wish I could get those." Finally, she asked, "Why don't you?"

Emily looked at Anna, who looked back at her, as if both were keeping a secret from Bailey and had just been caught. Latent envies reemerged along with a dormant resentment.

Bailey noticed the look. "Whaaat?"

Anna waited and looked at Emily, who looked at Bailey. "Bailey, we didn't want to say anything since you dress in all the nice things, but we can't afford them."

Bailey was stone-faced.

Emily piped in. "No offense, but your dad makes really good money. You can get nice stuff. We look at Lululemon and dream big, but Target is about all we can afford, or Amazon or Walmart online."

Bailey was slightly offended, but then she really thought the whole thing through. It had never occurred to her that she dressed better than Emily and Anna. It was just what she wore. The mansion was just the place where she lived. But as she thought it out, she began to realize that because she had nice things, she thought Emily and Anna could afford them too. It took Bailey a long time to understand her own assumptions.

With the prolonged silence, Emily was increasingly worried she had hurt Bailey's feelings. Anna looked like she could cry.

Now Bailey looked hurt, but it was for her friends and how she had treated them. "I didn't know," she said, her eyes tearing up. "I'm so sorry."

Emily and Anna scooted over and took her hands. It was a moment of deep sharing, of truth and honest hurt between friends. A time of coming even closer together as outer layers of assumptions and misperceptions were shed, revealing new images and emotions and intimacies. The three were becoming one.

The economic lesson behind them, their chatter went back to clothes and soon settled on bras and bikini tops. Emily, ever skinny, was proud she could finally fill out an A cup … kind of. Anna, more curvy than Emily, complained that a B was kind of okay, an A was too small, and a C was much too large. "I'm either mushed or bouncy," she explained, with appropriate manipulations of her chest before throwing up her hands in mocked frustration. "It's so difficult being voluptuous!" she sighed sarcastically. Emily rolled her eyes. Then they both wondered what Bailey would make of her joke.

Now it was Bailey's turn, and although a bit uncomfortable with the topic, she smiled embarrassingly as the other two apologized for bringing the issue up. *Awkward!* Then they demurred until Bailey, having surfed through her list of imagery and vocabulary, finally found the right words to explain her body. She thought about her conversations with Maria, her blessing from Miss Hattie, the words from Frederick. She looked down in mocked sadness but then looked back up with a smile. Emily and Anna each exhaled in relief.

"My ladies are currently under the care of Prince DD Charming."

Emily looked at Anna, and both stared back at Bailey with confused faces. Then it hit them, eyes big with astonishment first, and they smiled and laughed, Bailey joining them.

Later, despite her pep talk to Jason, Maria could not sleep, so she quietly wandered out onto the deck, stood in the shadows (just in case), and looked over at the trailer. The island was quiet, the ocean lazy, and the breeze warm. The slight sliver of a moon with the help of a zillion stars brought an odd, even eerie, pall to the trailer. It was past two o'clock in the morning. No lights were on, and all was quiet. "Good," she whispered to herself. Just as she turned to go back inside, she saw the trailer door open, and three figures emerged very slowly, as if they were escaping from the penitentiary. In the darkness, she could not make out the details, but she figured it was the three girls heading out the boardwalk and over the dunes to the beach. Then she saw it: Beach towels covered their bodies.

Maria had secretly worried about Bailey after the incident, and she even blamed herself for what had happened. *Maybe I crossed the line too much.* She wondered if Bailey would ever get her self-esteem, her courage, her *self* put back together after the incident. But now, a tall shadow was leading the way over the dunes.

"Back on the horse again."

Curious, Maria had waited a long time. Then three giggling specters ran over the dunes on the boardwalk and scurried back into the trailer. Lights came on, and a whisper of music was soon audible over the faint crashing of the waves. She saw shadows dancing on the curtains. Relieved, Maria had turned and headed for bed, knowing Turtle would take care of the rest.

Recollection over, back to her morning stupor in the Parker Palace, Maria heard clunking sounds on the steps, and in walked an energized, sweaty yet relaxed Jason, fresh from a morning bike ride around the island. His hair was tousled by the winds, his body wrapped tightly in a multicolored jersey and black cyclist tights.

"Thought I'd get back before you woke up." It was an admission of embarrassment rather than a "good morning" greeting. "Didn't know you were an early riser."

Maria, still distracted by every defined muscle on his body, didn't hear him. Her college human anatomy class suddenly roared back from years of being stuffed in the Closet of Who

Cares. Delts rounded, taut; biceps slightly bulging; veins in his forearms swollen with pumping hot blood like rivers from the spring thaw; the traps of his neck introduced the pecs, flexed, flowing into lats that moved from wide to narrow as they merged into a slim invitation to his abs. The advertisements of his jersey then ended where his black shorts took over. They were too tight for her morning comfort, emphasizing every bit of his masculine lure in amazing, distinct detail. She quickly moved downward to his clearly defined quads, past his knees to his striated calves that bulged out from his shins.

"I apologize, I must smell like a horse that's been ridden hard and put up wet."

Her heart quivered, her nerves pulsed, cold chills emerged from somewhere, and trembles raced around her waist, spiraling down into her intimate depths. A tanned Adonis morphed into Michelangelo's nude *David* who transitioned into a montage of Henry Cavill, Scott Eastwood, Liam Hemsworth, Cole Hauser, Jason Momoa …

She did not realize she was staring until she saw he was trying to bite back a smile. She swallowed the dry lump in her throat. "M … morning," was all she could stammer out.

Jason, too, stalled at the woman sitting in front of him. Her morning hair, brushed only with fingers, was still untamed. The oversized pajama top, one side alluringly hanging off the shoulder, and baggy bottoms hid mysteries that suddenly needed solving. Painted toenails brought to mind a Saturday night of watching TV while his devoted wife prettied up for the next day. Her face, still not quite ready for the sun to rise, radiated something mesmerizing—color, joy, life, *warmth*. A long, warm cuddle under a fluffy fleece comforter in a quaint mountain cabin on a cold morning raced to his head.

Suddenly, unexpectedly, he was aware that Plain Maria had lit a fire his biker shorts were not going to hide. He turned quickly and headed for the stairs, hoping she hadn't noticed. "Give me a few minutes, and we'll whip up some breakfast. Coffee maker should come on soon."

She watched his tight, taut butt leave the room too hurriedly. Caffeine was the last thing she needed right now.

Fresh from the shower, dark curly hair still a bit wet, a clean Jason emerged from the back of the house. He sniffed the air and wondered who'd cooked breakfast. When he turned the corner, he looked out on the deck and saw a morning spread on the table.

"Coffee?" a tender yet now-in-control voice asked.

Jason turned, and the pajama woman stood in front of him. "Thought I'd beat you to the punch," she said. Cup in hand, she nodded to the deck. "Meet you outside."

The humid, salty air, delivered by a slight breeze, wafted in the fresh hint of fish. Jason looked down and saw breakfast fare that reminded him of trips to visit his grandparents years ago, as well as the morning breakfast at the expensive hotels he stayed in while on business. "How did you ... I didn't know ... *you* did all—"

Maria interrupted him, nodding to the chair across from her. "My grandma could make a five-course country meal in thirty minutes. I learned from the best."

Jason sipped his coffee and stared in amazement. Omelet with spinach and tomatoes, granola bars drizzled with chocolate syrup, sliced apples sprinkled with cinnamon and sugar, orange juice, hash browns and onions fried up crispy with some kind of spice on them, and ... "Biscuits?"

"Angel biscuits, from scratch."

Jason sat down and shook his head. "This is quite the spread." He reached for the biscuit first. "Bet this is good with jelly."

"They're good with anything," Maria answered. "Eat, Mr. Parker." She answered his next question before he could ask. "I just looked in the cabinets and fridge and cooked up what I saw."

Jason shook his head in amazement. It had been a long time since he had seen a breakfast table like this. Since a woman had treated him like this. Before he could stop himself, he mumbled, "I could get used to this."

Maria mumbled back, "You could if you'd let those bimbos go."

Jason moved the conversation forward. "So," he started with a mouth full of biscuit before finally swallowing. "What do you think the kids did last night?"

Maria crunched a granola bar, thought about the possibilities, and then answered. "Jason, we may not really want to know, right?"

He nodded, reaching for another biscuit. "These are really good."

For the first time in years, both sat back and relaxed, surrounded by the warmth of the morning, the life of the ocean, a hint of romantic tension in the air, and the aromas of breakfast on the deck.

Three cups of coffee later, both realized the day was moving on without them. "Best get these dishes in the dishwasher, huh, Jason?" Both stood, Jason more reluctantly than Maria, and reached for the same plate, hands bumping into each other, a brief spark of intimacy suddenly arcing between them.

"Sorry," Maria whispered. But she wasn't. Neither was he. Both knew what they felt but weren't ready to admit it.

Still, something else, something deeper than breakfast with a neighbor, needed to be said.

Jason stepped back and looked at Maria with an almost helpless face of genuine care, compassion, friendship. "This was nice, Maria. Really nice. Thank you." He paused and reached for a plate. "We should do this again." He paused again, wanting to do something else. A hug? A kiss? He just wasn't sure what that "else" was. "Soon" was the only word he could get out.

From out of nowhere, the old adage popped into Maria's head: *The way to a man's heart is through his stomach*. Though at the moment, it was more the way to this particular man's body than his heart. "Country breakfast, my place, anytime. Let me know when you're ready."

Maria slid the key into the corroded lock—*Surely, I can afford a new lock*—and breathed in. "Time to face the teenage music." She quietly, hesitantly opened the door and then saw the mayhem of the slumber party. Three girls in a knot of blankets, bare feet and arms sticking out, lay on the floor, popcorn strewn about everywhere. There were enough empty and half-filled drink glasses about the place for a catered wedding party. Red licorice stick figures stood on the end tables like odd artifacts from an ancient civilization. The stereo was still on, the turntable going round and round, and old albums were scattered about.

"They listened to that stuff?"

Flip-flops and beach towels were the incriminating evidence that Turtle had inspired a new sisterhood. On the kitchen table, the sea turtle figurine was surrounded by open bags of chips, dips, soda bottles, and some lingering effects of hotdogs made during the night. "I'm scared to even go to the back of the trailer." The small bedroom was covered in bath towels and backpacks and enough discarded clothes to outfit a room of teens.

One shower and fresh clothes later, Maria decided it was time for the teens to wake up. She found an album with "Johnnie B. Goode" and placed it on the turntable, set the needle, and turned up the volume.

Three sleepy-eyed girls slowly converged at the table and stared at each other. Then Emily woke up, eyes wide open. "Ship, Bailey?"

Bailey, not even back on earth yet, hair everywhere but straight, looked up, rubbed her big eyes, and squinted. "Huh?"

Anna, rubbing her eyes too, suddenly realized what Emily was asking and, now wide awake, beamed bright. "You know, *ship*."

Bailey, normally lost as she processed whatever was happening before her, was totally out to sea. "Ship?"

Anna recalled the conversations they'd had for the last few days as Bailey began opening up and sharing how she secretly hoped Maria and Jason would marry.

"You don't know what *ship* means, Bailey?" Emily asked incredulously.

Bailey was stupefied.

Maria came into the kitchen. "You mean a boat?"

Anna corrected her. "No, Ms. Gowins. *Ship* means boyfriend and girlfriend."

"Oh. Bailey, aren't you and Frederick still boyfriend and girlfriend?"

Anna and Emily snickered.

Bailey, now cognizant of the moment and the new slang as well, smiled and wondered—hoped, really—that the *ship* had indeed come ashore.

TWELVE

Check Yes or No

At the next meeting of the Fourteens Club, as they now called the upper deck of the trailer, more plans were concocted to get Bailey further out of hiding. Various ideas were tossed around, but then Anna called out, "Horse rides!"

While the girls and Frederick had lived on the island all their lives, they had never taken the island horse rides. One reason was the expense. Their parents weren't rich by any standards. Another was the horses were such a part of the everyday life on the island, it just had never occurred to them. Now it was time. The only thing standing in their way was Bailey.

Her generally stoic face had a mixed bag of "oh my!" in her big eyes, but her pursed lips said "hmm" as her cheeks glowed.

Even though all the rich kids spent at least a few years learning the English riding style at expensive stables around Greenville, Bailey had never gone that route. It was more a status thing than a desire to actually ride. Most of the girls lost interest after the novelty faded away and their parents' egos had been satiated. Bailey had never had an interest, period, and Jason, ever attentive to Bailey's every need, honored her wishes.

"Baaaiiillleeeyyy?" Emily cajoled, looking at her with daringly eager eyes.

Anna jumped in. "You know you want to! I can see it in your face, Mona Lisa!"

Bailey was hesitant, but there was a latent cowgirl in her who wanted to don a corseted Victorian dress and serve up drinks at the saloon while trying to catch that lonesome cowboy's eye. If anything, this could be another experience that would come out in her writing.

Frederick was excited. He had always wanted to take a beach ride.

About that time, Maria topped the summit of the stairs. "What's up, Fourteens?"

Emily took the lead. "We're trying to convince Bailey to go on that island horse ride thing."

"Oh yeah?" Maria answered, taking the last seat on the deck. "You know, I used to ride when I was a teen. Mountain trails. Spooking deer. Got caught in a thunderstorm one time. Owned a nice chestnut gelding. Kind of tall. Name was Spirit."

"What's a gelding?" Frederick asked, not knowing what he was about to hear.

Maria pondered the answer as the irony of the male asking the question hit her. "What the heck, you're all teens. They cut off the man parts of the horse to make him more tame."

All the girls instantly stared at Frederick, who turned as red as his hair. "Oh my God!"

"Well, girls and boy, what's it going to be?"

All looked at Bailey for their answer, and she looked back at them with one of her patented "What?" faces. She ran the idea through the trails of her brain while the girls and Frederick whispered, "Buffering, buffering." Maria looked at her and mouthed *Turtle*. Finally, she gave in. "Okay."

"Yipee ki yo!" Frederick called out.

"Uh, wait, not so fast," Emily answered.

"What?" Anna responded.

"How do we pay for this?" Emily asked with an uncertain expression. It seemed so unfair the tourists could afford such luxuries, but her mother couldn't.

Anna solemnly nodded her head, red hair wafting like a plume on a warrior's helmet. "It's really expensive. I forgot about that part."

Maria stood up. "Saddle up, Fourteens. I'm buying."

"Yee haw?" Bailey said in her best southwestern drawl, still not sure this was a good idea.

The next day, the Fourteens anxiously piled out of Maria's SUV and stood about the horses. The smell of fur, leather, and poop mixed together as the teens hesitantly waited for instructions. The girls sported ball caps and tank tops and shorts. Frederick, decked out in jeans and a shirt, arm now in a soft cast, was the most enthusiastic. Emily and Anna were next, and then it was Bailey, whose face showed more worry than excitement. They giggled and smiled to cover their anxieties and cooed over the horses who stood calmly, tails swishing at flies, ears turning from front to back. Maria tossed Bailey a bottle of sunscreen. "You all lather up."

The horse rides began at the end of the main portion of the island right before the long, sandy trail began. No cars, golf carts, errant big-tired bicycles, or four-wheelers to spook them on the trail that belonged to the National Park Service.

The owner of Island Trails Stables, "Gringo Sam," as he called himself, was a weathered, range-worn, thirtysomething cowboy. He sized up each person but mostly stared at Bailey's chest as he talked with the group, coaching them about how to ride, how to be quiet and not rowdy, and how to respect the horse. "They know the route, so just let them do their thing. If you're not sure, just hold the saddle horn." He tapped the protrusion at the head of the saddle.

Maria, having been raised around horses in the mountains, showed the Fourteens how to feed the horses the bites of carrot she had brought. "Hand flat, no fingers sticking up." They were hesitant at first but soon caught on, the soft muzzles tickling their hands as each horse crunched the treat. "You folks get familiar with the horses," she called out. She patted one horse firmly.

Gringo Sam was still fixated on Bailey. Maria, tired of the stares, had had enough. She walked over to where he stood on the other side of the horses while the teens took selfies and posted them on social media. "Time to pay up?" she asked.

That got his attention. For a moment.

"Gringo," she said rather softly yet sternly. "You can make three hundred dollars today, or you can keep looking at that young woman's breasts. And don't you *dare* make some dumbass male comment that you weren't looking, or they're really big, or how old is she. Got it?" She glared right at him and took another step closer and made sure he saw her worn and scuffed cowgirl boots, one scraping the sand like an angry bull about to charge. "If you do say something like that to me, I'll turn you into a gelding right here in front of them."

Gringo Sam looked a bit stunned. Tourists didn't talk this way. Women didn't talk this way. His inner cowboy was ready for a gunfight at the Banker's Point Corral, and he started to retort but then thought better of it. There was something about Maria that scared him. And her scarred boots suggested she was not a greenhorn. "Cash, check, credit card. I take them all."

Anna was paired with a bay mare named Sweety. Frederick, the shortest of the five, got Milky, a small white gelding. Emily was placed by Sam, a gelding paint. Bailey was matched up with Zeke, who stood tall at sixteen hands, and Maria was given Lady, a buckskin dun. Gringo Sam, now paying more attention to the girls' faces and their horses, made the appropriate changes to the stirrups on each horse and tightened the cinches once more. "Had a horse one time who would breathe in when I cinched him and then breathe out, leaving the saddle loose. Not good when a cowgirl or cowboy falls onto the sand." When he got to Maria, he saw her cinching up her own horse saddle. He led the horses over to the mounting block and helped each one mount up, except for Frederick, whom he ignored until Maria glared at him. Caught red-handed, he helped the "one-armed bandit," as he now called Frederick, mount his steed. Maria grabbed the saddle horn, stuck her left boot into the stirrup, and hopped right up on Lady.

The sandy trail wound through the dark expanse of twisted and gnarled cedars and live oaks with thick limbs crawling outward from large stumps like eerie tendrils of monsters. Then the trail emerged onto the back tail of the island on the sound side. The tide was high, and he led the horses through a small inlet that had about three feet of water in it, but it looked like it was fathoms deep to the inexperienced riders. Sensing their fear, Maria informed them that horses knew how to swim. "Let them do their job, kids." She smiled as the horses stepped right through the water.

Gringo Sam regaled them with a mixture of tales from the Southwest, a brief tour on the rodeo circuit where he received more broken bones than gold buckles, island lore, and ecological wonder. "Quit my job when them four-wheelers came out. Used to ride the range, mending fences out in Arizona. Miles and miles of fences. But I just couldn't get used to them four-wheeled horses. I like my horse. Guess I'm old school. Tried teaching folks how to ride, but that was boring. So packed up and went east. Wound up here. Got me some horses, set up a stable, and here you are."

Bailey was laser-focused on Zeke, and white-knuckled; she held the saddle horn like Gringo Sam told them to if they were not sure of themselves in the saddle. One-armed Frederick was at home on the range. Emily and Anna, riding just behind Gringo Sam, talked quietly to themselves.

After half an hour, they turned back for home, this time on the ocean side of the island. The horses ambled along, staying clear of the fishermen, as Gringo Sam continued his banter. He told stories of shipwrecks, hurricanes, hidden treasures, and tourists. "True story, honest to God, one time, three cuties showed up in chaps and shirts and brand-new boots. When they turned around, all they had on was them thong things under their chaps. I ain't kiddin'."

Maria was curious, so she took the bait. "Okay, Gringo, what did you do?"

He glanced back in his saddle and continued the story. "Well, I told them that cowboys and cowgirls always wear jeans under their chaps because, after riding awhile, their butts would be sore and full of blisters. *That* got their attention. I told them to go back to their hotel or house or whatever and get some clothes on."

"Huh … guess he's not all that bad," Maria muttered to herself. She noticed Bailey had let loose of the saddle horn and, reigns in hand, was now more relaxed and enjoying the ride. "How's it going up there, Bailey?"

"Well now, Miss Maria," Bailey answered in her best cowboy drawl. "The back forty of the island looks mighty fine, so I'm a-guessin' we'll head back to the ranch, whoop a mess of beans and corn bread, and have a hoedown tonight."

Maria smiled. "Another small step for womankind."

Back at the stable, Gringo Sam, once again ignoring Frederick, helped the girls off their mounts. They all were initially stiff-legged until they got their land legs back. He then showed them how to lead their horses to the shady stables and tie them up. Bailey, still feeling a little full of herself, continued walking like a bow-legged cowboy fresh off the cattle drive. Emily and Anna and Frederick followed suit.

Gringo Sam took a hay bale out, broke it into flecks, and showed them how to feed the horses. "Now if you ladies will grab a bucket, we'll get 'em some water." It was like Frederick did not exist. The slight did not go unnoticed. Chores done, he announced, "Now you are all official cowgirls," making sure he looked at their eyes.

Maria complemented Gringo for the ride and then called the Fourteens together. "Let's get that pic, folks. Gringo, why don't you kneel in front of the Banker Gang." Pic done, Maria sent the Fourteens to the "Toyota buckwagon," as she now called it, and then pulled out a one-hundred-dollar bill.

She looked at Gringo Sam as she made her point. "You go apologize to Fredrick, in front of the girls, for ignoring him this afternoon, and you'll get your tip."

He did as she instructed, then walked back to Maria who was now settled in the driver's seat, engine running. "Apology made, ma'am."

"I'm sorry, were you talking to me?" Then she hit the gas and sped away, dirt flying all over Gringo Sam.

The Fourteens, now weathered buckaroos, were scarfing down homemade pizzas on the patio at the trailer. Maria had just taught them how to take canned biscuits, flatten them out, roll up the edges, pour in spaghetti sauce, and add pepperonis and grated mozzarella cheese to make the fare.

"Back where I'm from, the closest pizza place was fifteen miles around three mountains, and it took a day and a half to get there and back."

It took the Fourteens a moment to catch her exaggeration. "A day and a half?" they all asked together.

"Two weeks if there was snow," Maria said with a smile.

They finally caught on, Bailey bringing up the rear.

"We just didn't have the options you all have these days. So we did what we could. We learned how to make 'em like this."

Another lesson learned for the spoiled teens about how some people grew up in poverty, with less.

Pizzas fresh out of the oven, they munched until the music stopped and it was time to turn the album over. The teens had brought the stereo outside. They were listening to 5th Dimension and the "Age of Aquarius." Maria, ever the historian, was filling them in on the '60s and '70s. Sex, drugs, rock 'n' roll. Vietnam. Riots. Gas shortages. Civil rights.

Anna was lost in thought. Slowly, she looked at Maria. "I guess we do have it good, don't we?"

The teens paused for a moment and pondered Anna's comment.

"Yes, we do," Emily answered.

Maria said, "I never saw the beach until I was in college. Spring break."

"Seriously?" Frederick asked incredulously.

Bailey was still buffering.

"There are a lot of kids who will never see the beach because their parents can't afford to take them there," Maria continued.

"I never thought of it that way," Emily said, a bit despondent. An introspective pause filled the patio. "'Course, I've never been to the mountains."

Still buffering.

"That's sad," Anna continued. "Not about the mountains, though I would like to see them one day, but about kids never seeing the beach. They're missing out on so much fun. I wish we could do something."

Emily and Frederick both answered at the same time, "Me too."

Maria glanced at Bailey. "Bailey, you there?" She waved her hand in front of Bailey's face then lightly tapped her on the head. "Knock knock. Anybody home?"

Bailey, buffering now over, timidly answered. "I have a plan."

Thirty minutes later, the plan was written down. It was simple, yet it would take some help from others.

Beginning the second week in June and running through the last of July, five kids would come down to Banker's Point for a week. They would stay in people's homes, free of charge. Each day, they would do one beach activity and, on Tuesdays and Thursdays, one community-service project. That could mean cleaning up the beach, helping with seniors who needed yards spiffed up, or maybe doing a supervised building project. They could enjoy horseback riding, paddleboarding, kayaking the bay, walking the nature trail, collecting stories from the locals, attending a concert at the local theater, taking the ghost walk, and riding on a sailboat. There would be picnics, one nice restaurant meal, and a gift of fifty dollars to buy knickknacks and souvenirs.

The Fourteens were proud of the plan. Maria applauded their creativity.

However, Frederick, ever the businessman, threw a wrench into the cogs. "How do we pay for this? A lot of these activities cost money, and we can't expect locals to give up valuable season money."

Ever the optimist, Emily shot back, "But couldn't they give up *something* to help these kids have a good time at the beach? Why can't people just help without expecting anything in return?"

Anna nodded in agreement. The glare she gave Frederick roared, "Don't you care?"

Bailey, caught up in the sudden conundrum, was buffering again.

Frederick countered, "I'm not against the plan. It's just …" He paused to get his words right. "Think about it from a businessperson's perspective. Fifty bucks a kid for each week for six weeks … that's *fifteen hundred dollars*. Captain Hook's sailboat ride only offers fifteen spots for a ride. Some days, he's full; some days, he's not. But five people out of fifteen every week means he loses a small chunk of his profit."

Anna, the balloon of bright hopes now leaking, butted in. "But that's just *one* night. Why can't he just help us out? It's poor kids we're talking about here."

Maria let the teens talk it through. It was a lesson in poverty, economics, benevolence, and the needs of the locals. They had to figure this one out for themselves.

Eventually, the three teens started talking in circles, and the conversation was going nowhere.

Bailey, now emerged from another bout of buffering, brought them back with a laconic conclusion. "Grants, scholarships, investments, donations. It's not hard."

Maria jumped in. "Brilliant, Bailey!"

Emily derisively mocked Maria—"Brilliant, Bailey"— then laughed.

Maria rolled her eyes and continued. "I know a grant writer. We can look up some foundations for scholarships."

Anna picked up on Bailey and Maria's train of thought. "We could put out donation boxes on the island."

Emily jumped in. "Maybe network through social media as well."

All then jumped in. "A GoFundMe page!"

Bailey brought it full circle. "Investments. Hmm ..." She looked at Maria. She knew Maria had money. She knew her father had money. And her father knew people who had money. Convincing her tightwad father would take some doing, but Maria would be a piece of cake.

Inside the Island Folk Crafts store, Maria and Bailey sat in front of Hattie, mesmerized by her deft, aged hands weaving pine straw into what seemed to be a simple coaster. Hattie had not spoken to them when they gathered around her. Maria, already having taken a few "lessons" from Hattie, was used to this, but Bailey worried about the silence.

Maria, at the insistence of Hattie, had coaxed Bailey into coming to see her work. "She got the gift," Hattie said. "I see it in her. Kennedy ain't interested in the craft. She likes the business side a things. History, sales, culture. But I need to pass the gift on. Maria, you do okay. It does you some good for that temper and all, but Bailey got the gift. I knowed it the first time I met her."

"Grammy's in the zone," Kennedy said, having silently walked up behind them, nearly spooking Bailey. She stood by Maria as Hattie continued her work. "We got in a new shipment of longleaf pine needles yesterday, and she jumped on them this morning." Hattie nodded, "Um-hm," but never looked up.

Maria and her former student talked about the history of basketmaking. Indigenous, African, African American, Anglo American. "Don't forget Latino," Kennedy reminded Maria. Maria recalled the simple white oak baskets in her mountain community. "They used whatever they could find: corn shucks, ash, hickory, and oak woods, vines."

Kennedy added, "Now some Asian basketmakers are making them out of plastic strips."

Bailey, though silent, was taking it all in. Kennedy pointed to her and whispered to Maria, "Look at her." Maria did so and then, glancing back at Kennedy, whispered, "Mentor and protégé?" Kennedy nodded. "I think so. Just like you were to me."

Hattie finally looked up, reached for a handful of pine needles, and handed them to Bailey. "Here, pretend it's your hair. Take three needles and braid them together. We call that plaitin'."

Bailey, slowly, as if caught up in a dream, followed Hattie's instruction.

"Good. Now do a bunch more." Bailey picked up more pine needles. "Maria, what you waitin' for? Get to work." Kennedy walked away to help a customer as others gathered around to watch the elderly Black master and her two apprentices.

After a while, several plaits of needles lay on the floor. Hattie put her work down and looked up. "Good. That's enough. Now we gon weave these together into kind of a flat plate." She showed them the technique, laying some crosswise and then weaving others through them, like the threads on a sheet. "There. Maria, you do a few, then Bailey." After half an hour, the semblance of a flat, somewhat square plate emerged. Maria noticed that Bailey's strands were much neater, closer together, precise. She thought to herself, "Yep, she's got the gift."

"Now see what y'all done?" Bailey thought they had messed up, but Maria caught the import of Hattie's observation. "That's the bottom of a small basket. Or one messy coaster." Hattie slapped her hands on her legs and laughed out loud, making Bailey jump.

Hattie looked over to Kennedy and called out, "Kennedy, get these two a bag." Then she looked back at Maria and Bailey. "Here yah homework: Get you a bag full of needles and make a whole bunchaf plaits. Then practice makin' longer strands by plaitin' some together, kind of like Kennedy's braids. See if you can figure that part out."

With that, Hattie picked up her work and resumed her weaving.

Maria looked over at Bailey. "I think class is over, Bailey."

On the way home, Maria looked over at Bailey, who seemed deeper in thought than normal. She wondered what planet or galaxy Bailey was floating in. But Bailey was resting on solid earth, in a village long ago, fingers reaching for another blade of grass to finish her basket.

Maria noticed a peace on Bailey's face that she had never seen before. Indeed, the SUV seemed filled with calm. She had felt that once, a long time ago, resting on a mountaintop, the whole world below, the heavens above. Perhaps baskets woven with the lessons learned generations ago in a land far away held that same Presence.

Maria once again sat in front of Jason in his plush office. Legs crossed, fingers tapping on her knee, she waited impatiently for the Summer Break for Kids Program plan to sink in. Again. She knew Bailey had broached the idea to him, and Jason had initially given it the cold shoulder. Bailey, disappointed but not surprised, decided it was time to bring in the artillery. Major Maria now was in full force, staring him down as Bailey waited in her room.

Jason was not budging. "Maria, that's asking a lot from these people. Why is it that folks just assume the haves should just jump in and give it all away? We work hard for our money. You don't know what it's like to have people constantly begging for your money. Life is hard. Some people do well. Others just get by. Some don't work at all, and then they just look for handouts. We live with the hand that we are dealt. If you work hard, then you move up the ladder. You sit on your butt, then you deserve to starve. That's the way the financial world works, Maria."

The coldness of his words made Maria hot with anger.

Jason paused to stand up, then he turned around and looked back at Maria. "Okay, I know some people just seem to get only bad breaks, but not everyone can enjoy the beach, the mountains, or the summer trip to Europe. You just learn to get over it and enjoy what life brings you." He paused one more time, as if making a final point. "Can't we enjoy our earnings without giving it to people who just won't work? At the same time, it's hard to enjoy the fruit of our labors when everybody wants a handout. Life. Is. Tough." He walked away, exasperated more than was necessary, throwing his hands up in the air and yelling, "Jeez!"

Maria realized she had now touched his one fresh nerve. But the fuse on her temper had just been lit. Therapy be damned. This time, it was personal. She rose and slowly stalked him through the house. "First of all, Mr. Jason Parker, I know about poor. I grew up poor. I lived among people who were poorer than me. Don't you *dare* preach to me about the poor!"

Jason tried to escape the storm following him by moving to the kitchen.

"Second of all, Mr. Jason Parker, where I come from, we try to live by a code, an ethic. Look out for others; do unto others; those who have give to those who don't. Do you know what it's like to see a jar full of cornmeal that would feed the family that night be cut in half so that the ones down the road who fell on hard times could eat something? *Do you?*"

Jason aimed for the den.

The tempest pursued him. "And finally, Mr. Jason Parker, if you don't have a caring bone in your fit body and bulging portfolio, then do what all you rich people do: Find a damn tax write-off! Get a bunch of your broker buds to plunk down a hundred thou' apiece into a nonprofit. Maybe *that* will get your attention! Nothing like a tax break to stir those never-benevolent types, right?"

Jason turned, face red, veins throbbing on his neck. He'd had enough. "A hundred thousand? That's a lot of—"

Maria cut him off at the pass. "What? Another Land Rover? A down payment on yet another property? How about one of those mansion things on top of a mountain, ruining the view, raising up tax values so the poor have to move away from the homes their families owned for generations?" She stomped away and then turned back and glared at him. "Bezos and his five-hundred-million-dollar boat. *Five hundred million,* Jason. For what? So his friends who only had hundred-million-dollar boats could be intimidated?" She stomped around the den, hands in the air. "Don't you rich people ever get enough?" It was now category-five anger.

Jason tried to calm down from her stinging insults. "Maria, try to understand—"

She cut him off again. "What I understand, Mr. Jason Parker, is that sometimes, you can be such a colossal ass, and right now, you are braying really loud!"

Jason was now fighting back. "I'm not the only one with money, you know!"

She came right back at him. "Well, Mr. Investment Guru, you're about to be less a million of yours. I'll start my own damn nonprofit!" Then she turned and headed out the door. "We're done!"

Jason was fuming. She didn't understand the constant assumptions people had about those who were wealthy. How difficult it was to say no again and again. How, if he gave to every cause that was asked of him, he would eventually have nothing left to give.

Then Maria's words suddenly hit him. "We?" he repeated. "When did we become a 'we'?"

The argument now over, Bailey rushed out from her room, tears barely hidden from view. It was all too familiar. The fights her father and mother had. Usually over money. But there were tears for something else this time: her dream of having a new mother named Maria. "Way to go, *Father*." She stomped by him and out the door.

"Bailey, wait! Surely, you aren't taking *her* side?" He rushed after her out to the deck as she headed down the stairs.

She turned back to him, and he saw something on her face he had never seen before. Fear in her eyes, sadness on her lips, and anger all over her face, all at one time. "I'm taking *our* side!" She stomped away, shaking the whole deck.

Way up the beach, she found Maria quietly sobbing. Bailey softly sat beside the woman who, a moment ago, she'd hoped would be her new mother in the near future. That dream now seemed hopeless, but Bailey, desperately trying to keep together what was breaking apart, now considered herself to be a counselor to both of them. It had been fun being fourteen … at least for a few weeks.

Maria, now somewhat collected, apologized. "Bailey, I'm sorry you had to hear that, but I'm *not* sorry for what I said. I'm just sorry for making a scene."

Bailey, ever stoic, sat in silence.

"Your father is a good man, but when it comes to his money, he becomes something else. I just don't like that side of him."

Bailey continued her silence.

Maria wondered if she was off in Bailey Land, lost in space, wherever it was she would go when she was quiet.

Bailey, mentally leaving the short life of being fourteen for the role of counselor, was scrolling through her long vocabulary list, carefully choosing her words. She took a line from Maria: *What would Turtle say?* She knew her dream depended on every word. The first was a polite reprimand for the woman whom she wanted to be her mother. She stared off toward the ocean, hoping its long life of wisdom would fill her with the right words. "Ms. Gowins, there's something you don't know about my father. He doesn't share it because … well, I don't know why. Maybe he's embarrassed by it. Maybe it just hurts too much." She shifted to look directly at Maria, who turned to look at her. Bailey told the story she had only heard twice in her life.

When her dad was a teenager, his father died. Since Jason was the oldest of the siblings, he felt it was his responsibility to take care of his mother and the family. He found odd jobs and looked for opportunities to help in other ways. He cooked meals and supervised the younger siblings while his mother worked two jobs, kept his grades up so he could get a scholarship to a good university, and continued working a job during his college days in order to send money home. And from that point on, he worked his butt off to make what he felt had been denied him as a kid. He still sent money to his mother and lent money to his younger siblings.

"He wants me to have the life he never had," Bailey said as she finished her father's story.

Maria was stunned. "I didn't—"

Bailey uncharacteristically cut her off with the wave of a very adult-like hand. "My father is a lot of things, one of which is blind as a bat, but … he is definitely not a colossal ass."

Sometimes it took the words of a babe to humble the masses. "Bailey, again, I'm—" Then Maria caught herself. "Wait, what do you mean? Blind to what?"

Now it was Bailey's turn to sob quietly. Back to being fourteen, the dream officially over, maybe she should just admit it. "He doesn't see a good thing when he's looking straight at it."

Maria was confused. "Looking at what?"

Bailey now saw she was dealing with *two* people who couldn't see the truth. "Looking at *whom*, Ms. Gowins," she corrected. "I know my father well, and he likes you a lot. But you're strong, and that scares him. He's had to be strong and in control all his life, and he can't let that go. He's too proud to admit it, but he wants to be with you." Bailey paused for round two.

Maria now fidgeted like a schoolgirl who'd suddenly learned the boy she liked actually liked her too. Was it time to check *yes* or *no*?

Bailey continued, "And … I think it works the other way too." Then she looked right at Maria. "I know I'm slow as Christmas and come off as dumb as a post when I'm circling the moon, but I see it in your eyes."

Maria was stunned that Bailey, whom she still deemed clueless at times, had seen the obvious.

Counseling session now over, Bailey cried. "I guess that's out the door now, huh?"

Maria, shocked by the fact that it had taken a teenager to state what should have been obvious to two adults, scooted over and put her arm around the shaking girl. "Bailey, I am so sorry. I didn't ... what do you need from me?"

Bailey's cries rang out over the waves. She cried a long time, and Maria waited as patiently as she could. Finally, Bailey admitted what she had hoped and schemed for. "I ... I need you to be Mrs. Jason Parker"—she was crying so hard, she was heaving, gasping for breath, shaking all over—"so that you can be my mother."

THIRTEEN

The Plan

Mother? *Wife? Mother. Wife. Mother. Wife.*

"Hello, anybody home?" Tara tapped the table as if knocking on the door, but Maria continued staring into an unseen conundrum behind a bank of dark clouds far out over the ocean. Fishing skiffs roared back home. One sailboat, sails packed away, tacked into the bay after a long journey.

After several more knocks, Maria opened her mental door back to the present discussion. She sipped her brew as Tara, now leaning forward, waited for the response to her question.

Maria put the biodegradable cup on the weather-worn table, contemplated the scalloped, frayed, flapping canopy edges now disturbed by the looming, potential tropical depression off the coast. A couple, maybe newlyweds, based on their affections and smiles, settled next to them on the deck.

Motherhood was not the plan when she moved to the beach trailer. She had wanted children when she married, but now, in her thirties, it seemed far off, impractical, if not impossible. *Face it,* she had convinced herself, *who at my age wants to marry and have kids? By forty, you want kids out of the house, not in it.*

Marriage. That was a possibility somewhere down the Yellow Brick Road. She had daydreamed of snagging an island hunk—tanned, curly blond hair, old truck full of tools as he handymanned his way through a carefree, seemingly irresponsible life on the island. Several on the island had enjoyed more than their fair share of Maria's attention. The more realistic angle was another teacher, colleague, or a responsible, educated professional. Then there was the idea of a tall, dark-haired stranger, mysterious, aloof, a cause to solve through a summer season, one who could actually afford to move into the mansion next door. It did not dawn on her how close Jason fit that description.

But now it was starting to sink in. In one way or another, parts of all three shone through Jason. But Maria had lived the life of money: the glitz, the glam, the country club, pocketbooks that cost hundreds of dollars, jewelry from the upscale boutique—the right kind of jewelry, mind you, the kind advertised in the pages of the trendy upscale magazines— the manicured yard, the backyard patio with a grill that rivaled kitchens in most houses, outdoor furniture that cost three times as much as a modest homeowner's living room set, parties, gossip, social expectations, envy, materialism, superficiality, wearing the façade of happiness, and being the look-the-other-way dutiful wife while filled with despair, loneliness, and emptiness. She had lived the Eagles's "Lying Eyes" once, and that was enough. Money was not what she had originally thought it was. Lastly, she was not the trophy wife either. Yes, she could afford a breast enhancement, and a tummy tuck would be heaven, but that wasn't happening.

With the therapy after the divorce, Maria realized she'd been born simple, rooted in dirt and family and generations of lore and love.

Tara touched Maria's hand, and Maria jumped out of her thoughts and chair. "You scared me!"

"You're scaring *me*, girl. It was a simple question: You want a scone or not?"

Scone acquired, Maria shared a piece with Tara who then moved to the deeper issue. "Why do you care, Maria? If he is such a jerk, why do you care?"

The answer was stuck somewhere between her past hurt and her current independent pride. She didn't want to screw up another time, another marriage. It ... he ... would have to be perfect before she took another leap.

Maria shared the litany of good things. Of course, the body was the most obvious one. "Agreed," Tara nodded. "You and half the eligible ladies on the island see that. You ought to hear them in here after they see him running or biking."

Maria looked at Tara with an "and?" face.

"Okay, guilty! If you don't land that fish, I'm gonna toss my line in!"

Maria pointed out how Jason loved Bailey, loved to dote on her, and wanted only the best for her; how he got along with her new friends; how he enjoyed serving dinner and hosting parties for others. She remembered how Jason loved the breakfast she cooked for him, how he really wanted people to succeed in their financial goals. How he bent over backward to help her settle in. How he even seemed attracted to her, even though she knew she was not his type.

"But?" Tara responded.

Maria leaned back and sighed. "It's just that, when he gets to the money part, he becomes a real ..."—she caught herself before the expletive could burst out—"butt."

Tara sat for a moment, then leaned back as well.

Maria filled the long silence by filling her mouth with the last two bites of the scone. A goose with goslings in tow wandered by, honking and causing a stir for tourists who had never seen such an endearing site. Two rental golf carts scooted down the road, followed by a family on white rental bikes.

"Maria, I'm thinking about changing the menu here, and I need your help. What five items do you *not* like?"

Maria, off her usual rationalistic game, took the bait, turned around, stared at the menu chalkboards for a while, and then called out five. "That cauliflower crust pizza. Avocado toast. It looks like pureed peas for babies. Kale chips. Broccoli tots. Yuck. And pumpkin coffee." Then she added two more and made a face. "I really don't like those at all."

Tara rested her chin in her palm, elbow on the table, and looked far away, like she was thinking about the selections. "Hmm ... didn't know that. So help me to understand my customers here. Out of curiosity, why do you come here if the menu is not totally pleasing? Be honest with me, okay?"

Maria talked about the atmosphere, friendliness, companionship, other foods, rustic setting, view across the road to the ocean, the conversation, and the contentment. "It just feels like home, you know? It makes me feel good."

Tara leaned forward and looked Maria directly in the face. "Boy, I sure am glad that you didn't dump me for a few bad items on the menu. Look at all the good things you would be missing."

Suddenly, Maria's face twisted into a quiet yet embarrassed face. She had not considered that aspect. Still, she was not ready to give up. "But—"

Tara brusquely interrupted. "There is no *but* here, Maria. You have cable TV, but you don't watch all the channels. You have satellite radio, but you don't like some channels. You love Reddy Freddy, but you disagree with his fatherly penchant to save the store and the family business, right?"

Chastised, Maria nodded her newly contrite head.

Tara went for the jugular. "Name one thing that you don't like about Bailey."

Without even thinking she responded, "Her OCD."

"Entirely frustrating," Tara agreed. "Yet it is what makes her unique, endearing, *Bailey*, right?"

Maria leaned back and thought about the times Bailey had been annoyingly OCD. The times Maria had wanted to shout out, "For God's sake, Bailey, just eat the blasted sandwich!" Then she smiled. "I would call it quirky."

Tara relaxed as the tension settled back down and changed directions. "You know, I get requests all the time for donations. Charity, causes, poverty, concerts, campaigns. I have to tell most of them no. It's not that I don't want to … there is just only so much that I have to give. My profit margin here is minimal. If I give it away, what happens if I hit a rough patch and have to let my employees go?"

The hair on Maria's neck was beginning to bristle. "Are you defending Jason Parker? I get your dilemma. You're protecting your employees. But Jason is just protecting *himself*!"

Tara reached over to take Maria's now-shaking hand. "Maria, right now, you're protecting *yourself* with your fear of commitment, fear of failure, and fierce independence and defiance. I imagine Jason is not too fond of that either."

Maria recalled her discussion with Bailey and how she'd intimidated Jason.

Tara's calming touch slowed Maria's temper down. "You don't throw away the nice blouse because a few buttons popped off, do you?"

Maria pondered the last comment for quite some time. "Scone's good, Tara."

"So is Jason." Tara paused to let that sink in. "Now let's talk about these tantrums you keep throwing. Time to call the therapist?"

Maria let that one soak in. Then she stood. "No, not yet. Hattie would say, 'Sit your butt down and let that basket carry your anger away, Maria.'"

Tara stood up. "She's the best therapist I ever met."

When Reverend Tate answered the very tentative knock on the church door, she was surprised to see who was on the other side. "Jason Parker?" Well, that came out all wrong. "I'm sorry, Jason, it's just that … I know church is not really your thing, and … well, this is about the last place I'd expect to see you and …" She sighed. "Sorry, foot in mouth. Let me try again." She shut the door and then opened it again. "Hi, Jason, what brings you by this afternoon?"

"Reverend Tate, how are you today?" he responded, half a smile on his worried face. Without giving her the chance to answer, he continued. "Have you got a moment or two to offer some advice?"

She motioned him outside and then to a picnic table behind the church. "If you don't mind the humidity, I like this office better than the one inside. And some folks will gossip if … well, you know."

Jason nodded as he settled onto the old picnic table bench. The winds felt confused, anxious, unsettled, and palmetto fronds smacked each other as he worked up the courage to cross a masculine line and bare his soul. A golf cart loaded with four vacationers and one large barking dog whizzed down the sandy side road. Breaking the silence, a marine Osprey plane thundered overhead, heading to the nearby base. After it passed by, both staring at it, Reverend Tate waited patiently as Jason breathed in and out several times, seemingly on the verge of tears. Strands of her dark hair flitted about in the breeze, but Jason's perfect hair stayed in place.

"You know, I have some clients on the island, but I don't really have any friends to confide in. Well, I guess I could call Maria a friend, but …" Reverend Tate crossed her thick legs, pulling one up over the other, rested one elbow on the table, and listened as Jason related the whole incident. "When she said, 'We're done,' I was flabbergasted, Reverend Tate. I didn't know we were a 'we.' Maybe she meant the business deal was done? She's really not my type, you know?" His face was a sullen, black-and-white kaleidoscope of emotions. Sadness, a faint smile, raised eyebrows of confusion, wrinkles of worry. He shook his head slowly, as if trying to remove all of them.

Reverend Tate rested her hands in her lap and skipped the obvious question of what was Jason's type. She had a good idea anyway. "But now you seem caught off guard that the 'we' is no longer a 'we,' right?"

Jason, looking off to the right, nodded his head, as if not wanting the minister to see his admission. "I had no idea that we were a 'we.'"

Reverend Tate wondered how he had missed the obvious. Emily, Anna, and Frederick all thought the two of them got along fine. They once shared that Bailey wanted them to marry. "Tell me how you came to be single, Jason."

As Jason leaned back, seemingly exhausted from his confessions, he began his sad tale. Reverend Tate observed his face and body language carefully. What she saw was a very successful man who, as the book of Ecclesiastes expressed it, had realized he was chasing the wind. It was time to quit chasing the winds of fortune and success, but he was not quite there yet. The emotional push-and-pull was palpable; the stress of this emotion was all over his face.

A few minutes later, Reverend Tate had the full picture in her mind. Then she made an observation to the fit man in front of her. "Jason, I see three things here. First, from looking at the buff athlete in front of me, I see someone who is trying to become the pool man so as to prevent this from happening again. Second, why do you hold yourself responsible for the actions of your wife? It looks to me like this is sort of a macho thing. 'If I had just worked out more, had better sex, bought her more stuff, drove a bigger car.' See where I'm going here?"

He looked a bit lost.

"You were doing the right things, Jason. Taking care of your daughter, putting meals on the table, making sure your wife had what she needed. Maturity means letting go of some things in order to take care of increasingly more important things. Two become one as this process grows. You were doing your part. You were being an adult. But your ex was still being a teenager. Nothing satisfied her. She was not maturing. She would not let go of things. It was not about you pleasing her; it was only about her pleasing herself."

Jason now looked less lost and more comprehending.

"You did your best, but it seems like you're punishing yourself with a bent toward becoming the perfect man so that you can do better the next time."

Jason nodded in agreement. He spent a lot of time exercising, working, and worrying about how to be the best.

"Lastly ... well, your daughter, Bailey, is a beautiful young lady. Now as I understand it from Emily and Anna, men and boys are attracted to Bailey because of her breasts, her long legs, her pretty hair." She let that sink in a minute.

Jason, smiling, answered yes and that Bailey just wished people would see *her*, not her attributes.

Like a lawyer making a feint and then moving on to another topic to mislead and confuse the accused, Reverend Tate tacked a different route. "So Maria is not your type. No judgment here. You may, indeed, be quite correct, but for my own sake, may I ask why not?" As he described what he would like in a woman, Reverend Tate saw the connection she was looking for. "Jason, I think you're working very hard to, ironically, be the very man you want to keep away from your daughter."

Jason leaned back as if dodging a fist to the face.

Reverend Tate played off the reaction. "Hurts, doesn't it?" She waited. "Jason, I'm not trying to make you feel guilty here, not trying to embarrass you. But you asked for my opinion. A relationship has to have some physical qualities. And let's be honest, you're a handsome man who is indeed eligible and would be a fine catch here on the island. Surely, handsome deserves pretty, beautiful, even sexy. But you're living the very standards that caused your ex to leave you. And you unwittingly work hard at being the very person Bailey deplores."

Jason leaned forward, as if with a question, but he did not know what it was.

Reverend Tate cut to the chase. "So back to the real question, Jason. If Maria is really not your type, then why are you here? Why do you care?"

He was having a hard time answering.

"Let's try it another way then. If she's not your type, then why do you *care* enough about her to reach out for help?"

The Fourteens were licking ice cream cones outside the Ice Cream Shack, trying to stay ahead of the melting treats. It was a lost cause.

"We need more napkins," Bailey said.

Anna and Emily missed her nod to the shack.

Bailey tried again. "*You two* need more napkins," she stressed, nodding to the shack. "You know ... *him.*"

Anna finally got the point and then rushed over to the counter, beating Emily by two yards. Caden was the latest teen heartthrob. He played baseball on the high school team, walked with a cocky swagger, and most importantly, had blue eyes and long blond hair. And muscled legs. And a fine butt. And that smile ...

Standing right in front of the napkin dispenser, Anna tried her best to look like a woman in need. "Can I have some more napkins, please?" she asked, eyes bigger and more pleading than a new puppy, staring right at Caden. When he wasn't looking, she undid another button on her blouse.

Caden, loving the attention but also noticing that Anna was looking right over the dispenser, tapped it gently. "Right there, ma'am." He laughed out loud but smiled at her and wondered what another loose button might reveal.

Enraptured by his smile and encouraged by his eyes that looked her up and down, Anna missed the sarcasm.

As she and Emily walked back to their table, Emily tormented her. "Seriously, Anna, you were standing right in front of the napkins. Brilliant, just brilliant."

"Hey!" Anna retorted. "At least he looked at me and talked to me!"

"Oh, he looked at you all right."

Anna had been proud of his interest, proud that some boys looked at her just like they looked at Bailey.

Bailey, now torn between her love and adoration of her father and Maria's apparent disdain for him, had convinced Jason he would now be, using her new phrase, the "chauffer du jour" for the group. She had been proud of her new words, especially since it rhymed.

Jason had dropped them off and then "skedaddled," as instructed.

"No adults allowed," Bailey had reminded him as she closed the car door.

"*Please,* General Bailey," he had whined out in his best mocking teenage voice.

She had stuck her tongue out at him as he drove off.

The Fourteens had talked about school coming up, what to wear, bullies on social media, jerk guys, stuck-up girls, celebs, new shows on Hulu and Netflix. All tried to stay away from the main topic: the big fight between Maria and Jason. And how Bailey was caught in between them both.

But now, Bailey needed a shoulder to cry on. "It's like I'm their parent now." She rolled her eyes. "They won't talk to each other, won't look at each other. We live beside each other. Awkward. It's like they're children." She paused and sighed. "If only they could be with each other again ..." She trailed off, exasperated that nothing she did seemed to bring them back together.

Ice cream cones done, fingers licked, and elbows on the table, the Fourteens looked about at each other, waiting for someone to have a moment of inspiration or, at least, something fun to do next. A coast guard rescue helicopter caught their attention, thundering overhead as it flew down the beach line.

Suddenly, Emily looked at Anna, who then looked curiously at Emily. Frederick looked at Anna looking at Emily, then looked at Bailey who was looking at Anna who was looking at Emily, who was about to pop. Emily leaned in real close, like she was sharing a secret or relaying information from a spy ring. "Doesn't your dad do those finance things? You know, those parties?"

Bailey leaned forward as well, mostly mocking Emily's pose. "Yes," she said a bit suspiciously.

"Quit mocking me!" Emily laughed, sticking her tongue out at Bailey.

Bailey, Frederick, and Anna all stuck their tongues out and squealed, "Quit mocking me!"

Emily's face looked like it could blow steam out the ears. Then she continued. "When is the next one?"

Still not sure where this was going, Bailey answered, "Tomorrow ...?"

Emily grinned. "Doesn't he usually ask you to be the hostess or something?"

Bailey nodded her head, her hair bunching up on her shoulders with each movement, finally falling down in front of her.

"Bailey, can you act real sick?"

"Why would I do that?"

"To get Miss Maria and Mr. Jason back together again."

"I don't get it."

Five minutes later, Bailey and Anna and Frederick now in the know, Emily crossed her arms over her chest and leaned back, proud of her plan.

The following afternoon, Jason was in a stir as preparations fell into place. He was excited since twenty people had signed up for the seminar/party. Dips for the appetizers were chilled. The veggie and meat plates arrived on time from the One and Done, and the drinks, both soft and hard, were iced and ready. Firm, clear plastic plates and fancy yet functional plasticware resting in pine-needle baskets from Hattie's store completed the spread. All he needed now was his hostess.

He knocked on his daughter's bedroom door. "Bailey, you ready in there?" Bailey could take a year and then some to pretty up for an occasion, so Jason was used to the pace of her preparations, but still, by those standards, she was running behind. "Bailey?"

"Daaad?" she called out from her room. "I don't feel good."

Jeez, Jason thought, *not now.* "Bailey, don't bail on me now, girl. I need you tonight." He laughed nervously at his pun.

Bailey emerged from her room, wearing long sleeves and sweat pants, like it was wintertime. She sniffed and wiped her nose.

"You look fine to me, Bailey. What's wrong?"

She sat down, sighed in a tired way, held her stomach, and coughed. "I hope it's not contagious. Wouldn't want your customers to wake up with it tomorrow. You know, a spreader event or something." She sighed again and wiped her brow with her arm.

Jason sat beside her and placed his wrist on her forehead. "You don't seem feverish. Do you really feel sick?"

She cleared her throat, saying she had some chills and felt nauseous and a little dizzy.

Jason, not quite sure what to do next, took a logical leap. "Is this, like, the summer flu, or is it the woman thing, Bailey?"

"I'm not sure, Dad. Maybe I should ask Ms. Gowins?"

Jason looked at his watch, then at his daughter, and then at all the food. "You run over there. I've got an hour or so to get my act together. I'll manage here."

Once she was out of her father's sight, Bailey practically bounded down the steps toward the trailer. Part one had worked well, but convincing sharp-as-a-tack Maria would be more difficult.

She knocked on the metal door and waited patiently. Soon she heard the doorknob creak, and Maria's puzzled face appeared. She looked at Bailey's fake worried look, winter clothes, and most notably, her messy hair and asked, "Bailey, are you okay?"

Bailey explained the situation as best she could. Maria invited her in. The trailer was filled with the sweet aroma of peaches. Earlier, Maria had rushed to the mainland for a shopping trip, mainly to stay away from the tense situation next door, and had found a roadside stand with ripe peaches. Now she was making peach jam. "Want a biscuit with some jam on it?" she asked.

Bailey pointed to her stomach and shook her head to keep up the ruse and then dramatically plopped on the chair at the table. Then she went through the list of ailments, not quite aware that, short of death or a dramatic crash, there was really no way one person could have so many things going on at one time.

Maria listened attentively and, her teacher radar now on, wisely but incorrectly assessed the situation, figuring Bailey just did not want to play hostess and wanted to be a teen. Why didn't Jason understand this? Was he so caught up in his money that he ignored his own daughter's needs? *Jerk!* "Well, Bailey, just make yourself at home while I tidy up here." She washed out the pressure cooker and wiped off the jars on the counter, just in case there was more sticky goo on the outside. There was a loud clink as the top on one of the cooling jars sealed.

"Ms. Gowins?" Bailey asked pitifully. She did her best to look forlorn. "Mr. Father Jason Parker Certified Financial Planner is having another party tonight, and he has twenty guests coming over. He's going to be overwhelmed without me being there. I feel really bad letting him down."

Maria folded the dish towel over the oven door handle and sat down across the table.

Bailey continued, "I know you two are having a spat and all, but is there any way you could fill in for me? It's a really big party, and he's hoping to get some good clients." Her big green eyes grew larger and sadder with the request.

Maria sat back. *Spat? More like a war.* She could care less for Jason's *feelings*. He could hire a hostess with all his beloved money. *Tightwad!* It would be fun to watch him sweat, trying to juggle presenting and serving. Then she remembered a Confucian teaching: Before you start on the road of revenge, dig two graves. Revenge aside, she considered Bailey. It was not fair to make her be the hostess, and it was obvious she was so tired of this chore—not to mention the advances and stares of the male guests and the glares of the females—that she was feigning illness to get out of it. If she filled in, Maria would be around Jason for several hours. How awkward would that be? Then she recalled her discussion with Tara. Now she was conflicted. Did she really want a man who was this absorbed in his money? Maybe he was too good-looking for her? It was short notice, but Maria agreed to fill in ... for Bailey. She rose up from her chair. "Okay, Bailey, what do I wear to one of these things?"

Bailey, trying not to smile, thought a moment. "Didn't you order some wide-leg pants and a crop top?"

Maria, normally quite practical and very plain in dress, had not had any reason to spiff up while on the island. No one, especially Jason, had seen her decked out. She just wore shorts and a blouse or shorts and a T-shirt. But in a fit of Turtle, she'd decided to order the outfit. "Might as well go with the trends," she acquiesced. "Might have a need for it one day." But when it arrived and she tried it on, she shook her head no and placed it in the closet. It just wasn't her. Too much flare, too much tummy.

Now she thought about it. Why not make Jason feel awkward for a while? On top of that, why not go in style and watch him squirm? Put it right in Jason's smug little money face. Be the flirty thing he had no hope of ever getting into his Mercedes. "I'll shower up. Don't tell him I'm coming. We'll let it be a surprise."

Bailey smiled as Maria headed to the back of the trailer. "Your gold thong sandals would look real good with the outfit."

With Maria now in the back of the trailer, Bailey took a biscuit and carefully loaded it with jam. All the way to the edges.

FOURTEEN

The Date

The look on Jason's face was priceless when Maria showed up at the deck door in her new high-waist, wide-leg floral pants and matching crop top, the small glimpse of her tummy inviting more curiosity, like that of an exotic belly dancer. Her earrings dangled enticingly and glistened like the sparkles in the ocean waves in the late-afternoon sun. He had never seen her in makeup, and now her face radiated a soft and lustrous glow. He looked at her feet, and the gold thong sandals highlighted her painted toenails. With the way she was dressed, it was like he had never seen her at all.

She didn't give him time to respond. "Bailey's sick, so I'm the hostess." She moved right by him and headed to the kitchen, suddenly in full command. "What's the order for the night?"

Jason was taken aback. "Is Bailey okay?"

Maria assured him his daughter was fine.

Next question. "Maria, are you sure this is a good—"

Maria whirled around, and Jason prepared for the lightning bolts from the storm. She paused when she saw the look of shear panic on Jason's face. Catching herself—*temper, temper*—she forced a smile. "Never look a gift horse in the mouth, Jason." She paused to breathe in. "And to be clear, I'm doing this for Bailey, got it?"

Jason nodded his head in understanding, but a small part of him was disappointed. Seeing her, he had wondered if … okay *wished* she had dressed up to impress him.

And Maria now wished she had shown more compassion in her choice of words. *Who's the jerk now, Maria?* Her new clothes might have to make up for that.

As guests arrived, Maria did her duty as hostess, offering drinks and introducing them to Jason. She watched him at work. He was so good with people, making them feel at home and hanging on their every word as they talked of financial dreams. College funds, a retirement place in the mountains, travel around the world. There was no slick sales pitch, no hint of how much he could make from their investments. Whomever he talked with, he was focused on their specific needs. *He loves his work.*

As she greeted guests, the first question from all of them was, "Now are you his wife?" She had to catch herself before she angrily shot back, "There's no way in hell I'd marry someone like him!" Instead, she would politely answer that she was a neighbor helping out a neighbor.

"Oh, how nice" would be the response. Then, "Now do you live in that big house beyond that trailer?"

It was the way they said *that trailer* that made her mad—condescending, as if the trailer were an eyesore between the two mansions. After the fourth derisive comment, she'd had enough. "No, I got three million in my divorce settlement from a sorry-ass-banker husband along with that trailer," she fired back. "Jason handles my money for me."

It was funny watching them walk away.

The party over, one guest—*Pamela* was written on the name tag she had attached enticingly by her cleavage—still chatted with Jason. She was petite with coils of perfect silvery-blonde hair somehow defying the ocean and evening humidity. She was obviously, perhaps obnoxiously, delighted to have his attention. Her way-too-short skirt fought a close battle with the sudden, unexpected bursts of the evening breezes; her blouse was unbuttoned for full effect; her stylish cork platform sandals, earrings, and bracelets showed her affection for clinking attention; and her dark tan and slim figure were the result of hours of self-attention. Clearly, she had her sights on this eligible man. And poor Jason, trying to be polite, looked like a cornered cat.

Maria watched him waver between enjoying her attention and tolerating the awkwardness of her obvious goal to land her a man for the night. Maria was tempted to just wave goodbye and head down the deck stairs, but something somewhere between whimsy and jealousy stirred deep within her. She walked over to Jason, hooked her arm through his, and looked adoringly at him. "Dear, we need to straighten up and then check on your daughter. I hope she's feeling better."

Pamela looked disappointed, even affronted, that someone should dare interrupt her conversation.

Jason looked relieved. "Yes, you're absolutely right. Pamela, you have my card, so let's chat soon. Thank you for coming tonight."

She faked a smile and nodded politely, but her eyes sent a direct glare at Maria as she turned and headed toward the stairs.

After she was gone, Jason breathed a sigh of relief into the lingering scent of Pamela's strong perfume. "Thanks for the save."

"Let's get cleaned up," Maria answered, her tone making it sound more like a command than a comment. She caught herself and wished, yet again, she had watched her tone and choice of words.

Dishes, bottles, food, and utensils now out of sight, errant napkins and out-of-place chairs addressed, Jason crashed onto a lounge chair and sipped a glass of wine. "Maria, would you like to relax a bit before going home?" he asked hopefully.

Maria was caught off guard by his hospitality but wondered, *Why not?* If anything, it was free wine. She poured herself a glass and settled (a bit apprehensively) into the chair beside him.

Together, they looked like two lovers in an island getaway ad. The ocean crooned soft background music, and the breeze brought scented gifts of salt, fish, and a slight whiff of a leftover barbecue up the beach. Each quietly reflected on the evening, not quite sure of whether to engage in small talk or continue the feud.

Jason took the plunge. "Thanks again for coming to the rescue with Pamela. I couldn't get away from her."

Maria teased him just to watch him squirm … and to see how he would respond. "Not up for a one-night stand with cutie pie?"

Jason sipped then turned to look at Maria. His face was serious. "Not so long ago, that would have been on my mind. But now, I want to be a good example for Bailey. And to be honest, it doesn't have the allure it once had." He looked back out over the dunes. *And you look far more alluring tonight,* he thought.

Maria was stunned by his honesty, humility, and candor. His sudden confession brought to the surface emotions that she had tossed overboard after the big fight. And, to be honest to herself, yes, they felt so good. And hidden in the knotted cords of her skepticism and hurt, she was slightly encouraged.

Jason, now relaxed from the drink, looked back over to Maria and then turned his whole body her way. *Why not?* "You look wonderful tonight, Maria. Add one of those stylish beach hats, and you would be the talk of an evening soiree. Or the belle at the horseraces."

Maria was surprised he had noticed, given all the beautiful, sexy, fashionable women he saw that evening. "You have Bailey to thank for that. She picked out my outfit." She was beginning to sense a change in the evening air, the feel of the breeze, the vibe of the handsome man next to her. Rather than admit the truth, she blamed it on the wine.

They enjoyed the quiet, the stars dancing in and out of the clouds, the sea oats waving on the dunes.

"Maria, can we please talk about the other day?"

Maria slowly stood up and leaned on the deck rail, looking out, as if contemplating the request.

When she'd gotten up, Jason wondered if he had crossed the line too soon. "I was just—"

Maria quickly turned around and threw up her hand.

Jason readied himself for the second round of the riot act.

Instead, she explained how Bailey had informed her of his past, how he had worked hard to take care of himself and his family, and how he still helped them out. She reminded him of her upbringing as well. "We were both poor, Jason, in our own different ways. Back home, we sacrificed to help others. In your life, you worked hard to help them. It's a different point of view to solve the same problem. We're alike in very different ways."

Jason, exhaling, was relieved the tension had somewhat dissipated. Still, there was another matter to attend to. He joined her at the deck rail, making sure to keep some distance between them, just in case.

Both defensively turned away from each other to look out over the dune. The breeze, however, knew what to do and wrapped them in a warm blanket of introspection.

Remembering the fight, Jason asked the next question. "So when did you want to come by and withdraw your funds?"

Maria turned back around to face the house, raised her wineglass, rested her elbow on her other arm, and then looked over at Jason. "That depends." She paused and sipped once more, mostly for effect. "I know you can't legally and professionally guarantee this, but aren't there some socially responsible funds that predictably, consistently do well out there?"

Jason turned and looked at the house as well and answered her question. He rattled off several funds and stocks that were quite dependable. "Why do you ask?"

Maria now faced him directly, looking all business. "Jason, I've been thinking. Can you set up an account where I can average, say, four percent a year? I would take it out annually for a project I'm working on."

Jason did the math, thought of scenarios, possible plans, ratios of stocks to bonds to funds. After a few minutes of silence where Maria wondered if he was going to blow his top, he answered her question. "I think that is doable, Maria. Why?"

She talked of her plan to invest her million into the scheme of the Fourteens to provide beach trips for impoverished children in North Carolina. "I think the kids have a good idea, and I want it to work. I would like you to handle the money end, if possible. I don't know a thing about nonprofits, taxes, stuff. That's your deal."

Jason breathed a quiet sigh of relief, not so much for keeping her funds under his management but for keeping a neighbor, a friend. He also felt something else. A melting of the ice, a warmth in the cool of the evening. A shift in the breeze.

Maybe it was just the wine.

But Maria felt something too, something strong enough to cause her to look deeper *into* Jason rather than *at* him. To see his skin glow in the darkness, his eyes glint in the lights of the mansion, his lips slowly transform into a hesitant smile. He looked at her, but his face had changed from all-business to something she had not seen before. Suddenly, she was squeamish, anxious, nervous.

"Maria?" he whispered

She paused and wondered what waited after the question. It was the tone, the inflection, the way he'd said her name.

It was different, almost pleading. She waited. It was an electrifying pause in the evening.

"Would you have dinner with me? We could, I don't know ...."

Maria was suddenly two people, the ecstatic high school girl and the wary divorcee. The girl who dreamed of dating the high school quarterback and who hurt from that same jerk. She wanted to jump for joy, and then she wanted to turn and run. Just to make sure she heard him right, she warily asked for a clarification with a stutter. "Jason, are—are you asking me out on a—a date?"

Jason paused as he pondered the significance of his next words. It was a big step, and it implied a potential commitment. Or the risk of a big letdown. It was like they were little hatchlings heading to the ocean. Sink or swim. Life or death. He took a first step. "Yes, I am."

The Fourteens insisted on chaperoning, and given that both Jason and Maria still were not quite sure about the whole thing, they agreed ... as long as the Fourteens sat at a separate table. That necessitated two vehicles since it would be hard to fit six people in Maria's Land Cruiser and impossible in Jason's Mercedes. There was the possibility of stuffing Frederick into the back of the SUV, and when he objected—"Why me?"— the girls answered quickly, "Because you're a boy!"

Not missing a lick, he fired right back, "Sexists!"

Maria, at Bailey's insistence, wore the same outfit she'd worn at the party. "It got you a date, Ms. Gowins," she'd reminded her, hoping it might get her a mother this time. The girls all wore short skirts with Spanx underneath—"Like the golf women do," Anna had said—and Frederick sported a pullover and cargo shorts. The Fourteens all wore Converse high-top shoes as a show of solidarity, even if they didn't quite complement the attire. Emily's yellow sneakers were laced backward with blue strings. Anna, still goth, predictably wore black ones that matched her black skirt and T-shirt. She had taken a marker and blacked out all the white places on the shoes. Jason, beaming with the entourage all around, turned heads with his tight olive-green T-shirt and khaki shorts. Maria, caught up in the moment of her first date since the divorce and wondering how she had become the mother of four teenagers, forgot how pretty her new outfit was.

The line at Fish Tales was long, but after a bit of a wait, a cute boy with long, curly blond locks and devilish brown eyes seated "the family," as he called them, at two tables. Emily and Anna watched him walk away and dreamed out loud of meeting him at the pier for a date.

"O. M. G!" Anna called out.

"He is *so* cute," Emily responded. Both turned their heads as he walked away.

Frederick quickly reminded them that the pier smelled of dead fish.

"So much for that dream," was the collective reply.

Lining the rough wall panels inside the restaurant were pictures of old boats, fish factories from the past, and other nautical memories, along with antiques from the island. Their server, Olivia, took their drink orders and returned a short while later with their drinks served in canning jars, and each table received a flowerpot with a loaf of bread cooked inside. Bailey, face scrunched up as she pushed the pot toward Frederick, questioned whether the pots were clean or if they ever had dirt in them. Anna took the dare and pulled out a piece of hot bread and loaded it with butter. Still alive after the first bite, Anna pushed the pot back to Bailey, who used her knife to push the pot back toward Frederick and then wiped off her knife.

The menu was pricy, and Emily, Anna, and Frederick stalled at what to order. Should they keep it low or go whole hog? Once or twice a year, their families came to this restaurant, but it was really beyond their budgets.

Jason noticed their reluctance and called out, "Get whatever you want, Fourteens. This one is on Frederick!"

Frederick, ever thrifty and quick-witted, jumped right in. "As long as you get the child's plate, I'm good!"

Olivia stood patiently, hoping that whoever paid for it would at least leave a good tip. Customers were getting more and more stingy with their tips. And she had a new Jeep on her mind.

Maria ordered the fried platter while Jason stuck to his healthy regimen and ordered the broiled version. The teens varied. Emily, the skinny one, ordered the three-item platter; Anna wanted a burger and fries; and Frederick got the shrimp plate. All looked at Bailey.

"What?"

They wondered how and what Bailey would eat in public.

She ordered the two-item plate but wanted a salad instead of slaw. When the teens asked why, she pointed out that the slaw would touch the other food. "Salad comes in a bowl."

"Bailey," Emily answered, exasperated. "You know the other seafood touches, right? Like, they put the shrimp on top of the flounder."

"Emily," Bailey responded after what seemed a long time to process such a simple observation. "It's so obvious. It's all fried. So fried batter touching fried batter is just fine."

Bailey rolled her eyes, and Anna shook her head in disbelief at Emily. "Duh. Seriously? You couldn't figure that one out?"

Bailey, statuesque, unwittingly gorgeous as always, walked over to the salad bar. Despite her sneakers clashing with the rest of her outfit, the older boys and young men stared. Jason, ever protective, waited to see what would happen. The teens also paused, fully aware of how Bailey drew men like flies to honey. Sure enough, one smitten young man took the Bailey bait. The family watched as he strutted over to her and, making sure all could see his toned arms and chest in his tight Henley shirt, stood by as she carefully filled her bowl, making sure each veggie had its own special section in the bowl. Apparently, salad items touching together was fine. From a distance, it was obvious he was talking to her, and it should have been as obvious to him as it was to everybody else in the restaurant that she didn't care for the advance.

Jason was about to be a protective father when Maria grabbed his arm. "Hold on, Jason, let's see how she handles this." She continued to hold on to him.

Suddenly, Emily had a plan, just in case. When she told it to Anna and Frederick, they both laughed.

Bailey handed her bowl to the man, as if asking him to hold it for her like a real gentleman. His eyes grew with excitement. At the same time, the teens rushed over to Bailey.

"Mommy, can we get puddin' tonight?" Emily led off.

The man looked stunned.

"Please? You promised if we were good." Anna gave her best puppy dog eyes.

Jason and Maria could see him mouth, *Are these really your kids?*

Bailey nodded yes.

"Perty please?" Frederick asked once more.

Jason and Maria saw Bailey moving her mouth, and then the puzzled young man walked off, shaking his head and still carrying Bailey's salad bowl. As Bailey came back to the table with a new salad bowl, she smirked and told Maria and Jason she'd explained to the man she was from West Virginia, she'd married at thirteen, these were her triplets, and her husband was special ops and personally killed Bin Laden.

Emily, Anna, and Frederick came back with bowls full of pudding from the dessert bar.

Soon Olivia brought the food, and the Fourteens dove in while Jason and Maria made small talk. Jason related the good news of a few more clients. Maria worried about the upcoming school year at the community college since funding was short; the legislature, as usual, had not approved the state budget, and she was the low instructor on the hiring pole. There was talk of taxes going up on the island. Maria stuck a big fried shrimp on her fork, parked it in front of Jason's mouth, and told him to enjoy life. He returned the favor with a broiled shrimp covered in cocktail sauce.

The Fourteens stopped and stared at the dating couple sharing food. Bailey smiled and hoped.

The increasing din of the myriad conversations throughout the dining area rose as the evening progressed. Maria and Jason laughed at the antics of "their children" who were now watching Bailey to see how she handled her food. Salad done, it was fries first, ketchup applied from the bottle to each individual fry before she ate it, then shrimp, then the flounder. She used her knife to apply cocktail sauce to the shrimp. Emily was the first to finish and then started stealing fries from Anna. Frederick, scarfing down shrimp, joked about how much of a man he was, as evidenced by his harem. Three tongues stuck out his way. Then Emily tried her hand at a sculpture with the salt and pepper shakers, ketchup bottle, sugar tray, and leftover plastic containers for the cocktail and tartar sauce. Anna, now finished with what Emily had left of her meal, leaned over and whispered something to Emily. The secret was passed along to Frederick and then Bailey who, having processed it thoroughly, finally smiled her approval. Phones appeared and thumbs went into overdrive. Soon Maria's phone was dinging. She took it out from her purse and started laughing. She showed the texts to Jason.

Anna: No holding hands on the first date!

Emily: No kissing on the first date!

Frederick: Two feet distance at all times!

Of course, Bailey, ever the slow one, finished her text last. Maria's phone pinged as she was placing it back in her purse. She looked at the message, glanced at Bailey in confusion, and then looked back to the cryptic figures in front of her. The word *mobile,* then the emojis of a house, turtle, cup of steaming something in a saucer, peach, bread loaf, then the word *deck,* then a chair, star, and moon. Then: I'll go to the mansion.

Maria, finally having deciphered the message: "Go to trailer, listen to Turtle, make some coffee or tea, serve him peach jam and biscuits, go to the deck, and look at the stars and moon." Maria put her phone away, looked at Bailey, mouthing, *Got it*, and looked back at Jason. When he asked what the text was, she lied and said, "Bailey says you have lettuce in your teeth."

The laughter broke the first-date jitters, but Maria and Jason were still nervous, skittish, even shy. There was so much they wanted to say, yet they also knew some boundaries needed to be heeded. The ice was melting, but Maria broke it when she smiled and touched Jason's wrist. Despite the previous tensions and disagreements, a tingle zipped between their hands from the spark of her touch.

"Hey," she said, "let's play a game. We are in high school, our friends set us up, and we know nothing about each other. I'll start." She stuffed a shrimp into her mouth and started talking with her mouth wide open. "And so, like, I'm on the weightlifting team and, like, so totally into it."

Jason, wiping his mouth after sipping his tea, kept up the game. "Wow, so totally awesome, dude. So, like, I'm fourth clarinet in the marching band—"

Maria interrupted. "No, wait a minute, like, OMG, I'm a jock, but even I so *totally* know there's no such thing as fourth clarinet. There is only first, second and, like, third clarinet."

"Lol," he answered. "I know, right; I'm that bad!"

With the bill paid, Olivia smiling as she counted her big tip, and the children loaded up, it was time to head home. Sadly thinking the date was over, Jason headed a bit dejectedly to his car where Frederick waited. Maria, girls packed in, paused and looked over at Jason. As the two stared at each other, each held a longing in their faces, as if they had been separated a long time, and even though they were standing close to one another, they feared that this might be their last time together, like the ending of a sad movie.

Maria stepped off the sand dune of reluctance and fear of rejection into an ocean of deep and dark unknowns. "Uh, Jason, I got some peach jam and some leftover angel biscuits. Come over when I get back, and we'll have dessert."

Jason nodded, glad the night was not over, and answered, "Thanks, will do!"

As Maria closed her door, the girls gave her a hard time and reminded her of the First-Date Rules. "Bailey will keep watch over you two!" Anna called out jokingly.

Maria nodded but thought, *Bailey set this up, so I wonder what she will really do?*

"Bailey's going to sleep," Bailey answered. *Turtle will do the rest.*

On the trailer's deck, the winds were strong enough to keep the mosquitos at bay yet soft enough to whisper romance into the ears of expectant listeners. Maria set the tray of jam and biscuits on the table between the two Adirondack chairs, and Jason set down two wine glasses ... actually, red cups. Each settled into a chair, leaned back a bit, and breathed in. The stars twinkled their silent wishes down to the earth, and the waning quarter moon shone just above the ocean. Maria spooned out the jam on two halves of one biscuit and handed one to Jason. The silence between them was filled with words left unspoken.

Jason, mouth full of the evening dessert, finally mumbled, "The kids were fun tonight."

Maria thought back over the scene at the restaurant. They were quite comical, especially when helping Bailey. "They are so creative, so ..." She paused, searching for the right words.

"So fourteen?" Jason completed for her, making the matter simple. "They've been so good for Bailey"—he paused a moment before continuing his thoughts—"and you."

Maria was puzzled. "The teens have been good for me?"

"Well, yes, but that's not what I meant. You've been good for Bailey. Like a mother."

Maria froze. *Mother.* Which implied *wife.* The word scared her; the implications frightened her more. Was Jason implying, asking, hinting? Was this the big moment when …? *Where's he going with this?* Had Bailey told him of her wish?

At the same time, there was something sweet and calming about the term *wife.* As if all the fears and tensions and upheavals of the past few years could be wiped away. But *wife* implied *mother.* And oddly, even that felt comforting.

The long silence worried Jason, and then he realized what he'd said and how it might have sounded. It had indeed been a thought Bailey had hinted at, wished for. Him asking Maria out was a hesitant first step. But that was not what he'd meant. Still, was it a Freudian slip, a testing of the waters? Did the waters suddenly turn cold?

The breeze wafted all about the deck, as if confused like the couple it caressed. A cloud slowly hid the stars and then covered the moon like a veil. The darkness enhanced their fears yet released their previous mistrust and covered their secret, latent hope of something more.

Maria gathered her nerve. *Take a chance, Maria.* "Walk on the beach?"

Jason was caught off guard but found himself more than willing to do so. He stood up and gallantly offered his hand to Maria. Pulling her up with the dramatic swagger of a medieval knight, then bowing low, he answered, "Sure."

A warm breeze sailed in off the waters. Shoes off, the sand was just a bit cool. Lights from the beach houses were low, and the beach was romantically dark. Jason assumed the role of the gentleman and offered his arm to Maria, who then hooked her arm around his. She could feel the strength of his muscles, yet his arm was amazingly relaxed. Jason enjoyed the warmth of her touch, the touch of a woman, the easiness of the night.

They arrived at a dark swath of the beach where a long stretch of large dunes separated two rentals. There was a magical feel in the air, as if the spray from the waves were coating them in a perfume of romance. Out of view of others, hidden in the dark from their own anxieties and fears, Jason stopped, pulled Maria close, and held her in his arms. Then he lifted her chin up and kissed her lightly, as if testing to see if the stove was hot or not. Maria did not refuse his advance and, wrapping her arms around him, pulled him close, feeling his taut frame against her now-quivering body. He kissed her again on her cheek, then the nape of her neck, then back to her lips, slower yet deeper this time, the hesitancy now gone. Maria, inhibitions freed, returned his kiss with hers, and their tongues met halfway. Jason pulled her closer, tighter, and Maria let herself go, feeling vulnerable, needing, wanting the strength of a man.

Jason sensed her fierce independence drift away on the receding tides and her unexpected longing for intimacy swell as the incoming waves touched their feet. Finally breaking apart, she rested her head in the crook of his neck. Desire arose, passions increased, and longings for more than company overcame previous hesitations. Maria nibbled his ear playfully, then temptingly. Jason's hands, strong yet tender, tentatively held her bare waist and waited for permission.

"It's okay," she whispered.

His hands then caressed her hips, rose back up to her waist, then inched down again, like a child's first attempt on a sliding board. He tenderly squeezed her and then moved his yearning hands around her bottom.

Maria hummed her approval and then whispered for both of them, "Jason, stay with me tonight."

The request, while secretly shared, was spontaneous, sparked by Maria's loss of caution and need for closure from the past. Jason was again caught off guard. It was the way she said it. She wanted him to stay with *her* tonight, not her with *him*. Suddenly, all of Jason's condescending feelings, attitudes, and stereotypes about trailers and their occupants rushed to his head, crowding out the passion he now felt in his beating heart. Despite all the fun and games of the summer, he was still prejudiced and even embarrassed about the faded, rusty, aluminum eyesore next door.

Maria felt his hesitation. "Please?" The way she held him was a desperate plea.

It was then he realized just how much the old trailer had brought them and the kids together that summer. Like an old, weathered, and fabled lighthouse guiding hesitant sailors through dangerous shoals, it had opened its doors and welcomed them to something that was slowly becoming home. Passion—or was it the first pangs of love?—trumped all his eccentric estimations of those lesser than him. "I would like that very much, Maria."

It was a simple text from Maria to Bailey: a turtle emoji. Bailey smiled and left her post on the deck, leaving the two alone for the rest of the evening and, apparently (hopefully), the night as well. Still, after a few hours of fitful sleep, she slipped on a long sweatshirt and tiptoed out on the deck, hiding in the shadows.

As she listened to the waves rhythmically pat the shoreline, she looked up and thanked the heavens for what she hoped was becoming a reality. A meteor streaked across the night sky, leaving a brief trail that seemed to connect other stars together into a romantic love story that would last a lifetime. It was a story she had been slowly writing, both on her computer and in her manipulations, of two adults who could not see the forest for the trees. She breathed in the warm salty air and turned to go back inside, ready to let go and trust Turtle to do her magic.

Then out of the corner of her eye, she saw something.

Two figures headed away from the trailer on the boardwalk, then disappeared over the dunes. Bailey covered her mouth before she laughed out loud and then pulled over a chair and, knees and legs now deep inside her sweatshirt, settled in. "Well, I'll be."

The skinny-dippers hugged each other, standing in the cool sand, towels wrapped around them. As they kissed and quietly laughed, they suddenly felt things crawling on their toes. Both jumped, thinking sand crabs were after them, but then Maria whispered loudly, "Be still!" She held Jason tightly to keep him from moving.

Barely perceptible in the darkness, little shadowy circles skittered their way to a new life ahead of them in the vast ocean. Turtle hatchlings headed to the ocean.

For the next hour, they sat and watched the whole dole wander into the deep blue seas.

Two hours later, Bailey fast asleep in the deck chair, two giddy adults snickered their way back into the trailer.

A while later, Jason tiptoed up the wooden steps and quietly opened the door.

"Busted, Mr. Father Jason Parker! You are grounded for two weeks."

Jason nearly jumped out of his skin as he sheepishly looked at his smiling daughter, who devilishly stared straight at him. His sleepy eyes said, *You caught me,* but his face glowed with joy. Jason was not sure how to respond. Acknowledge the obvious? Offer a stuttering and embarrassed excuse? "Bailey, I—I, um—"

She cut him off with a wave of her hand. "Mr. Father Jason Parker, be it known forthwith that from this moment forward, everything you say can and will be used against you in the Bailey court of law." She backed away from the door as Jason entered the house.

"Will I be granted leniency if I thank you for setting up our date last night?"

Bailey cut to the chase. "Will I be getting a new mother sometime soon?"

The abrupt question stalled the exuberant Jason. As he pondered his words carefully, knowing he was on the verge of jumping into a great unknown, Bailey shook within, hope fighting fears. His answer even surprised him. "That's a good possibility, Bailey."

Bailey's hug was instantaneous, nearly knocking her father down. "You're the best father I ever had." And then she broke down and cried.

FIFTEEN

Shifting Winds

That same morning, breakfast was prepared by a beaming Maria in the trailer kitchen. There was a new energy, like a bright-yellow aura buzzing unseen yet bouncing off the cheap cabinets. Father and Potential Mother both quietly radiated something new. Was it the sex, the budding romance, or the relief of the past tension between the two lovers? Turtle?

Maybe it was the aroma of breakfast.

Jason breathed in as Maria ladled out a heaping helping of steaming grits onto his red plastic plate. Then she forked a thick slab of real country ham, bone in, and set it beside the grits. Doing the same for herself, she set both plates on the table and shoved a bowl of brown juice toward Jason.

He beamed. "Is this what I think it is?"

"If you think it's genuine redeye made-with-coffee-not-water gravy, then yes, it is," Maria proudly answered. "Bailey, I set out your bowl for Froot Loops and the peanut butter and jelly as well. Figured you were staying traditional today."

Bailey, green eyes sparkling with joy, was in happy la-la land, dreaming about breakfast with a mother and father forever. Sticking to routine, she poured out the milk first and then added the cereal and munched away as the twosome chatted about whatever. After another serving of grits and gravy for Jason, Bailey suddenly felt emboldened. She cautiously reached over and spooned out a small portion of the grits and tried it. "Hmm." She spooned out more and then another big spoonful as well.

Jason and Maria, jaws dropped, stared in utter disbelief "Bailey!" Maria called out. "We can get you your own plate, you know."

Bailey, mouth full of the new fare, muttered, "I'm doing fine with this one, Ms. Gowins."

Standing up slowly, as if not to spook Bailey, Maria went to the oven and took out a pan of hot buttermilk biscuits. She pushed off several with her fingers onto a plate and then set the plate in front of Jason, who licked his lips. Then she retrieved a fresh jar of molasses from the cabinet and a jar of her homemade peach jam from the fridge and placed both with some theatrical culinary aplomb in the middle of the table.

Maria took a biscuit and opened the jar of molasses. "You ever see someone do this?" She took her pinky finger and poked a hole in the side of the biscuit and then slowly drizzled some molasses into the hole.

Jason was spellbound. Bailey, mesmerized, was stuck somewhere between *yuck* and *hmm*.

Maria took a bite and then held the biscuit in front of Jason's mouth. He took a bite and smiled. "Oh yeah, that's the ticket." He grabbed one and carefully stuck his finger into it. "Like this?" he asked. Maria nodded and then slid the molasses over to him. He filled the hole too much and a trickle of brown goo driveled down the side of the biscuit. Licking it off, he took a bite and smiled. After swallowing, he exclaimed, "Heaven!"

They nearly fell out of their chairs when they saw Bailey slip her hand over, grab a biscuit, and poke a hole in it. Lacking any manners or even grace, she reached over and grabbed the molasses. Still not sure, she carefully poured some of the dark goo into the biscuit and then took a tentative bite. Talking with her mouth full, she asked, "Got any more grits and gravy?" Then she pushed the peanut butter and jelly jars aside.

The Fourteens were busy digging in the sand, preparing the soil for Maria's small garden. It was too late for vegetables, but spinach, kale, and lettuce were good for fall weather. After a serious talk, Emily and Anna had explained to Maria that they appreciated the many times she had bought them things and taken them out, but sometimes, it felt like they were the poor waifs in a Dickens novel, helped by the rich. Maria apologized and then offered a suggestion. "You two help me with some chores, and that way, you can earn your keep."

The metal sections and parts for several raised beds were strewn about the small yard. A large mound of topsoil rested just beside the driveway. A new wheelbarrow, shovel, rake, and hoe complemented the work scene. Maria set down her new tool bag in the shade of the trailer. Bailey brought their shovel over as well and then stared at it, as if confused. Several bags of compost lay ready for use.

Anna sported old cutoffs that seemed ... no, *were* a bit too short and a raggedy shirt, both black, of course. Emily, always making a statement, wore cutoffs and a Black Lives Matter T-shirt. Bailey's hair, coiffed in long pigtail braids, draped down one of her father's old shirts, sleeves cut off at the shoulders. Her jean shorts reached to her knees. When she saw the stares of the other Fourteens, she scrunched her eyebrows, pouted her lips, and then explained, "You know, pigtails for that farm-girl look, right?"

Frederick, pretty much useless because of his still-healing arm, showed up in cargo pants and a One and Done shirt. "I'm supervising, ladies. Get to work!" He pantomimed cracking a whip, and handfuls of sand landed all around him.

Even in the early morning, it was a hot and humid day, and the winds were calm, a good prescription for heatstroke. As gulls flew overhead, Maria pointed to the trailer door. "Plenty of water in the fridge, y'all. Stay hydrated." She walked to the end of the trailer and looked about, as if to decide the precise location of the new garden beds. "Okay Fourteens, where do you think we should put it? Think geometry, how the yard works, the flow, aesthetics." When the gang looked lost, Maria realized that *fêng shui* was not in their vocabulary. She rebooted. "Where would it look good and blend in with the trailer and yard and not get in the way?"

Their faces shifted to I-got-it-now looks. They walked about and eventually agreed on a good spot.

"Excellent! We'll start here, gang," Maria announced, pointing to their patch of sand. "Girls, let's take the shovels and loosen up the sandy soil. Then we'll add some dirt to it, mix it in with the hoe and rake, and then we'll assemble the raised-bed bins and begin filling them with dirt and mulch. Frederick, look over the instructions for the raised beds and see what you can do with one arm."

Bailey and Anna each grabbed a shovel. Bailey, still seemingly stymied by the whole concept of a shovel, paused and then stared at it once more. Frederick looked over at Maria and smiled a devilish grin. "Bailey, I'll get an electric cord so you can plug it in."

Bailey answered, "Okay," and then, appearing somewhat more confused, stared at the handle of the shovel and drifted off. Emily, Anna, and Frederick began counting Mississippis as Maria turned away to laugh.

At thirty-two Mississippis, Bailey's assessment of the situation was finalized. She smiled. "Frederick, I don't think this one is electrified."

Anna, taking a break, stood by as Emily took over. Soon Emily felt an odd sensation at the end of her shovel, like it was poking a stiff balloon. She stooped over and dug in the sand with her hands. Then she pulled out a plastic bag with what looked like a stuffed rabbit and a big, discolored, decomposed glob of something. She held it up with two fingers. "Ew!" she screamed.

Frederick replied with, "Yuck!"

Anna looked over at the bag. "Ugh!"

Bailey thought Emily was talking about the dirt.

Maria came over, considered the bag and its contents, and suddenly, something foreboding overcame her. Despite the summer heat, cold chills raised goosebumps on her arms. Mountain intuition took over. This was evil. *Peter Rabbit*, she remembered from the diary and letters. And something that looked vaguely familiar from biology textbooks and antiabortion ads. *Is that a fetus?* "Damn!" Maria yelled. The festive mood of outdoor work flew away with the gulls and profanity. The Fourteens looked at Maria, not used to such curses coming from her. "Emily, put that back in the dirt, will you?" It was more of an angry command than a friendly request.

Emily, first looking puzzled and then hurt, did as she was told. Anna and Frederick looked worried. Now Bailey was focused on the bag. All five cautiously moved over to the bag in the sand, staring at its contents and wondering silently to themselves.

"What is it, Mr. Gowins?" Frederick finally asked.

Maria took out her phone and dialed 911 but waited before touching the call button. From out of nowhere, she recalled Simpson family reunions where Blane and his cousins would go off to the side and reminisce about the beach trips they'd taken as teens ... and rabbit hunting, of all things. They would mimic their cousin Nina who had Down syndrome. They'd mocked her, and Maria recalled how offended she was of this juvenile behavior from supposed adults. It had disgusted Maria. Then she also recalled the hushed talk of a family member who resided in a "home" and how Nina had never attended the reunions.

Then it hit her.

"They called Blane by the name Peter," she hissed to herself. "And I never knew why." The Fourteens looked bewildered. Maria recalled the box of letters and the references to Peter, Peter Rabbit, and rabbit in the hole. "Disgusting!" she hissed again, this time louder. Then she looked at the plastic bag, and it all made horrific sense. "That bastard!" Maria shook her head and told the gang to take a break. She hit the call button as she walked away from the Fourteens.

"Nine-one-one, what is the nature of your call?"

A short while later, still incensed, she called her attorney, and suddenly, the salty breeze turned into a nor'easter that howled invectives the kids had never heard before. Sailors would have been embarrassed as Maria railed so loud that Jason looked out his window in shock. The kids feared that an angry, dark cloud would shoot lightning down, searing open a dark hole into the sands, swallowing Maria and then closing back up.

Bailey, now back up to speed, wondered aloud, "I hope we didn't do something wrong."

Emily's eyebrows rose as she looked at Anna and Frederick. All three looked anywhere but at Bailey, who was aware enough at the moment to ask, "What?"

Anna spoke for the rest. "The curse, Bailey, the curse. We never told you about the curse."

Jason ran out to see what the matter was, and then he tried his best to calm Maria down. Anger, fear, disgust, shame, and a host of other emotions swirled out of Maria. "How could he?" she cried out over and over, waving her arms, stomping her feet. *"How could he?"* Jason offered a hug, but right now, Maria hated all men. Again. "Not now!"

Jason looked affronted but honored Maria's command.

Finally, Maria ran out of steam. She looked at Jason and waved him over. "Sorry."

Jason held her close while Maria cried. The kids watched, still confused.

"Wow," Anna whispered. "It must be really bad."

When the sheriff arrived, Jason corralled the kids off to the side. Maria pointed to the bag and explained how the kids had found it. The sheriff shook his head. "So?"

"Look at it carefully, sheriff," Maria asked.

The sheriff did so but still did not see anything worthy of his service.

"Doesn't it look like a fetus to you, sheriff?"

He stared at it for a while. "It's so decomposed … but I guess so. I don't know. Why do you ask?"

Maria explained the letters, the diary, the possible connection to her former husband, and the unfortunate rape of a defenseless and innocent young girl.

The sheriff shook his head, not convinced of the story. "I know that family was weird, and the boys had some run-ins with the law, and there was that odd girl, but I just don't know, Ms. Gowins."

Maria tried to clarify. "I think that the father of this fetus was my ex-husband, who was raping that little girl. I can show from dates in her diary and letters that an eighteen- or nineteen-year-old boy was raping an under-age, mentally handicapped girl. The only way we can find out for sure is a DNA test, Sheriff."

The sheriff, wiping off his brow with a handkerchief, still was not convinced. "This seems very circumstantial."

Maria, increasingly impatient at what she felt was a stonewalling sheriff who had better things to do, was now trying not to explode. "Kids, would you or Jason get the sheriff some water, please, while I make a call?" Maria pointed to the patio and motioned for them to get in the shade, and then she walked over to Jason's driveway, stood in the shade, and called her attorney again. After a short, hushed discussion, she came back to the patio and handed her phone to the sheriff. "My attorney would like to explain this to you."

The sheriff took the phone, introduced himself, nodded his head a few times, and then concluded the call. "Yes, ma'am, I'll get on that immediately." Then he walked out to his cruiser, opened the trunk, and took out several stakes, a hammer, and a yellow roll of plastic tape. He motioned to the teens who had followed him. "Would you folks please step back? This is officially a crime scene."

As he cordoned off the area, Maria stalked behind him. The island gossip and hints of a crazed family now added up. "Sheriff, what do you *really* know about this place that nobody is telling me? It's like there's this big secret that nobody wants to let loose."

He stopped and wiped his brow again. "I was deputy sheriff then. From what I recall, there was that time when the Simpson family called the paramedics. A girl, maybe fifteen or so, she seemed what we used to call retarded, and ... I don't recall exactly. She was screaming and wouldn't stop. There was blood on the bed, and for all they knew, she just had her period. But she would not stop screaming, something about rabbits, Peter Rabbit."

The sheriff paused and looked at the small hole where the bag rested. He took off his hat, as if allowing the breeze to refresh his memory even more. Then he set his hat back on his balding head. "Damn." He shook his head, remembering something. "Now I remember it like it was yesterday. She stood right where that bag is and wouldn't move, crying and crying and calling out, 'Poor Peter Rabbit.'" He paused as if lost in time. "She was so crazy that they took her to the island clinic, and we never saw her or the family again. Rumor was she went insane. Took her to Dix, that asylum in Raleigh, where she stayed."

Maria resumed her previous conversation. "Sheriff, my former husband at that time was about nineteen. If I'm right, that would be statutory rape, right?"

He wiped his brow again. "Guess we'll know after that DNA test."

Anna looked at the others with eyes opened wide, like she had just seen a ghost. "I guess that's why they say this trailer is haunted, huh, Emily?"

Frederick, ever stoic but looking more confused, answered for a stunned Emily who slowly stepped back from the trailer. "I didn't think that story was true."

Jason cautiously stepped closer and put an arm around Maria.

Bailey quietly walked over to Maria and spoke in hushed tones. "Ms. Gowins, one night, right after *the event*, when I couldn't sleep, I looked over here and saw three rabbits jumping around this spot." She paused for a moment, possibly for effect, or a sideroad of bewilderment, or a descent into fear, or just to collect her breath. As she finished her thoughts, the sun hid behind an ominous dark cloud that appeared out of nowhere. "Then they disappeared."

What looked like the beginnings of a sweetgrass basket lay beside Hattie's feet. She sipped a fragrant brew from an old mug. A shopper walked up, paused, then wandered off to look at the pewter plates.

"Tara and Kennedy done got me hooked on that fancy brew from Tara's store. I guess old Hattie is a addict now." She laughed and slapped her knee. Bailey flinched, still not used to Hattie's boisterous laughing and knee slapping. Hattie laughed again and then set the cup down on the wooden floor and picked up the basket she was working on.

"Maria, you gon tell me why you came here this mornin'? It's obviously not for weavin'. You ain't done nothin' since you sat down." Pausing, Hattie looked over at Bailey and pointed at the blade of grass in her hand. "You 'bout got it. Now pull that one tighter, then loop it around that end piece." The window unit air conditioners hummed in the background.

"It's that sorry-ass former husband of mine," Maria said as she looked up and continued. "I guess you heard from the Banker's Point gossip mill?"

Hattie nodded and then corrected Bailey again. "Look at mine. Now look at yours. See the difference?" Looking back to Maria, Hattie said, "You back to profanin' again. Hattie done told you 'bout that."

Maria was in no mood for correction. "Every time I get that bastard out of my head he comes back."

Hattie put her basket back down, sipped her coffee again, and then, just like Bailey, seemed to disappear somewhere. While she was gone, another customer paused to stare at the three basketmakers. Now back from her mental break, Hattie ignored the shopper and looked at Bailey. "Bailey, when you leave your house to see Maria in her trailer, what do you do?"

Bailey's face scrunched into confusion.

"You know, you go to her trailer and ..."

Bailey then, kind of, caught her train of thought. "I knock on her door and—"

Hattie interrupted, "And what does she do?"

"She opens the door, and I say something like, 'Hi.'"

"And what does Maria do after that?"

"She says, 'Come in, Bailey.'"

"Um-hm." Hattie looked over at Maria but said nothing for a moment. Kennedy walked by to restock some new kaleidoscopes. Hattie looked back at Bailey and then another long pause ensued. "Why do you think she lets you in?"

Bailey waited a moment. It was the kind of question that people never think about. "Well, I guess it's because she likes me, or she wants some company, or she thinks I need something, or something like that."

"Um-hm." Hattie sipped her coffee again. "Hattie addicted for sure!" She laughed again, put her cup down, and resumed her basketmaking. What followed was a long delay. Then she looked directly at Maria.

"When that Blane scoundrel come to your door and knocks and you open the door, why do you keep inviting him back into your life?"

Maria began to speak, but Hattie sternly waved her off. "Ain't finished yet."

Maria was about to explode at what she perceived as a rude reprimand.

"Before you go off on one of those Maria conniptions, I got more to say." Then she wove a few strands while Maria impatiently waited for round two.

As Hattie wove, she continued. "Sometimes, when Hattie is makin' a basket, Hattie runs into a problem. Sometimes Hattie can fix it. *Most* times Hattie can fix it. But sometimes Hattie runs into a problem that ain't fixable. Hattie keep tryin' and tryin', but it just don't work. Then Hattie gets madder and madder." She paused while she worked around an edge of the basket.

"That messed-up basket keeps callin' Hattie's name, and Hattie keeps openin' the door and invitin' it in, and Hattie gets really mad." Corner resolved, back to weaving, she suddenly stomped her big feet on the wooden floor. The old building shook. Maria, Bailey, and two customers reeled backwards.

"So I just slam that door shut and start me a new basket." Hattie reached down for her cup and took a last swig. "Hmm, that is so good. Kennedy?"

A voice called out, "Yes ma'am?"

"Kennedy, I need another one."

"In a minute, Grammy."

A shopper walked up, looked over at Hattie and then her basket-in-progress, and commented about Hattie's weaving. Hattie related about the history of the woven baskets in her culture. Then she nodded over to a section of the store. "Got plenty to choose from."

As the shopper walked away, Hattie stared directly into Maria's eyes. "If you don't learn to shut that door, you ain't never gon make a basket."

It was Man's Day In, as Frederick called it. The crime scene was now cleared for the garden, the rape case in the capable hands of Maria's attorney, the raised gardens in place, and fall veggies planted. Maria took the girls to the mainland for manicures, pedicures, and some shopping as a reward for their hard work. Girl's Day Out, she called it.

Jason, with the mayhem of the summer, realized he had not really thanked Frederick for his role in the event. He also realized, without Maria's help, Frederick needed a father figure. And so, with the girls "out of the way" as he described it, Jason spent a day with Frederick, who grinned the whole time.

Ever the entrepreneur, Frederick had some questions about finance, investments, and even the future of the island.

They shared a healthy smoothie in the shade on the deck of the mansion as Frederick asked question after question about Jason's line of work, how he started it, and how financial planning operated. Jason was amazed at the youngster's vision of the future and his keen understanding of business. He was about to make Frederick's future a little brighter. "It's getting toasty out here, Frederick. What say we head inside, and I'll explain my job some more? Show you how it's done on my end." He walked into his office and patted a seat for Frederick. "Let me show you what I do."

Unknown to Frederick, Jason had talked with Fredericka about setting up an investment account for her son. "He's done a lot for Bailey, maybe even saved her life, and I just want to say thank you," he'd said to her. Fredericka balked at the suggestion out of politeness, but deep inside, she jumped for joy. Even though the store was prospering, she still worried about college. She eventually humbly nodded her consent and thanked Jason with a load of free steaks for dinner.

Jason opened up a window on one of the screens. "Let's set up a pretend account, Frederick. Pull your chair over here."

The budding financial planner was all eyes as Jason inputted, clicked, scrolled, and filled out the online program with Frederick's personal information. Graphs appeared out of nowhere.

"So let's say you begin with a thousand dollars, Frederick."

"Man, I *wish* I had a thousand dollars, Mr. Parker."

"Now look at this curving line on the graph here." The cursor paused at forty years after the initial investment. "Like what you see?"

Frederick was astonished. "I'll be a millionaire."

"Put a little bit into the account each month, and you'll be more than that, young man."

Frederick was amazed. He wanted to be like Jason, to make money by helping others make money. By investing shrewdly so he could enjoy the good things in life and take care of his mother. But he also wanted to be like Maria, using her money to help others.

"There you go, young man, your account is all set up." Jason patted Frederick on his back.

A huge grin exploded all over Frederick's freckled face. But then it subsided when he realized it was only just a demonstration. "Well, I'll start saving up to get that thousand dollars, and then we'll sign that dotted line, Mr. Parker," Frederick said, beaming with a can-do face.

Jason leaned forward, his elbows on his knees, and looked Frederick in the eyes.

Frederick was afraid he had done something wrong. He had only kissed Bailey once. He thought holding hands was okay. They had wrapped their arms around each other once when they were sitting on the steps on a cool night. He was frightened.

"Buddy," Jason began. "I need to apologize to you. I never took the time to give you a proper 'thank you' for saving Bailey. I guess I was so busy being a father that I forgot you were there too. I am sorry, and I hope you will forgive me."

Frederick, relieved he was not going to be banned from seeing Bailey, exhaled, but then he saw a tear on Jason's face. "Mr. Parker, are you …?"

Jason wiped his eyes and settled back in his chair. "I'm fine, Frederick. Just thankful is all." Now composed, Jason continued. "So Frederick, as a thank you, I have set up this account for you and—"

Frederick interrupted in disbelief. "Seriously, Mr. Parker? *For me?*" Now it was Frederick's turn to cry. He tried to be manly, but in Jason's act of kindness, many barriers had been broken: the still-faint wall between Jason and Frederick, his need for a protective father, his worried hopes about his future, and his deep-down lingering sense that, indeed, in all the fray, he and his wounds had been ignored and then forgotten.

Jason, the father figure, stood and opened his arms wide. "Come here, buddy."

The hug was eternal.

Next on the Man's Day In list was, ironically, lunch out. Frederick wanted Mexican at the Nacho-Taco stand nestled inside an old wooden fence and rows of scrubby, sandblasted bushes. The sun-bleached umbrellas standing up in the tables blocked the oppressive rays, but the wind was only a slight deterrent to the summer humidity. The pair were quite the attraction for all the tourists and locals. Women, both young and not-so-young, dreamed of walking on a sunset beach with the handsome dark-haired man dressed in casual yet obviously expensive shorts and shirt, sitting beside the epitome of the redheaded stepchild. Islanders walked over and patted Frederick on the back and reminded him he was a hero.

Jason raised his bottle of grape Nehi and called out, "A toast to my newest client!"

Frederick raised his bottle and called out, "To men!"

The clink confirmed their new relationship.

Halfway through a burrito, sweat on his brow from the hot sauce, Frederick braved a plan he had been working on. "Mr. Parker, I have an idea."

Jason, mouth full of burrito, nodded for him to continue and mumbled, "Listening."

There were quite a few trailers on the island, most in decent shape, others not so. All were owned by families who had frequented Banker's Point for three generations now. As the families died, some of the mobile homes were sold to developers who quickly removed the outdated domiciles and then built yet another cookie-cutter condo. What Frederick picked up on in his deliveries and at the store was that newcomers deemed the trailers as obsolete, ugly hindrances to the future progress and tourism of the island. "We can't attract the kinds of tourists we want with those things around," was the general sentiment. But after all the good times he'd had in Maria's trailer, Frederick wondered if the other trailers, rather than being eyesores, were actually more good times waiting to be enjoyed. "So you see, Mr. Parker, what if we could buy them up as they become available, restore them to their fifties look, advertise them as retro, and then rent them out? Airbnb or Vrbo?"

Jason put down his burrito and looked at the old trailer resting among some weeds across the road. He mentally cleaned up the lot, repainted the rusted aluminum siding, added air conditioning, pictured retro furnishings inside, set out unique patio furniture, and surrounded it all with simple gardens topped off with a small firepit for s'mores.

"You know," Frederick continued. "We could have fifties week, old-car shows, beach bands, and—what were those things called? Sock hops?"

Jason, a bit surprised by Frederick's entrepreneurial savvy and vision—not to mention that he actually knew about sock hops—took another bite of his burrito and said, "Frederick, tell me more about this idea of yours."

When they arrived home, the new business partners now sharing ideas, Frederick saw a new bicycle under the mansion. "Mr. Parker, I didn't know you had a new bike. Is that for Bailey?"

Jason did not answer but instead walked up to it and patted the seat. He had secretly arranged for the delivery and setup with some of the local firemen while they were out for lunch. "This, Frederick, is my new advertising campaign. Check it out."

It was shiny, the aqua and forest-green metallic colors reflecting those of the One and Done logo. On the back was a large basket with what looked to be a cooler. On the sides of the basket were signs for the One and Done. Jason continued as he walked to the back of the bike. "And there is a sign for Parker Investments."

Frederick's eyes grew bigger, but he was afraid to say what he was hoping.

Jason patted the seat again. "All for you, pal."

"You're kidding!" Frederick called out, jumping on the seat. "Really?"

Jason stepped back a bit, allowing Frederick to explore the new bike. "And I'm putting one hundred dollars a month in your account to advertise for me."

It had been a fun Man's Day In, and now the men were relaxing in the Adirondack chairs on the deck of the mansion, enjoying the last bites of two twelve-ounce ribeye steaks fresh off the grill. "Man food!" Frederick called out as he stuffed a big bite into his watering mouth.

The shadows from the sea oats were long gone as the sun settled for a night's rest. The breeze circled around the deck, stirring up the lingering smell of meat on the grill. Two pelicans soared westward over the mansion. Jason sipped his beer and pondered about Maria and their first night together. Things were not hush-hush, but there was definitely something different now between them. He worried things had gone too far too fast. A one-night stand with the next-door neighbor would be awkward. Friends with benefits was intriguing and even salacious, but that would put Bailey in an awkward situation. The beginning of a long relationship? That was more like it, but how long was "long"? Marriage? The very word was scary but also inviting. Settling down, breakfasts on the deck, and a companion, friend, and lover bringing warmth and joy to an often-lonely mansion.

He stood up and walked over to the siderail and looked over at the trailer. Maria's Toyota was parked beside it, and only the kitchen light was on. Jason considered walking over and knocking on the door. Nothing more than just to say hi. But would she see it as a desire for more lovemaking?

Bailey quietly walked up and wrapped her arms around her father from behind. As if privy to his thoughts, she asked, "So what's next, Dad?"

Jason looked around as Bailey sidled up beside him and glanced at the trailer. There was a long silence as the ocean lapped on the shore like a clock keeping time.

Then Jason picked up the conversation again. "Bailey, I know you want us to get married and all, but you know, there are things we have to discuss and figure out."

"Liiike ...?"

Jason turned and faced Bailey. "*Like,* we've only had one date. It went well, and I think there is chemistry between us, but we need more time to ensure we are compatible. We've had a few spats and can be bullheaded and stand our separate ground. Will that be a recurring problem? If not, then what about work schedules, like her during the day and my evening sales parties? Can you accept Maria as a parent and mother, not just a beach friend? Can the three of us blend together into one family? Are we over our divorces enough to move on to the next phase of our lives? If so, then when would the ceremony be? This fall or next spring or summer?"

Bailey shifted from one foot to the other. "Didn't know it was so complicated."

Silence again.

Jason put his arm around Bailey's shoulder and pulled her close. She wrapped her long arm around her father's waist as a rogue wave crashed onto the beach.

Out of sight on her deck, Maria lay back in her chaise chair and stared at the stars in the sky. She was still shaken by the conversation on the way home from the shopping on the mainland. The girls had been curious about the date, and they danced all around the big question of, "Did you do it?" Of course, the question was out of bounds, and Bailey was sure she knew the answer. But *doing it* in their minds really meant getting married. So the unspoken question then morphed into the spoken question of, "When you get married, where will you live?"

The question, like the continuous waves of the ocean, crashed again and again on the shifting sands of Maria's mind. "Where *would* we live?"

The answer was obvious: the Parker Palace. And for some reason, that scared the hell out of her.

SIXTEEN

All Together Now

The Fourteens convened on the trailer deck one evening when Jason and Maria were on a date. While they waited for the pizza to be delivered, Frederick was given the precarious task of judging whose tan was the best so far. Anna, much to her emerging moxie, won. A horn blew, and the girls rushed down the steps only to realize in disappointment that Skylar, not Ricardo, was delivery person for the day.

"I have an idea," Frederick said, munching his second slice.

The Three Amigas leaned in toward him. "And?" Emily answered impatiently as Frederick finished chewing.

"I think we should have an End of Summer bash."

Eyeballs lit up. Emily sat back in her chair. "Hmm."

Anna stared at the ocean, as if her answer might arrive as a message in a bottle. From a muscled-up pirate who needed a scantily clad lass.

Bailey was more concerned with semantics. "We who?"

Frederick explained. "You know, the Fourteens, Ms. Gowins, Mr. Parker." He paused for effect. "We could invite Reverend Tate, Miss Tara from the coffee shop, Miss Hattie, you know, since they were significant parts of our lives this summer."

The mention of adults initially brought scowls from the girls. However, afraid of hurting Frederick's feelings, nobody said anything.

"Might cramp our styles," Bailey finally observed.

The other three weren't sure if Bailey was being her usual sarcastic self or was being serious. Or even if she was answering Frederick's question at all. Sometimes, things just came out as she remembered a conversion that really ended, say, yesterday.

"Bailey …?" Emily asked in a tone that requested more information.

"Emily …?" Bailey mocked in response.

Anna, moving forward, interceded. "Frederick, whatcha got in mind?"

Frederick outlined his plan. "The Fourteens will gather at the trailer in the afternoon for a beach party—"

Anna stood up, did her best model pose, and responded, "You just want to be seen with us beautiful girls in our bikinis on the beach, right?"

"Have a Low Country boil cooked in a big pot—"

Bailey interceded, "I bet Ms. Gowins knows of a recipe. She cooks cool stuff."

"Then a campfire on the beach. Maybe s'mores. Or at least marshmallows over the fire."

Anna chimed in, "We'll need permission for that."

Then Frederick finished his spiel. "I think we could all share what was special about this summer."

He was rewarded with stares that bordered on glares. Then Emily and Anna fake yawned.

"Lame."

"Boring."

Dejected, Frederick sat back.

Stalemate. Three against one.

Bailey came to life. "You know, girls, I know we're boyfriend and girlfriend and stuff, and FYI, I was not in on this plan, but it *has* been an interesting summer. I had my stuff, Frederick had his, you two got us through it, and even the adults helped out. Then there's Mr. and Potential Mrs. Jason Parker."

The Fourteens thought about it as the sun settled in for the night. It was another classic sunset. To the east, a bank of clouds billowed low on the horizon, like a blend of different-colored cotton candy, from white to orange to light blue. To the west a zigzagged line of clouds reflected white and gray above as the sun sunk below them, turning the clouds into deep oranges as it settled into the gray ocean. As pizza was swallowed and sodas sipped, for the first time the whole summer, each realized how significant it had been for all four of them.

Anna leaned forward. "You know, Mrs. Tara is pretty cool."

Bailey was next. "Mrs. Hattie scares me a bit since it seems like she knows everything, but I would like her here."

Emily responded. "I know, right. She scares me too!" Then she leaned back. "But in a good way, you know?"

Bailey sent a *duh* face toward Emily. "That's an oxymoron, Emily."

"What?" Emily exclaimed, looking exasperated.

Bailey explained what an oxymoron was.

Emily, now somewhat clear on the idea of an oxymoron, observed, "Frederick, you left out your mom."

Frederick mumbled, "Oops."

"Who's paying for all this?" Anna wondered.

"I can convince Mr. Parker," Frederick said with a grin.

The Three Amigas relaxed a bit.

Emily called out, "To the beach, Fourteens! We got some details to figure out."

Bailey snickered. The word *details* reminded her of a joke. "Defeat of deduct went over defense before detail."

Confused looks all around.

"A teacher once asked a student to use the words *defeat, deduct, defense,* and *detail* in one sentence. Get it?"

Three incredulous, lost faces silently replied, "No."

Two days later, Maria decided it would be a good time for another bikini party. This time, it was homemade tacos and burritos with fajitas. The girls, draped in their oversized tees, walked down the short counter in the trailer, now a buffet of Mexican fare.

First round completed, they sat down, and immediately the interrogation began. "Sooo Ms. Gowins," Emily asked with a bit of a smirk and a wink to Anna. "It's been two dates now. How's it going with Mr. Parker?"

Maria's eyes lit up, and Bailey looked over at Emily with a sharp look that said, *Don't spook her.*

Anna, crumbles of taco shell on her lips, joined in. "C'mon, Ms. Gowins, just us girls here. Give us the real scoop."

Maria was caught off guard. *Not again.* She laid down her burrito and leaned back in her chair, as if pondering quantum theory.

Bailey was curious as well. Up till this point, she had deliberately stayed away from the subject. Some details she did *not* want to know about her dad. Was Maria going to spill some beans she would have to clean up in her mind?

Anna cut to the chase. "Is he a good kisser?"

Maria turned red.

"Is he a good hugger?" Emily continued.

Maria looked at Bailey with a crimson face that asked if she was okay with this conversation.

Bailey was finishing her burrito that, unnoticed by the others, was made with all the ingredients mixed together. Still chewing, she looked at Maria and mumbled, "I'm good. Might as well answer the inquisitors."

Maria breathed in. "Yes to both questions."

Anna and Emily both called out, "Oooh, Ms. Gowins!"

Cat out of the bag, Maria cut the discussion off with a smile and wave of her hand. "And, girls, that's all for right now."

But Anna was not done. "Ms. Gowins, how does it feel to be dating the best-looking man on the island?"

Maria's face turned thoughtful, introspective, then became serene. "Like I'm the luckiest woman alive."

Thankfully, no one asked where they would live.

Interrogation done and kitchen cleaned up, it was time to work on the tans. Towels laid out, Emily and Anna wriggled out of their tees and reached for the sunscreen. When Maria removed her wrap, the girls squealed. Her new bikini had surprised them.

Anna smiled devilishly. "That'll keep Mr. Parker's attention! Right, Bailey?"

Bailey, oblivious to the commotion over Maria's new bikini, looked all round, as if she were a spy on a mission, and sheepishly took off her tee.

"*Bailey!*" all three screamed.

Bailey grinned. She was wearing her new bikini.

When she turned around, Emily, eyes still wide open, observed, "Hmm, a bit cheeky there, Bailey."

Anna was now even more envious.

Bailey smiled. She finally felt like she was part of the island crowd and a true member of the Fourteens.

It was a simple third date. Bailey had been shooed off to hang with the girls at the pavilion, so it was just Maria and Jason as they had dinner and drinks on the mansion deck and then took a long walk on the beach with, as agreed upon earlier, no expectations of anything else. Still, there were some latent desires, but none were spoken out loud. Oddly, each was not quite sure if there was anything here, and if there were, where it was going, and if it were going somewhere, where they wanted it to go.

"Let's just see where the night takes us," Jason finally offered, but he, like Maria, hoped for more.

The evening fare was superb: grilled shrimp and cocktail sauce, kale salad, corn on the cob, lobster tails, and cherry cheesecake. With their tummies full and the dishes placed into the dishwasher, they settled into the Adirondack chairs as they sipped two glasses of wine, talking small talk while the breeze encircled them like a soft blanket.

"Maria, how about a slow walk on the beach?" Jason asked.

"I would like that very much, Jason." Maria kicked off her sandals and extended her arm as Jason stood up.

When they crossed the dunes, Maria paused and pulled Jason close. She stood on her tiptoes and kissed him softly. Maybe it encouraged him too much. He pulled her even closer, and his hands began to roam. Strong fingers touched her shoulders, her neck, and then began to tickle their way down her blouse. Maria shivered and then pulled back.

"I'm sorry, Maria, I shouldn't—"

Maria cut him off with a finger to his lips. "We'll get to that soon. Let's walk first."

Bailey came bounding up the stairs at ten o'clock that evening, the agreed curfew time. She saw her father sitting alone in a chair, beer in his hand, never looking back to see who was on the deck. She had wondered if they would wind up in the trailer like on their first date. She didn't expect to see her father alone this early in the night. Still full of expectations and wanting to hear all about his date, she wrapped her arms around his neck and kissed him on top of his head. "Sooo?" When Jason turned around, she saw a glum face. "Uh-oh." She sat down beside him, suddenly afraid of losing Maria. She waited for her dad to offer an explanation. And waited. And waited some more. Now she was getting *really* nervous.

Jason breathed in and then looked straight at his daughter. "We had a fight, Bailey."

"About?" She turned to face her father and placed her elbows on her knees.

Jason explained how he had tossed out the idea of Maria moving in with him when they felt comfortable doing so.

Maria had shot back, "Why *your* house? Why not move in with me?"

It had started as one of Maria's funny feminist retorts, but soon the conversation devolved into a heated debate that ended with Maria's observation that Jason was embarrassed by the trailer and felt it was beneath him—and also his possible future wife—to live in it when they had the choice of living in the mansion.

Bailey nodded but remained silent. Her disappointment in her father and the fear of losing Maria as a mother slowly festered into anger. She stomped her big shoes onto the deck, stood up, and marched off to the glass door, leaving a befuddled and even sadder father alone on the deck. Recalling his initial reactions to the old trailer next to his fine house, she stopped and called out, "I hope your inner snob enjoys living alone in your wonderful palace!"

The clap of the sliding glass door hitting the jamb hard echoed all around.

Meanwhile, Maria was sitting on the beach and letting the tears fall. Jason had wanted to move ahead with their relationship, and his offer of moving in with him was so enticing. But it was the finality of how he'd said it that caught her off guard. Once she moved in with him, then it was goodbye to the trailer. For some reason, she did not want to let it go. At least, not yet.

The old trailer had become home. It was her safe place … the place where she had begun her new life. It was like her childhood home—simple, rooted, with the hint of a haunted past, just like the mountains. She was not sure she was ready to leave it all behind. Plus, the Parker Palace would put her right back into the very place she had left behind: a life surrounding money and affluence.

The way Jason had talked, it was like he couldn't get her out of "that old trailer" fast enough. As if it were somehow hurting her, holding her back, and he had to help her escape and find a new home in his mansion. The knight in shining armor and his grand castle. As if she was not good enough for him until she lived in his domain on his side of the tracks.

She had never been good enough for her ex, and now she wasn't good enough for Jason.

"It's just a damn trailer, Maria! Why can't you just let it go?" he had called out in exasperation.

Why can't *I let it go?* Maria now wondered to herself.

As she sat on the sand, she recalled how this was the place where she and Bailey had discovered Turtle. She was laying her eggs at the time, and then the hatchlings crawled over Maria and Jason's bare feet.

Turtle. Sea Turtle. Hatchlings. Wide open sea.

The trailer was Maria's turtle shell. She lived in it, hid in it, returned to it when threatened or frightened. Living by the beach, she had, in many ways, emerged like a hatchling from Turtle's nest. Her new clothes, her tan, her friendship with Bailey, and yes, her relationship with Jason, wherever that stood now. Even the daring bikini top. Life outside the shell.

Strength. She sighed, wiped her face with her wrist, and listened to the waves, inhaling the breeze. *It's like he wants me to live away from my shell.*

Then it suddenly dawned on her. The female sea turtle always returns to the same site every year to lay her eggs.

Turtle. Shell. Hatchlings. Return.

She had come to the beach for a new life. The trailer was her shell, and she was Turtle. She went in and out of her shell, depending on life's whims. She had nested and produced eggs with potential for new life. The new life meant new births—the new Maria, Jason, Tara, the Fourteens, Fredericka, Hattie—like hatchlings heading to the sea. And she could come home to lay new eggs and give birth to new lives, including her own in a spiritual way.

Home.

Thank you, Turtle, she prayed. Then she whispered ... or more like hissed, "You want me to live outside of my shell, Jason Parker? Then you're gonna come out of yours!" Then she laughed out loud. "Hell hath no fury like Turtle scorned!"

Maria stopped by the trailer to grab what was now affectionately called Turtle before barreling over to the palace and storming up the steps, a feminine tsunami on a mission to take out whatever stood in her way. She banged on the glass door and then waited, bare foot tapping loudly on the deck boards.

Soon a bleary, weary, and obviously shaken Jason appeared at the door, wearing shorts and a wrinkled tee. Reluctantly, he opened the door. "Maria, I don't think I—"

Like an eel snatching its dinner, she grabbed his hand. "Out here, Jason Parker. Now!"

He stalled, tired of this stubborn woman telling him what to do, and yanked his hand out of hers.

"It was not a request. You want this to work? Then out here." She pointed to the deck.

Bailey wandered up to the door, aware of the ruckus, still in her pajamas, rubbing her eyes, and hair in a mess.

"Not now, Bailey!" Jason uncharacteristically shouted.

"She comes too," Maria commanded. She turned and pulled three chairs into a circle and then yanked over a small table and shoved it into the middle. Turtle was then placed on the table. The queen and her court. "Sit!"

All settled into their chairs, and then Mother Maria Turtle breathed in and exhaled slowly. As she gathered herself, she assumed the slow, measured pace of a turtle on a mission. Then she began laying her eggs. She repeated the revelation she had on the beach to both Jason and Bailey. She methodically noted each point, allowed time for it to sink in, and then moved to the next egg. The clutch laid, she began covering up her nest.

"The trailer is my nest that I have to periodically visit. It may not meet your expectations, Jason Parker, but it does mine. It's all I need. I don't *need* anything else. Got it?" She paused for effect and then continued. "But I *want* you, and you come with your house. So"—she motioned to the house—"this is the sea that I go back to."

Maria paused once more.

Bailey was trying to keep up with the logic and analogies.

Jason was trying to restrain his impatience.

"This beach, this island, is my home. It's where I lay my eggs, dream my dreams, reach for my hopes, and live my life. And that could include your mansion if that is the path we choose, but I don't *need* this house. I do, however, *need* my trailer. That is my shell."

Okay, the analogies were not precise, but she paused to let them sink in.

Jason was stoic.

Bailey was quivering. She looked at Turtle, as if hoping to hear what to say next. Then, three steps ahead, she spoke. "Daaad, please. She isn't saying no."

Jason stared at his daughter. His heart understood what she was saying, but his ego was not there. Then he looked back to Maria.

Maria helped him out. "A relationship means two people becoming a couple. You and I become a couple. My trailer, your mansion, one relationship. You need this"—she motioned to the mansion—"and I need that." She motioned to her trailer, paused, and then, like a new hatchling, headed out to the dark and dangerous unpredictability of the wide-open sea. "And, Jason, we know that both of us want each other." She paused to catch her thoughts. "The question is: Do we *need* each other enough to give up something that means everything to us?"

Jason, confronted, castigated, and cajoled, stood up and walked over to the side of the deck overlooking the eyesore trailer. It was ugly and so out of place next to the lavish rewards of his hard work, but he was lonely within the huge place. He smiled when he recalled the good times they'd had that summer within and without the trailer's aluminum walls. The strength the flimsy structure had given them. The aroma of homecooked meals. And that wonderful night of pleasure in Maria's bed. How she had brought so much life to all of them despite the pains deep within her. He recalled her feisty temper, which reflected her passion for justice and a love for the oppressed. The way she worked with the Fourteens and brought them together and taught them so much about the ways of the world. The new garden. And yes, those green triangles, her shorts, and the glimpse of a tummy between her high-waisted pants and cropped top. And sunglasses.

There was so much more to Maria than a rundown trailer.

He looked over at Bailey and realized she had fallen in love with the trailer too. It was a home away from home to her as well.

Then he stared at the turtle figurine on the table, and it hit him. If he really wanted this to work, then it was time to come out of his own shell—the shell of success that had been protecting him from his fear of failure and rejection.

He walked back over to the women and the circle of chairs and picked up the turtle. He eyed it like it was a Ming dynasty vase. Then he turned to Maria. "May I stay at your place tonight?"

Maria stood up but then paused. Was he just giving in to the emotions of the moment for what could very well turn out to be another one-night stand? Or was he implying they should move in together even though it meant living in two separate places? "Jason," she started, "what are you really asking me?"

He thought very carefully about his next words. "May I *live* with you in your trailer starting tonight?"

Bailey gasped. Was this for real?

Maria motioned with a hooked forefinger for her to get up. "Come over here please, Bailey."

Suddenly, Bailey was worried. What did Maria mean? Want? Like a dog with her tail tucked between her legs, she tentatively walked over to Maria and her father.

Maria looked her straight in the eyes. "Bailey, is this kind of relationship okay with you?"

Bailey was frightened of this new development and yet also delighted at the future this request might lead to. The tension between the two emotions caused her to shake, and tears leaked from her big green eyes. She couldn't find the words to voice how she was feeling, so she just nodded her head in silent hope.

Maria quietly, calmly walked over to Jason and placed her arms around him and lovingly pulled him closer. Then she motioned for Bailey to come join them, and she placed one arm around her. "Yes."

The following week was an odd one as Bailey learned a new word: *cohabitation*. When the Fourteens asked about the relationship, Bailey explained the Cohabitation Agreement she had drawn up and made Jason and Maria sign, just like Sheldon Cooper had done in *The Big Bang Theory*. One night in the trailer, two nights in the mansion, two nights alone for both, then the toss of a coin for the next night.

"Where do you stay, Bailey?" Anna asked. It seemed a simple question. When other couples moved in together, the kids came with them. Would Bailey stay in the trailer on Trailer Night, as it was now called, and then in the mansion on other nights? Where did she stay when Maria and Jason stayed in their separate homes?

Bailey, her face scrunched and twisted, was puzzled at what seemed so obvious. "In my room, silly. Where else would I stay?"

"Whatever floats your boat!" Emily called out.

SEVENTEEN

The Sea Turtle Basket

Maria was in full culinary swing that Saturday. She had looked for and found a large iron cooking pot on the internet. It had served many a Brunswick stew on the mainland, but now it would do coastal fare, beginning with a Low Country boil.

While on the mainland, she'd bought fresh-made kielbasa sausage from a meat market and then found late-season yellow corn on the cob at a farm stand on the side of the road heading back to Banker's Point. Then she stopped on the back of the island for fresh-caught crab and shrimp.

Frederick brought potatoes, seasoning, and charcoal for the outdoor fire from the One and Done.

Anna and Emily, standing in the kitchen in the "prep line," as Maria called it, having lived on the island all their lives, confessed they had never had any kind of boil.

"Seriously?" Maria asked incredulously. "Never?"

"Never even heard of it," Emily admitted as she and Anna shucked the corn.

Bailey was in charge of cutting the potatoes.

Frederick sliced up the kielbasa. "Real men love meat!" he called out.

"Let me get this straight," Maria said. "I lived in the middle of the state and had this several times, and you live here and never had it?"

Emily looked at Anna who stared back, and both shrugged their shoulders.

The crowded trailer kitchen soon filled with a smorgasbord of aromas. Jason was outside cleaning out the pot.

Ingredients prepared, the pot hanging from a tripod and filled with water, Maria dramatically added the ingredients as Jason stoked the coals underneath it. Now it was time to stir and wait.

As the fire roared and warmed the slight errant chill in the evening breeze, all sat around in chairs from the Methodist church fellowship hall and reminisced. Hattie smiled as she sat among folk who appreciated the deeper side of her. Tara reflected on her new friend, Maria. Fredericka silently rejoiced that Frederick was good as new. Emily and Anna were happy to have friends who were not shallow and mean. Frederick was now empowered by a new manliness. Bailey looked around and realized she felt stronger and more accepting of herself thanks to the Fourteens and Hattie. Maria glowed in her status as den mother of the Fourteens. And Jason felt fulfilled in his role as a father to the whole family. He took the lead in the next part of the bonfire, clapping his hands together.

"Folks, it's been quite a summer, right? At the risk of sounding like the closing night at the YMCA camp, can we all share one thing that was really special about this summer?"

The silence that ensued made Jason wonder if his request was a bit too sappy. However, all were just thinking, mulling over the past few months. The logs crackled and popped as the silence grew fretfully awkward. Late-evening beach walkers passed by, envious of the romantic fire.

Tara was the first to respond. "I'll start the show," she called out, recrossing her legs. "Sometimes, running the shop leaves me a bit empty, but this summer has taught me that we all have chances to help others. I'm glad I was here to help Bailey and, in other ways, Maria as well."

Maria, Bailey, and Jason all nodded their appreciation for Tara.

Reverend Tate followed up in her matter-of-fact voice. "Likewise. Jason, I was glad to be around when you and Bailey needed help the most. It reminded me that ministry is not always behind a pulpit on Sundays. It's also in the hedges and highways."

There was a lull in the moment.

Then Hattie leaned forward. "I'm glad to just be here among all y'all." She grinned a small smile. "Being here this summer without my family back home gets kind of lonely. I'm glad to be part of this here celebration. You's good people to be around."

After a moment, Emily squirmed. "I'm glad I met Bailey. She's quirky but cool. Mr. Parker, you've been like a dad to us this summer. Thanks." She choked up and then blubbered out, "Ms. Gowins, you've been a good mom as well."

Now it was Anna's turn. Even though she was a bit jealous of gorgeous Bailey, she had seen her struggles and learned a lot about life. "Bailey, I'm glad we got you out of your shell. Ms. Gowins, you cook the neatest food."

Maria was quietly sobbing. Jason took her hand, a move that all noticed.

Frederick cleared his throat and then, always himself, stood and spoke. "I want to thank you all for helping me out after my wreck." He paused for a moment. "Bailey, I'm glad I was there to save you." Bailey teared up, remembering what she had put behind her. "Mr. Parker ...." He couldn't go any further, so he sat back down.

Fredericka took up where he'd left off. "Jason, thanks for taking my son under your wing. You've been the dad he needs." Jason, wiping his eyes, nodded, but she wasn't done. "Maria, you've been very special to Frederick. Thank you. Bailey, Emily, Anna, you three have been so wonderful for my little Frederick." She looked over at her son, who looked back in embarrassment.

"Seriously? *Little* Frederick? C'mon, Mom." Everybody laughed.

She continued. "Other girls make fun of him, but you three have given him a confidence I have never seen in him before. Thanks."

Emily responded. "It's what friends do, right?"

Bailey reached over and took her boyfriend's hand. "I owe you everything, Frederick. I don't think I ever really said thank you for saving me." Then she sobbed.

The girls jumped up and gathered around her.

After a moment, Maria chimed in. "Fourteens, I never saw myself as a mom before. Thanks for being my kids this summer. Tara, your advice and brew gave me a new perspective this summer. Hattie, your wisdom is so special to me. Fredericka, how many discounts did you give me? Thanks!" Then she paused and looked at Jason and suddenly went dumb.

After a moment, he patted her hand. "You're welcome."

The fire crackled in the awkwardness, and all stared deep into it, reflecting on the summer.

Then Jason clapped his hands together again, and all jumped. "So folks, I'm dying to know what Hattie has in that mysterious bag she's been toting around all night. Hattie, are you going to enlighten us?"

It was Hattie's turn to speak again. She picked up and then reached into the mysterious bag she had not let out of her sight. "I made all y'all somethin' special. I wove and wove until I got 'em right." Then she laughed at herself. She reached into the bag. "These is for Miss Emily and Miss Anna." She handed Emily what looked like a hammer made from pine straw. "You full of justice, so here is your hammer. Bang it when the world needs straightenin' out." Then she handed Anna a wall hanging of a heart with a peace sign embroidered in the middle. "You a sweet thing who needs love, but your heart needs to fight for something, so fight for peace."

Anna and Emily looked at their gifts and turned them around slowly, as if taking in each strand of pine needle and grass. Both thanked Hattie.

Hattie continued, "Tara, your coffee keeps us going on this island, so I made you a cup."

She handed it to Tara who crooned over it. "Miss Hattie, this is so sweet. You shouldn't have."

Hattie waved her hand. "Never say such words to a gift. Miss Fredericka, I made you a little grocery bag 'cause you do us so much good with your store. And Frederick, here's your new bicycle."

Frederick held the intricate weaving in his shaking hands. Then he noticed the wheels turned. "Wow, Miss Hattie! How did you do that?"

"I don't give my secrets away," she laughed, her whole body shaking. She then turned to Bailey and handed her a flat disc. "Bailey, we done talked, and I told you you was blessed, so I made this for you."

Bailey stared at the disc, and after a brief wait, she understood. Into the light-brown plate, the dark letter *B* was woven, with white straw lines emanating out from it in all directions. After a brief trip into the outer reaches of Bailey World, she thought she had it figured out. "I am blessed, and my blessing goes out to the world?"

"Close, Miss Bailey. You is blessed, so go and bless others."

Bailey smiled and nodded her assent. "I will, Miss Hattie."

As the fire dwindled down, Hattie turned to Reverend Tate. "Reverend Tate, I made you a basket for all them fishes and loaves you serve up every Sunday."

The minister held it up and noticed that faint outlines of fish and bread were woven into the side of the basket. "Miss Hattie, thank you. This means the world to me."

"Then go into that world and feed us some love. Lord knows, we need some these days and times."

Reverend Tate nodded her head in agreement, and Emily, full of social justice, called out, "Amen," though a bit too loudly.

Anna suddenly realized something. "Miss Hattie, this is a lot of work. It is so special. It must have taken forever, and we just planned this party. How did you get it all done so fast?"

Hattie leaned back and sighed. They were all about to get a lesson on the ways of the Spirit. "Before June, before Kennedy asked me to come up for the summer, I started havin' dreams and visions and feelin's and such. When Maria came to the store, I suddenly knew what they was about. When I met Bailey, I already had a picture of her in my mind. I seen Jason scootin' down the road one day and felt a feelin' 'bout him too. I knowed Tara and Emily and Anna and Fredericka and Frederick already, but soon they was in the dreams too. Then images came to me, concernin' each person. So I began making all these gifts, knowin' that a day would come when I would need them all together. Today is that day."

There was silence as each person around the fire pondered the spiritual implications.

Hattie continued, "The wind, it blows the grasses and the needles that I use. When I weave them together, I feel the story, the Spirit, that the wind blowed into 'em. I wove that story into each gift you all holdin' in your hands tonight."

"That is just amazing, Miss Hattie!" Frederick called out.

"What an amazing gift," Reverend Tate responded.

Hattie, ever blunt in her ancient wisdom, huffed. "All us got the gift. Most of us just don't take the time to open it. That gift been 'round all you this summer. We just now slowed down enough to open it up." Then Hattie reached down deep into her bag. "Now Jason and Maria, the last one is for both of you." Hattie pulled out what looked to be an oddly shaped basket and placed it in Maria's hands.

Maria held it carefully, turning it around and around. The top had five little knob-like extensions and was arched in the middle and somewhat circular. The bottom half was the same size as the top circle and an inch deep. Then she realized it was a *turtle* basket. "Oh my God!" She showed it to Jason, who turned it around in his hands. "Jason, it's a sea turtle basket. Hattie, this is beautiful. It's so intricate. How in the—"

Hattie butted in. "Open the lid."

Jason held the basket nervously and nodded to Maria to open it. When she did, both looked inside. Then they looked up at each other, question marks on their faces. Maria reached in and took out a small object. Then she moved the box toward Jason. He reached in and took out something as well. They both looked at each other's objects.

The fire did not put out much light, and nobody could make out what the two held in their hands.

Bailey, curiosity at the bursting point, uncharacteristically took charge. "You two gonna share?"

Maria, eyes wide open, looked over at Bailey. "They're turtle hatchling figurines."

Bailey's eyebrows lifted.

There was a collective gasp around the fire. Then everyone looked at Hattie for an explanation. "They's three in there."

Jason reached back into the basket and then pulled out another one.

"That one goes to Bailey."

Jason carefully handed it to her. Bailey twirled it around in her hand. Then it hit all three.

From Turtle, a new family was being hatched.

Hattie saw the glint in their eyes. She looked around at the others, who were just beginning to catch on.

"Folk!" Hattie called out, looking around the fire. "Turtle came to me in a dream some time ago. 'It is time,' Turtle said. I wasn't sure what time she talkin' 'bout, but I thinks we all know now." She looked at Jason, then Maria, and finally Bailey. "It's time for you three to become one. Learn from Mama Turtle. She came in from the sea. She laid the eggs. Y'all done hatched, but you ain't gone nowhere. Don't need to rush. Take ya time and figure it out. But y'all taking too much time tryin' to figure out what already been decided. Get outta the nest and head to the sea. It's time for a new adventure."

Jason nodded. Maria silently looked up at him. Then she motioned for Bailey to come join them. After a long silence, Maria tentatively began the journey. "You ready?" she asked Bailey, who nodded yes.

Jason looked at Maria. "You ready?"

Maria looked expectantly at the man who, she hoped, would one day be her only man. She took his hand. "I'm ready, Jason."

Then Jason spoke for all three. "Hattie, you are right. It *is* time. Thank you."

Hattie threw up her gnarled hand. "Don't thank me. Thank Turtle. I had nothin' to do with this." She slapped her leg and then laughed and laughed. "You and Miss Maria best get goin'. Y'all got some turtlin' to do. Miss Bailey might want her a little hatchlin' to take care of."

Jason smiled, Maria turned red, and Bailey buffered on "turtling."

Then everybody laughed.

The kids had left with Reverend Tate after all had helped pack her SUV with the chairs, Frederick and Fredericka had scooted away, and Tara had taken Hattie back home. All was now quiet, the fire was dying out, and the three hatchlings were still huddled together on the sand. Maria stared at the basket and then opened and shut the lid. Jason and Bailey watched her fidget and began fidgeting deep within themselves as well. The weight of expectations was heavy upon their shoulders.

After the gift of the basket and Hattie's boisterous laughter, the mood was light, festive, and in some sense, congratulatory. All knew Jason and Maria were dating and that Bailey desperately wanted Maria to be her new mom. And, to use Hattie's spiritual imagery, all knew Turtle had laid out a plan of some sorts for the three to become one. But after the crowd left, Bailey, Maria, and Jason remained on the beach, the dying embers of the fire slowly giving reign of the night back to the stars.

Turtle may have known what the plan was, but it was not so obvious to the three people sitting by the fire.

Maria opened the basket and took out the three hatchlings, holding them in the palm of her hand. After a brief pause, she said what was on everyone's minds. "Now what?"

All three stared at the dying embers, all wanting to say something, but nobody saying anything. The ocean was quiet, as if pausing to hear what might come next.

Bailey sniffed as her eyes watered. "Could you two just hold me a bit?"

Maria scooted over and patted a spot on the sand.

Bailey clumsily got up and then plopped between the two. She was crying.

Jason, growing concerned at her sudden shift in emotions, hoped it was just a moment of teenage female hormones out of whack. "Bailey, what's wrong? You seemed so happy just a bit ago. Is this not something you want?" He put his arm around her, and Maria hugged her close. Bailey cried, then sniffed, whimpered, sniffed again, rubbed her nose on her arm because her hands were sandy, and then quieted down. The silence seemed forever. Jason was growing impatient and worried. As he was about to ask Bailey again, Maria tapped his arm, signaling him to wait some more.

Bailey started shaking. "I've been unhappy for so long that … feeling happy scares me. What if it goes away? What if you two can't get it figured out?"

Maria searched her mind for historical proverbs on happiness, but the ones she knew just didn't seem to answer Bailey's question or promise to calm her fears. Jason employed motivational quotes in his everyday approaches to success, but somehow, an inspirational snippet didn't feel appropriate. Maria, still holding Jason's arm wrapped around Bailey's shoulder, reached around Bailey, grabbed Jason's other wrist, and pulled it, making a circle of love around tremoring Bailey. She was worried too. So was Jason. She could feel it in his arm. But they could worry or take it one day at a time, enjoying the blessings and even the struggles as they swam in the seas of the future.

Then she started humming a tune from the past. An old Bobby McFerrin song. She adapted it just for Bailey. "Bailey, don't worry, just be happy."

At Bailey's insistence, Maria and Jason spent the first night of their journey in the trailer. Turtling practiced, the new couple-to-be lay in the back room of the dark trailer and wondered aloud. Maria rolled over and hugged her man and delicately kissed him on the neck. "Is it weird, considering that your daughter is next door, knowing that we are turtling together?"

"What does it say about two parents who obey a teenager's command to have sex?" Jason countered, pulling her tight.

Maria whispered into his ear, "I think it says we should do it again before she changes her mind."

The next morning, the trailer soon filled with the smells of breakfast. As if on cue, there was a tentative, quiet knock on the door, as if not to wake up anyone. "Anybody in there?"

"Come in, Bailey!" Jason called out.

The metal door opened slightly, and two big, twinkling green eyes stared through the crack. "Just making sure everybody has their clothes on. You know, not walking around naked or anything." She walked into the den, hugged her dad and, hopefully, her new mom, and sniffed.

Maria called out, "Breakfast is ready!"

They gathered around the aluminum-framed table, and Maria saw Bailey's eyebrows rise. "Cheese grits with real bacon bits, kind-of-homemade cinnamon raisin rolls, and fresh pineapple." She shoved a saucer of bacon bits and another saucer of cheese toward Bailey and then poured a bowl of plain grits. "You'll have to figure out the rolls on your on."

Jason smiled and enjoyed a big spoonful of creamy grits as Maria plopped an elbow on the table and looked lovingly at him.

Bailey was still doing the math on the grits, bacon bits, and cheese when she suddenly got up and went into the den. When she came back, she placed the turtle figurine in the middle of the small table. "There. Mother Turtle needs to dine with us." Back to breakfast, she sprinkled bacon bits on the left side of the grits and then dribbled the cheese on the right.

Maria looked at Jason, who looked back at her, and then both looked at Bailey.

"You know—Hattie, the turtle basket, Mother Turtle?" she finished. She waved her hand over her head and rolled her eyes. "Whew." One spoonful of grits with bacon bits done and the next spoonful of grits and cheese on the way, Bailey paused and smiled. "This is nice. Really nice."

Maria and Jason looked at each other, love all over their faces.

Jason answered, "Yes, it is, Bailey."

Maria took Jason's hand and looked over at him. Then she reached out for Bailey's free hand. Looking at Turtle, she answered, "Yes, it really is."

A SNEAK PEEK AT J.T. ALLEN'S NEXT BOOK

What Friends Are For

J. T. Allen's next beach novel, What Friends Are For,
is the sequel for his first novel, Love, Judie Kate,
and The Gift From Turtle. *Here's a sneak peak ...
See you soon back on Banker's Point Island!*

The two-lane road into Banker's Point was lined with live oaks for a stretch, and then suddenly they seemingly opened wide to the expected beach scenery. To their right was the beach, the lower end of the Outer Banks that stretched from Banker's Point right up to Virginia. There was an old, faded, rusty trailer, then a small beach shack, then a mansion. And the pattern seemed replicated up the road. To their left, sun-bleached and sand-blown old beach houses and trailers lay hidden beneath twisted live oaks. The old structures, cared for by their owners for years, held memories of family and friends who came and enjoyed the surf, sand, and sights year after year. On some of the deck rails, beach towels and faded shorts flapped in the wind.

"Should be around here somewhere, Judie Kate," Joe called out, as if taking soundings before making port. "Maria said look for the first public-access parking lot. It's on the left. They're across the street."

Judie Kate spied it first.

"Land ahoy, Joe!" she called out, pointing left.

Joe grimaced as he assessed the parking lot, looking for a place to park the sound trailer. An impatient traveler honked her horn.

Judie Kate jumped out to help Joe park the trailer.

She waved the car along and then gestured at folks to stop while Joe pulled up and then backed in carefully into a tight space. Now in the parking lot, Judie Kate signaled for him to back up and then made a halt sign. After Joe unhitched the trailer, they looked across the street.

"Wow, Joe, look at that place!"

Joe whistled his astonishment.

"It's huge, Joe. What if we get lost in there?"

Joe looked over at Judie Kate. "Google maps?"

She punched him in the shoulder then hopped back in the truck to wait.

In front of them stood a three-story beach mansion, and to the left of it was a newly painted yellow-and-white trailer. A woman came down from the deck on the mansion and waved at them.

"Is that Maria?" both of them asked out loud together.

Joe and Judie Kate had not seen Maria since her horrific divorce. Now she was trim, tanned, and wearing a faded yellow tank top and short jean skirt. Maria excitedly waved again, happy to see familiar faces from Greensboro. Joe scooted his truck across the road and into the sandy drive between two immaculately groomed green grass lawns. Maria, wearing cheap flip-flops, walked over to the passenger side as Judie Kate stepped out of the truck.

"Hi, Judie Kate. Welcome to Banker's Point!" Maria opened her arms and gave her a big hug, like they had known each other for years. As Joe came around, she turned and did the same to the man who had been both a colleague and supportive friend for years before she came to Banker's Point. "Joe Clark, you look good! Judie Kate has been so good for you!"

At that time, someone who had to be Adonis from Mount Olympus came bounding down the stairs and rushed over to greet the travelers.

"You must be Joe and Judie Kate! I'm Jason." He stuck out a hand, and Joe and Judie Kate reached out to return the greeting. Judie Kate had never shaken the hand of a god before. He was so good looking.

Joe looked at Maria. "Wow, Maria, how much do you pay this fine-looking man to stand beside you?"

"Joe Clark, still giving me a hard time?" She bopped him on the chest. "This, my old friend, is my hunk of a new husband."

Judie Kate did not realize her mouth was wide open.

Joe looked over at Jason. "Jason, you better take good care of this one. She's like a sister to me."

"Will do, sir! But let's get you folks inside before you melt. Gosh, it's hot! Joe, let me help you with the bags. Ladies, if you will, please lead the way."

Stopping at what looked like a large closet, Jason tapped a button, and the door of an elevator opened. Judie Kate faced Joe and mouthed, "Wow, can you believe this?" It was a tight fit with all four and luggage. "Thought we'd introduce you to the Big El, as we call it. Don't use it much, mostly take the stairs," Jason called out.

Arriving at the first floor, Joe and Judie Kate marveled at what they saw. Jason's success in financial planning was obvious in the exquisite furniture, the high-tech smart appliances, the fine art—not prints, but real art—on the walls, and the authentic folk décor on the tables and shelves. Yet there was this genuine sense of "Aw shucks, it's not much ..." that helped visitors feel right at home. After a brief tour, Jason led them up the stairs to their bedroom on the third floor.

"You two get the luxury suite this week," Jason said, plopping their bags on the queen bed. Joe, ever the chocolate buff, noticed the two candies on the pillows.

Judie Kate was still in "I can't believe it" land.

Jason pointed out the different amenities. "Bath is through those doors. Towels and robes included free!" he called out as if doing the voiceover for a hotel commercial. "There's a fridge if you need one, microwave in the kitchenette, wasn't sure what to stock in the bar, but let me know if you need something." Then he walked over to the full-length drapes and pulled them open.

Judie Kate froze.

Jason pulled the sliding doors open to reveal a large, private deck and hot tub.

"There you go, kids; make yourselves at home! When you get settled in, come back down and join us on the deck."

And with that, bellhop Jason disappeared.

Joe looked around and whistled again, missing the fear on Judie Kate's face.

"Quite the spread, huh, Judie Kate?" He walked over to her and hugged her close. The romance of the beach blew into the room on a salty breeze and then crept into his bones. My, how he loved the feeling of her body next to his. He craved every inch that she always felt insecure about. Her round hips, her soft shoulders, the way her neck hid behind her dark hair. He placed his hands on her waist and then playfully moved them up to her breasts. But Judie Kate felt frozen in time. The moment stalled, worry now interrupting bliss. He stepped back from her and placed his comforting hands on her shoulders.

"Sweetie, what's wrong?"

She pulled her man close and nestled her head under his chin. That was her safe spot.

"Demons from the past, Joe. I saw ·the deck and remembered that creep who broke into my room." She tried to hold back a sob, but Joe knew the signs all too well. He rubbed her back and ran his hand through her hair.

"Sorry, Joe. Didn't mean to ruin the moment. It's just, sometimes, you know …."

He did. And, while he had hoped the trip would be a time of healing, he knew it would be punctuated with occasional sadness and even repressed fears. And to be frank, the deck did indeed have a strong resemblance to the one on Ocracoke, the one the stalker, who broke into the house, had unlocked sometime during the day in the hopes of getting to her that night.

Joe led her to the bed, set the bags on the floor, and then sat down and pulled her tight against him. Judie Kate wrapped her arms around him and settled into his body. After a moment, she felt calm. She looked up and kissed Joe softly, cautiously, as if it were their first kiss and they weren't sure what came next.

Joe lay back on his side and patted the bed. Judie Kate knew what he wanted. She lay down on her side and backed up to him, pushing her bottom up against him, and then waited for his arms to wrap around her chest. Lovingly intertwined, she grinned in delight.

www.ingramcontent.com/pod-product-compliance
Lightning Source LLC
Chambersburg PA
CBHW030644020726
47493CB00006B/1866